WOOLLOOMOOLOO BAD

ALISON OWENS

This novel was researched and completed as part of a PhD at Central Queensland University. The author acknowledges the invaluable supervisory assistance of Prof Donna Brien.

The author also acknowledges the profoundly useful data and inspiring narratives provided by many historical texts, but particularly:

Peter Stanley (1997) Tarakan: An Australian Tragedy, Allen & Unwin

Capt. James Gaby (1974) The Restless Waterfront, Antipodean Publishers

David Wilson (1998) Always First: The RAAF Airfield Construction Squadrons 1942-1974, Air Power Studies Centre.

John Birmingham (2000) Leviathan: The unauthorised biography of Sydney, Penguin.

For Glenda and Keith

PROLOGUE

1945 Tarakan Island, Borneo

The young soldier lay breathing steadily but otherwise motionless.

"No signs of consciousness yet for Private Pace?"

"No, he still hasn't come around," the nurse shook her head. "Been twenty-four hours now."

"Hmmm," the Doctor approached the young man and took his hand to check his pulse. "It was a major explosion. He's lucky to be alive, I suppose." He stroked the stubbed fingers of the patient's right hand and wondered where the lad had lost them. It had clearly happened some years before he would have been old enough to enlist. He reached for the chart at the end of the cot and read the data before hanging it back on the bed railing. "He has every chance of recovering nurse. He's young and fit and I see he's from Woolloomooloo." The Doctor smiled. "I think we can assume he's a tough lad. Keep an eye on him. He will be very disoriented when he comes to."

The Doctor observed the pile of mail at the patient's bedside. "I see he has some reading to catch up on when he wakes. He may need some help reading at first. Concussion often affects their vision for a time."

"Yes, Doctor."

Little George Pace held tight to his mother's thin skirt, as he was told, and allowed her to lead him through the crowd at the entrance to Brisbane's Central Railway Station. He met the yellow eyes of a brown dog as they passed each other through the maze of legs, like endlessly parting curtains on a picture show. He had never been in the Station before and he gazed at the grand ceiling, so far above him that it made him dizzy. Electric lanterns lit the vast hall and the platforms where people gathered in the dusk and hugged one another and wiped their eyes. The smells of horse manure, fumes from motorcars and steam from the train were powerfully strong but the noise of the train was like nothing he had heard before. Finally, they reached the platform for the Sydney Mail where he saw the grand, steaming red and black machine and his heart raced. The train let out a fearsome sigh and he tightened his grip.

"I'll get these loaded for you," said Uncle Rob lowering for a moment the two suitcases of belongings they were taking with them on the long, overnight journey to Sydney.

"Ta," said Mum. She wasn't saying much today. She swung George's baby sister to her other hip and glanced down at him. "Keep a hold, son."

Uncle Rob returned from the luggage carriage and stood before them adjusting his hat, contemplating a suitable farewell.

"See ya', Rob." Sybil gave him one of her inside out smiles with her lips tucked firmly between her teeth. The smile that usually preceded bad news and indicated only forbearance.

"I'm real sorry about everything, Syb," Uncle Rob (who wasn't a real uncle but played drums in George's father's jazz band) muttered, studying his boots. "I sure hope it works out in Sydney for you." He bent down to confront George. His kind eyes with deep lines around them looked tired. "You look after your mum and your sister now mate." He followed George's gaze and brightened. "How's about that fancy train, eh? You're a lucky boy riding on that to the big smoke!"

"Bye, Uncle Rob," George smiled. He didn't know. He didn't know he was leaving Brisbane and his father forever. He didn't know that his father had taken up with Beth Randall, the barmaid at the Regatta. He only knew that his mother was taking them on an exciting journey to the biggest city in Australia to visit his grandparents. And that she was angry. With his dad.

Maggie said nothing. It was best if Jim were left to himself when his temper was up. She'd learned that over thirty-five years of marriage and four children. She kept peeling the carrots and potatoes she was preparing for the roast. As her small fingers worked the vegetables she thought over the meager furnishings they had collected in the front room for their daughter-in-law and her two children speeding their way to Sydney along the brand new single-gauge rail track from Brisbane. A double bed for Sybil and baby Anne and a single cot for George. They had a little wardrobe and some bedside drawers and the blue and white rag rug that she had made herself when the first of the babies came along. All four of them had crawled across that rug and she was secretly excited to know that the first baby girl in the family would soon do the same. Of course, it would be better if things were otherwise, but in the circumstances, she, being both a pragmatic and sentimental woman, was prepared to make the most of their chance to watch over the grandchildren they had so rarely seen. Jim, on the other hand, was not done with his fury over his son's selfishness and irresponsibility. When Sybil had sent news of Thomas' decision to go and live with his 'fancy woman', Jim lost his block.

"I won't have it! I'm going up there to knock some sense into him. The two-bob lair! Wasted half his life on blowing a bloody horn…., and now he shoots through on his family for a…. barmaid!… And we pick up the pieces." Jim's normally calm manner had been disturbed for days but he had come around and accepted that they were to receive new lodgers. It would take a lot longer for him to forgive Tom, Maggie knew that much. Jim was a hard worker and a hard father but he was a good and honest man struggling to accept the undeniable fact that his sons were trouble.

Maggie sighed as she watched Harry through the rear kitchen window lead his horse and cart into the row of old stables that stretched along the narrow yard of their Woolloomooloo home. They had been granted the two-story terrace at 107 Dowling Street by Public Housing just before the war. That was when there was more work than men and Jim had put in long, wearying days on the construction of the Finger Wharf where he still worked along with their youngest son, Sean. When there was work available, that is. It wasn't wartime anymore and the sense of urgency for the wharves to keep supplies of goods and ammunition constantly moving to support Australian soldiers was well and truly gone.

At sixty-one years old, Jim Pace, still nuggety and strong, was holding his own as an old hand foreman on the wharves where he was known as Big Jim due to his short stature, or else Jim-on-the-chin, in reference to a few stoushes he had when a younger man where he had knocked out men bigger than him with his famous right hook. But work was drying up now the guts had fallen out of the economy and the merchant ships just weren't coming. Maggie had never heard of Wall Street before Black Tuesday but she and everyone else she knew was learning fast about economics, the cost of the War and the price that had to be paid by the ordinary folk.

"It's a crying shame what happens to good workers in times like these, Maggie." Jim would return home an evening more shamed than exhausted at the selection he had to make each morning of a few handfuls of men from several hundred seeking a day's work and a wage at the end of the week to feed their families. "I can't see an end to it, that's the worst." His usual stoicism faltered at the sight of tough, grown men begging for work. He had even stopped flashing his new dentures.

"Ow 'ya goin?" Harry stood in his usual spot, hat in hand, outside the open back door. Having finished looking to his horse, his habit was to drop in for a cuppa at the end of his day carting groceries around Woolloomooloo, the Cross and Darlinghurst and chat with Jim or Maggie, or anyone who was home. Harry knew everything about everyone as he visited most kitchens in the district at one point or another. In the setting sunlight he was a sorry silhouette in his loose trousers and shirt, dirty from the horse and smelling of cabbage. "Jim at home, Maggie?"

"Inside, Harry." Maggie looked up from working the wood stove and waved a poker towards the living room where Jim sat cleaning his fingernails with his penknife. "I'll put the kettle on."

"You're a good woman, Maggie," Harry entered the gloomy room furnished with a simple bench sofa and two armchairs that they had been gifted for their wedding. He placed his hat on the solid timber table Jim had knocked together from wharf scraps.

"G'day."

Jim nodded and Maggie heard their infrequent murmurs as they shared a day's labour and waited for the kettle. She glanced anxiously at the extravagance of two stuffed chooks as she closed the oven on them. They had cost an arm and a leg, but it was a special occasion after all. They would be here in a couple of hours and they would be hungry after the long train journey. She pulled the kettle off the boil and filled the teapot, her small face shining with perspiration. As the tea brewed she closed her eyes and enjoyed the late sun streaming through the window above the sink. This was where she was usually to be found, looking out over the side fence across the other fences and yards of the row of terraces as she cooked and washed and sipped on strong tea. Her thick, greying hair was coiled at her neck and the lines around her small, brown eyes appeared as delicate, pale webs engraved by house spiders on her sun-darkened skin. Perhaps her most striking feature was the pronounced cleft in her upper lip so that it hung over her lower lip in an endearing and childlike manner. It expressed her innate gentleness. Thomas had it too.

"Are we having tea today?" Jim bellowed.

"Keep yer skin on!" She gathered the teapot and cups on a tray and joined them in the living room. Harry was describing the trouble in town yesterday.

"What do they expect?" Jim spat. "You either agree to work for less or you're out of a job altogether. Men won't take that forever. How many were there walking on the House?"

"There were over six hundred leaving Trades Hall yesterday arvo'," said Harry. "They marched on the House and told the coppers they wanted to interview the Premier." Jim couldn't help a little smile at this. "The coppers just charged them with batons and chased 'em off." Maggie gasped and Jim shook his head. "Most of 'em went over to the Domain and you can imagine the speechmaking! The Commies were in the thick of it of course. But it was later that things got serious. Over a thousand of them went back to Trades Hall to start another march but there were even more coppers there. They didn't even get it started before the wallopers laid into them. Bert Morrison's been bagged - you remember Bert - along with Fred Williams and many more. It was a royal blue. Plenty of police being bandaged up as well as the marchers." Harry accepted his cup of tea from Maggie with a nod.

"Have you seen the twins, Harry?" Maggie remained standing before him, her dark unblinking eyes reading his roughened face.

"Nope, haven't heard nothing about 'em", Harry sipped his tea and concentrated his gaze on the floorboards.

There were a few moments of quiet as Maggie took her seat again and sipped her tea. She was used to awkward silences when the topic of her eldest boys came up.

"Sean came home last night, love." Jim gave Maggie a reassuring wink. "Those other buggers are big enough to take care of themselves." Maggie quietly chewed the inside of her cheek.

"Will you be up at *The Anchor* tomorrow?" Harry looked sideways at Jim.

"Yep. Seen something I fancy in the 2 o'clock. And you?"

"Yep. I'm cockatoo for Roy." Maggie glared at Harry who avoided her gaze by folding his lanky frame sideways so he was almost off the sofa.

"S'truth. Getting a bit sharp, aren't you?"

"It's getting tough mate. I gotta' feed the horse and people can't afford the fruit and veg anymore. Everyone's scrimping. Never seen so much trouble for families." He shook his head. "The Marshall's house was the latest to go, saw the signage meself today. Another family got the bung. Bloody bailiffs got no feelings. Seven kids and a missus and no work, not enough on the sustenance payments to please the landlord. Out they go! Never mind the poor bastard fought the Johnny Turk!" Harry flung his arm in the air and his voice cracked.

"Where have they gone?" Maggie asked.

"She's gone to her family out west and he's on the road heading north. They just left what they had in the street ... and there wasn't much worth keeping. Poor bastard. I hope he finds something."

"Something'll come up." Jim looked at Maggie and back at Harry signaling the end of that topic.

"So, the Billy Lids arriving tonight, eh?" Harry took his point. "Bet you're excited about that, Mags. Be nice to have the little ones running round again." His smile showed the few teeth he had left in his head.

"Yep, Sean should be bringing them about now from Central Station," said Jim. Maggie smiled and collected the empty teacups.

"See ya' tomorrow then, mate," Harry rose and slipped through the back door past the stables and through the gap in the fence to the terrace next door where he lodged in the small rear room overlooking the laneway behind the row of terraces.

Like most laneways in Woolloomooloo, Judge Lane was to be avoided at night unless you were the dunnyman. The local push, roaming larrikins and petty criminals considered dark laneways as their sacred ground and even the locals thought twice about walking out at night down these grim corridors. More than a few bodies had been discovered come morning either beaten, drunk or dead, depending on their luck and their state of health. Woolloomooloo was a tough neighbourhood inhabited by an odd mix of wharf workers, fishermen, musicians, artists, layabouts and prostitutes along with the criminal elements who traded sly grog after the 6pm lockout from the pubs and supplied visiting sailors with the kind of hospitality they craved after months at sea.

Jim had lived here all his life having learned the sea trade on his father's fishing boat. But the fish markets had long ago moved to Darling Harbour and Jim had done his time on the wharves learning the trade and learning to tread a fine line between the demands of a ruthless management and the hard men on the wharves. So far, he had managed to keep the peace but he could feel things tightening and too many nights now he dreamt the winch slip and the crushing load fall into the dark hold.

"Stupid bastard!" Guy Pace pushed his brother ahead of him out the pub door. 'What d'ya get involved in that lark for?" Nick Pace was laughing uncontrollably and leant against the wall to catch his breath. As it was six o'clock the pub doors were flung open to belch out the rowdy clientele who poured into Palmer Street with their bellies full of beer and their spirits, however briefly, restored.

"You're just jealous." Nick grinned at his twin brother through uneven teeth and watched him roll a cigarette. "You didn't get to throw one at the coppers. And anyway, I was just minding my little brother."

"Sean's a dill but you're a bigger bloody dill. You know what we agreed. No trouble that doesn't pay. No free throws." Guy dragged hard on his smoke and watched Nick regain his composure. Nick was handsome with only a small slash scar down his left cheek. Guy could see Handy Mandy smiling at them from where she sat at the door of

Number 12 and Nick smiled back. "For Christ's sake..." He pushed Nick before him towards William Street so they could walk up the hill to Darlinghurst where they lived. Both were a little unsteady on their feet having been drinking for several hours. "What you looking at a moll like her for? You've got woman trouble enough!"

"I like her," Nick shrugged. "She knows how to have some fun and she doesn't mind I've got the clap."

Guy laughed. "You're all over the place like a mad woman's knitting, mate! Your bloody missus wants you dead, you're half crazy with clap and you still want more. I dunno'. Just do me a favour and stay out of the politics, okay? It doesn't pay and the baksheesh is what we need. You were bloody lucky you and Sean got away last night. They've got eight put away in the Academy from that brawl and you can bet they will be looking a lot worse when they come out than when they went in." Guy crushed his smoke underfoot and tipped his head sideways in greeting at Jerry Watson at the front of his pawn shop. "Closing late mate?" Jerry smiled silently and nodded at the two burly men before making his way carefully past them in the direction of the city.

The twins moved up busy William Street with its buzzing electric trams, horse carts and motorcars competing for space in the constant tidal rhythm up and down the hill between the Cross and the city. The jangling bells of the trams and the nasal moans of car horns provided a restless soundtrack to the darkening of the day. Electric street lamps had lit the place up at night so that it gleamed but the nightlife of Woolloomooloo was not always a pretty sight. As the brothers approached William Lane muffled moans, curses and the unmistakable sounds of a beating provoked them to turn their heads and glare into the dim laneway. Two women restrained another against a wall while a third assailant shoved something forcibly into the mouth of the spluttering victim, flinging wild, stockinged kicks at her legs.

"That'll teach ya' to keep your bloody mouth shut. If ya' wanna' root a copper, better learn to shut your gob."

"Evening, Maisie," Guy couldn't help himself. The aggressor

turned to face him pulling her furious red hair aside. Her two accomplices dropped hold of their victim who collapsed to the ground choking up whatever it was in her mouth, gasping for air.

"Fuck off, Guy!" Maisie smiled and the brothers skipped back into the William Street thoroughfare laughing and shaking their heads.

"She's game, that Maisie," Guy's admiration was clear. He was almost identical to his brother with the same thick, dark hair and small, brown eyes but slightly bigger and coarser all over bearing more scars including several bullet wounds one of which had taken off part of his left ear. Guy put it about that this had happened in the war but everyone knew he hadn't lasted more than a few weeks in the military before he was discharged on account of bad character. He was the elder twin by almost seven minutes and he was an infamous bully. It was said that he bullied his brother from in the womb and bounced him from his mother's breast. Nevertheless, the two were rarely apart. They were to be avoided unless you needed stand-over men and they were on the payroll of several bookies who worked the Woolloomooloo and Darlinghurst pubs on a Saturday. If you didn't pay up on your lost bet by Monday, you would become horribly familiar with the Pace twins. The evening foot traffic parted obligingly to allow them to swagger up the hill without incident.

They stopped as they reached the rundown row of cottages on Barcom Avenue. Guy lived with his wife and two sons in one of the dark and sorry looking cottages with a long strip of weeds and collapsed wooden fence out the front while Nick boarded with another family two doors down as Guy's wife wouldn't have him in the house. "Remember we're goin' home tomorrow to see Tom's mob. Better put your best clobber on for mum's sake." Guy examined the frayed and grubby collar of his brother's shirt. "That Tom must have a screw loose, if you ask me. Always was one for the sheilas. Sybil's not one to put up with it. God knows how she'll fit in down 'ere."

"I like her" said Nick.

"You barely know 'er!" Guy poked his incredulous face close to Nick's. Nick shrugged.

"She's family." He belched and turned his back on his brother. "G'night".

"Night, mate." Guy watched him move through the night then opened the stubborn front door to his house with a shove of his shoulder and closed one eye at the shrieking pitch of his eldest son.

"Get off it, ya' great moocher!"

"Oi!" His gravel warning reverberated along the bleeding stone walls of the dark and narrow hall and a careful silence immediately ensued.

Sean recognized Sybil the minute she stepped from the train. He hadn't seen her in a few years and she had put on a bit of weight but she had the same mass of dark ringlets that had a life of their own and were standing almost upright around the short brim of her hat in the sudden southerly blast that kicked along the platform driving the day's heat out of the city. It was getting dark and he could see her quick eyes scanning for a friendly face. With the toddler Anne on her hip and little George by her side, she looked vulnerable despite her tall, solid frame. Sean smiled and approached her with his hat in his hand.

"G'day, Syb."

"Sean," her eyes lit up and she hugged him to her causing Anne to squeal in protest. "Oh, it's good to see ya'. What a handsome young man you are these days!" She stepped back and studied him further noting the sun freckles on his long nose and the fresh bruise under his left eye. "Got your mother's eyes and your dad's smile there. Say hello to your Uncle Sean, son." George stared up at the young man before him and nodded dutifully.

" 'Lo, Uncle Sean."

" 'Lo, son. You remember me? Bet you don't. I remember you anyways. You were only two when I saw you up in Brisbane. My you've grown into a solid young bloke! S'ppose you're hungry, eh? Let me get the luggage Syb and I'll get you lot home. Ma's dying to see you." Sean jumped onto the train and soon returned swinging their cases and chatting over his shoulder as they followed him to the street. "Mind your step here, Syb. The tram stop's over the road. Hold your ma's hand Georgie. This is the big city here. They'll run over you as soon as look at you."

George looked around him in some wonder at the people hurrying, some running, among the train carriages and the trams, over busy streets packed with more motorcars than he had ever seen. Stallholders yelled their wares, fruit, newspapers and frozen ices. A man was arguing with one of the conductors on the trains and a police officer was talking to two young boys not much older than him at the exit to the station. Everywhere there was movement and noise and snatches of conversation blown about in the roughneck southerly playing havoc with hats and jackets but bringing relief from the damp heat of a Sydney February. Finally they boarded the tram on George Street that would take them to his Grandparent's house and he sat next to Sean on the wooden bench watching the streets with their tall, darkening buildings pass him by.

"So, how was your journey on the train, mate?" Sean bent his neck to hear George above the conversations of other passengers.

"A man fell off the train," said George his forehead tangled.

"What?" Sean leant further down.

"A man fell off the train!" shouted George. "We think he's dead."

"Crikey! Is that so?" Sean looked across at Sybil his eyebrows upright. "And how did that happen?"

"Poor bugger tried to jump the train outside of Taree," said Sybil. "We had to stop for a bit ..." They were all silent for a few moments. With the depression now biting hard 'jumping a rattler' as it was known was a common problem both for the railways and the men who mucked up their timing. A free train ride was for some men the only way out of a desperate situation and a ride to the city offered the prospect of work. At least, that's what they thought, but Sean knew differently. There was not enough work in Sydney for the poor bastards who lived here.

Anne was dozing off to sleep on Sybil's shoulder rocked by the motion of the tram. George had his face pressed to the window fascinated by the streetscapes passing him by. Sean studied Sybil's face as they moved along George Street and she watched Sydney, reconnecting with her past and thinking goodness knows what. She had an intelligent although not quite beautiful face. It was a little too round and her quick brown eyes a little too close together but she had a generous mouth with small, even teeth and fine, pale skin despite her years in the sun. He had always enjoyed her company especially when she and Tom were courting and still in Sydney. While Tom had largely ignored his younger brother, Sybil had always had a few words with him when she came to the house and had even tried to teach him some dance steps. She was a good dancer and it was her grace on the dance floor, despite her unusual height, that had caught Tom's attention as he played trombone in the Sydney Jazz Band at the Palais Royal on a Saturday night. They had taken up together pretty quick after that and it wasn't long before they married and moved to Brisbane where Tom had an offer in the newly formed Sampson Orchestra. Sean was only vaguely aware of what had happened from there but knowing his elder brothers as he did, he had no doubt that Tom had disappointed Sybil more than once as a husband. Tom had always been popular with the ladies and he was a real groomer, always combing his hair and checking himself in the mirror. His big brothers had called him *Princess* and said he was the girl Maggie never had. Although Sean smiled wryly to himself at this memory, he felt a deep sympathy for Sybil, knowing her own parents were dead and gone - her father taken by tuberculosis and her mother buried just a year ago after a bout of bronchitis and pneumonia. He leant across to pat her knee.

"I'm really glad you've come back to us, Syb."

She smiled gratefully, an escaped tear hurtling down her face before she could brush it aside. "Thank you, Sean. Thank you for coming to get us." She shook her head briskly to clear the emotion. "I'd forgotten how busy Sydney was! It makes Brissie look like a country town." She paused. "And how's your dad taking ... everything?"

"He can't wait to see you all!" said Sean smiling broadly. When

Sybil lifted an eyebrow he added, "Tom, on the other hand, he curses every day." They laughed and George looked quickly at his mother responding to the welcome sound of her laughter unheard for what seemed a long time.

"Righto, the next one is us," Sean got up and collected the luggage. "Follow me."

They disembarked at the tram stop at Bourke and William and walked slowly home to Dowling Street with Sybil pointing out familiar sights to George: Mr Greig's tobacconist, the old pharmacy, the Chinese laundry along with Mitchell's fish shop burning light and steaming oil. They turned into Dowling and encountered a few of the more colourful locals loitering just out of the circle of light cast by the street lamp.

"G'day, Sean," a young man dressed in black with a slouch hat on the back of his grinning face pulled into line with them as they strode towards the Pace home. Three other blokes walked along a few yards behind. Sybil pulled George closer and he stared in fascination at the high-heeled boots with mirrored toecaps that peeped from the wide ends of the trousers worn by this thin man with the high- pitched voice. 'Whatcha' up to, mate?"

"G'day, Johnno'," Sean continued walking seemingly unperturbed by the sudden appearance of this group of theatrically dressed young men. "Just bringin' me sister-in-law home." He kept walking but indicated Sybil and the children. "You'll be seein' them around. Syb, George, little Anne, these blokes here will do you no harm."

"Too right, M'am! And welcome home to the 'Loo," Johnno swept his hat from his head and bowed awkwardly as he attempted to walk backwards in front of them.

"Thank you," Sybil was not sure if she should laugh or cry at the sight of this odd mob which she knew instinctively were the local Push. The faces changed but they had always been here. "Johnno, is it?"

"It is indeed."

"Well, I am pleased to meet you and to be back in Woolloomooloo."

Johnno grinned broadly keeping step. "You were up at the Trades Hall last night, Sean?"

"And whose business is it, if I was or I wasn't?" Sean stopped walking for a second or two and waited for an answer.

"No-one's, mate." Johnno pulled his chin into his neck accentuating his resemblance to a goose. "I was just wondering, that's all."

"Well, wondering is all right, Johnno." They approached the front gate of the Pace terrace and Sean smiled. "Be seein' ya' later, fellas. Here we go, Syb." He pushed the gate ajar as the front door opened and an excited Maggie skipped into the street.

"You're here!" She held her arms open and flung them first around Sybil, then little George whose head was turned after Johnno and his mates as they slid quickly into the shadows. "And our baby girl!" Sybil heaved a sigh of relief as little Anne was taken from her hip where she had become almost a permanent fixture. "Maggie, it's so good to see you." Her eyes filled as she felt some of her burden lifted. Maggie placed her arm around her and led her through the front door.

"I wish we had a better son my dear but you are as welcome here as my own daughter," she whispered as they moved through the narrow hallway into the lamplight of the living room where Jim stood flashing his new dentures for all he was worth.

Once their suitcases were settled in the front bedroom and they had washed up in the basin Maggie had filled for them, the family sat down to eat at the kitchen table. Sybil nursed Anne who had eyes like a skipping rope swinging round in her head with barely the momentum to keep going but determined not to miss anything. Next to Sybil sat George and then Jim at the head of the table with Sean and Maggie on the busy side of the kitchen.

"This is a feast, Maggie!" Sybil exclaimed. "Your favourite, George. Chicken! We haven't had that for a good while. You shouldn't have gone to all this trouble for us." Maggie smiled as she served plate loads of chicken, potatoes, carrots and gravy across the table.

"It's a treat," she conceded. "We can't eat like this every night, George." They all laughed at George who stared lovingly at his plate of food entranced by the aromas and primed to start only awaiting the signal as was polite.

"Get into it, son," Jim winked at him and as he picked up his cutlery. "S'not so bad the rest of the time either, as long as you like snags."

"I love snags," George hurriedly assured him in between mouthfuls.

"We are very grateful to be here, Jim," Sybil said quietly, her brows drawing together. "I know I can get work in Sydney,… once I get the children settled. I don't think that would have been possible in Brisbane. Given …everything."

"Plenty of time to think about working," said Jim approvingly washing down his mouthful of potatoes with a sip of tea. "I am sure a capable girl like you will land on her feet. But you are welcome here for as long as you like." He smiled sideways at George. "You're a big fella for your age, aren't you?"

"I am taller then Fred McReeve and Dennis Marshall," George observed.

"Are they your mates?" asked Sean, laughing.

"Fred is, but I don't talk to Dennis Marshall … he killed my lizard." George continued to eat his dinner unaware of the smiles playing above his head.

"I see you were up at the Hall last night," Jim nodded at Sean. "Collected a new face decoration." Sean touched the bruise under his eye self-consciously. "You're wasting your time, you know that?"

"I know you think that," Sean replied. "And I know why, but this is a new era Dad and something's got to give. People are desperate. It's not just the rights of workers but it's the right to work at all now!"

"You're bloody lucky to have work down the wharf son and you want to be careful you don't lose it causing trouble for the bosses. Can't you stay out of it?" Jim's voice was tightening ut his face was a plea for reason. Sean sighed.

"All right you two," Maggie sang. "Time for politics on another night. Look at that baby, she's gone off with the fairies. Let's put her to bed, Syb." The women proceeded to the front bedroom leaving the men to finish off the meal.

"Can I go to the wharf, Grandpa?" George stared keenly at Jim. Jim sighed.

"You will go to the wharf, young George," laughed Sean. "There's almost nothing surer than that!"

George was overwhelmed by the smells and sounds of his new school. Baking wooden-hinged desks, scraping chairs, chalk dust and the combined noise and aroma of twenty-eight children hit him like a wall as his mother led him into his new classroom. He had not attended school before and had arrived a couple of weeks later than start of year so had to join a class already settled at Plunkett Street School, locally known as 'Plunko'. Mr Grant, their teacher, unclasped George's hand from his mother's and bade her goodbye, leading George to a free desk next to another boy with pale hair who smiled at him showing a row of gum and spit.

"Welcome to Plunkett Street, George," said Mr Grant before he returned to the front of the room and resumed drawing the letter 'S' repeatedly on the blackboard. "Copy this down, children," he yelled at the board.

"I'm Bernard," said the boy next to him. "You better do as he says." Bernard raised his eyebrows and started drawing wobbly attempts at the letter 'S' on a slate board in front of him. George lifted the pencil on his desk and moved it across the slate board conscious of the stares from other children but unwilling to look up. He had arrived a long way down the alphabet, he realised. His Ma and now his Uncle Sean had been teaching him to read and write and he was suddenly grateful. Mr Grant praised his writing before he sent the class to lunch break and breathed a private sigh of relief that this late addition to his class could at least use the alphabet.

"You're a Bananalander!" George looked evenly at the boy with red hair and ears like teacup handles who had been sitting across from him in class. He said nothing but the boy wasn't finished with him and followed him into the schoolyard along with a few of his mates who seemed to be enjoying the show. George's new friend Bernard edged away chewing his nails and squinting in the hard midday sun. George noticed that Bernard had a slight limp. "Bananalander, Bananalander," sang the red-haired boy.

"What's a Bananalander?" asked George turning to face the boy who was almost the same size as him. George had a direct and deliberative gaze beyond his years and tended to look at people longer than was polite. 'Don't stare, George!' was one of his mother's favourite sayings but he wasn't staring. He was just looking. Although his question had prompted loud guffaws of laughter from the group of boys around him, his challenger hesitated.

"It's a blasted Queenslander,…what you are!" spurted the red-haired boy.

"Righto," George nodded. "So, whadya' call people from New South Wales?" This caused further raucous laughter from the group of boys who looked to their red-haired representative for an answer.

"Nothin', you don't call 'em nothin'," he said with uncertain hostility.

"Let's think of something," smiled George. "Something real flash." That was how he befriended Reginald 'Bluey' Butler. The group of boys tried for some time over their lunch of bread and butter and apples to come up with rhymes for New South Wales but it was too difficult. They then attempted a series of rhymes for Sydney, largely dependent on the word 'kidney' which no-one particularly liked the sound or taste of. So, they gave it up and tried for a name that they could call themselves as locals. Mr Grant had been talking about local history and the Sydney Cove but they all knew 'cove' meant 'a bloke', so they took it for their own and preceded it with Plunko, as in *the Plunko Coves*. By the end of lunchtime Bluey had elected himself leader and appointed George his Lieutenant and another Woolloomooloo gang was formed.

Bluey lived two streets away from George on Forbes Street above his parents' pub. He had three older sisters and hated girls, largely because they couldn't or wouldn't wrestle. Bernard lived just across the back laneway from George with his parents and two brothers in a rundown weatherboard cottage with a broken roof. Tony, who had neatly oiled and combed hair and wore a smart black tie was Italian and the second son of the greengrocer on William Street. He was the best fed of the gang and provided supplies of aging fruit for the meetings that they held in Judge Lane to discuss the gang's plans and strategies or shoot marbles or play cricket with a piece of fence paling for a bat. Girls weren't allowed in the gang and Bernard was only in because he had had diphtheria and couldn't help being a weakling and he was a pretty good catcher anyway. Edward, or Lump, as they called him was the other standing member, an over-sized, phlegmatic child with poor reflexes but a clown-like capacity to make them all laugh. His dad was dead from what happened to him in the war and he lived with his mum, a laundress, in a room in the St Kilda boarding house near the school. His mum got the widow's pension and took in washing and ironing but they were still dirt poor. They were all poor and so they ran barefoot the daylong but it was only Bernard who had no shoes at all as he needed a special fitting for his limp and there wasn't the money to get him one. The rest of them preferred to be free of their ill-fitting and worn shoes which were usually hand-me-downs and were reserved for special occasions.

"Is your dad dead from the war too?" asked Bluey the day that he first visited George's house after school. They were climbing the fencing of the stables at the rear of the house watching for Harry so they could feed Winnie the horse. Bernard hung upside down from the wooden crossbeam with his pale hair brushing the hay strewn across the floor of the stable, listening intently.

"Nope," said George.

"Where is he then?" Bluey wrinkled his nose and cocked his head as he sought standing balance on the fence.

"He's working in Brisbane," answered George. This is what his mother told him and he didn't question it. Lots of dads were somewhere else 'trying to get work'. But no one wanted to talk about his dad much at home. He sensed there was something he was missing and whatever it was made grownups go quiet and nervy. Particularly around his mum. George hiked himself onto the crossbeam with Bernard and swung himself upside down banging his head against the hard dirt floor beneath the hay, forgetting he was several inches taller than Bernard.

Bluey spat laughter through his fingers while Bernard dropped to his feet next to George who had collapsed in the hay.

"Are y'all right, George?" Bernard's flushed and anxious face looked over George as he lay staring at the spinning sky observing with interest the black dots that swarmed like mosquitos across the pumping blue dome.

Despite the increasing hardships of the Depression, Sybil remained a fleshy, long-limbed woman of impressive stature.

"It's in the blood," Jim observed to Maggie. He genuinely liked his gregarious, mad-haired daughter-in-law the more he got to know her but it was the element of height that she brought to the family that he was most pleased with. Having measured a modest five foot six most of his life, he was deeply satisfied to see George stand taller than the other boys in his class with a strong build and a slow, purposeful nature. "A strapping boy!" he declared at the pub when asked about his grandson. "He's careful too, watchful, like his grandfather." Then he would start thinking about his own sons and quieten down.

George and Jim had formed a natural alliance with the boy shadowing his Grandfather about the house and them both chatting about ships, fishing, the wharves, the new Bridge, swimming, football, cricket, motorcars, anything, as long as it wasn't school or politics which were topics of aversion for one or the other. It had tickled Jim pink when he had reached out a finger to still the habitual shaking of George's right leg on the boy's first evening at the house. Jim had the same nervous habit and it bound them closer.

George was observant and endlessly curious. "What happened to your fingers, Grandpa?" Jim patiently explained the incidents involving zinc slabs and timber loads at the wharves whereby he had lost part of a finger here or there and George considered him the greatest man alive as a consequence and looked forward to losing a finger himself one day.

"He'll need to be told about his father sooner or later, you know" Jim was removing his work boots at the back door and not looking at Sybil or Maggie who sat at the kitchen table in the last light of the evening.

Sybil looked intently into her teacup. "It's a hard piece of news for the boy, and, if you don't mind me sayin', I think his father's earned the right to deliver it himself." Maggie nodded a grim agreement as Sybil went to her room. Several weeks later the letter from Tom arrived. As neither George nor Anne could read well enough Sybil realised that she would have to read it to the children, or at least to George, which really meant that she was back in the position of delivering the news herself so she read the 'blasted letter' silently over a bottle of beer and had a cry. Then she told George in her own words.

"Your father's not coming back to live with us, son." It was a quiet moment alone together in the living room on a Saturday when George brought up the topic of his dad.

"Why?" asked George looking up from his marble collection arranged in careful categories on a rag on the floor.

Sybil drew in a long, slow breath that she eventually and suddenly surrendered. "Because he's a bastard." She quickly added, "I don't want you repeating that love. I'm angry with him because... he's left us." Suddenly, George saw his mother not as young, strong and happy, as he had always thought of her, but as troubled and alone. He remembered that she was a girl. He walked across the room to sit next to her on the sofa and put his arm around her shoulder. As he was still only six years old, this meant he couldn't actually sit and so he leant against her silently and determinedly.

"I'll be 'right, son." He wanted in all his heart for that to be true and from that moment he understood and shared the quiet anger of the house. But in deference to his mother's sensitivity, his father remained 'working in Brisbane'.

Sean wiped the sweat from his eyes as he stared up into the sun and the swinging load of gleaming steel carried toward him by the winch. He gestured to the winch driver and guided the load through the hatch into the ship's hold: "I'm coming down, youse lot!" His gang of packers cleared the space for the sling to land with a deafening clang and within a couple of seconds the load was undone and the swinging hook recoiled and lurching hungrily over the side of the ship seeking the next sling. Along the wharf below, blinding piles of steel beams were gathering in the afternoon sun and truckers and stackers moved among them each with a purpose, busy as ants working disparately but together to keep the hook moving and get the ship out.

They were a gun team of stevedores, experienced men in their prime, known as bulls, and chosen daily by Jim from the sorry hundreds seeking any bits and pieces of work still turning around at Woolloomooloo. These elite wharfie gangs worked loads around at a rate that matched any port in the world. The easy calibration of the team trucking and loading on the wharf, driving the winch and stowing the loads was something to watch. And that was the hatchman's job; to watch. Sean had been stevedoring since he left school at fourteen resisting the urgings of his mother and his English teacher to stay on at school and exploit his natural talents in reading and writing. Instead, he chose to take his place among the working men at the wharf so that he could bring home a pay packet. As a result of his quick eye and reliable nature, Sean won the trust of his workmates and quickly graduated to hatchman. The hatchman worked as the eyes and ears of the men below the deck and on the wharf. Only the hatchman saw the total picture and could stop or start work with the smallest gesture if a hazard presented. Sean's job was to protect the workers, the merchandise and the ship as much as to guide the load.

Above the rattling of the winch and the groaning of the ship against the wharf, Sean could hear his father's familiar shouts of encouragement and denigration. Like a ringmaster at the circus, the foreman never stopped pacing and watching and shouting and directing the whole show. Stopping to discuss problems, gesturing to those out of earshot, conferring with his assistant foreman, the 'panno' or 'pannikin boss', arguing with ships' crew and most importantly perhaps, placating ship-owners. There was never a moment when Big Jim wasn't talking and walking. He was a very different man on the wharf to the man he was at home where the less he was required to say, the better.

Jim's panno, Keith Mackenzie, was known simply as Mac, or Mac the Stack, and the impressive size of the man made the origin of his nickname self-evident. Mac had arms like logs and shoulders that caused him to walk sideways through doorways. He had been a foreman himself for many years working the Darling Harbour wharves until the day his temper broke. That fight went down in the record books as the best entertainment seen along the harbour in a decade. Mac and another giant, a Scandinavian seaman, laying into each other. All hands stopped work across the wharves to watch the two heavyweights battle it out over what issue or insult was never quite clear. They ripped into each other neither able to get the best of the other until they were too exhausted to do more than sway and fall at which point they were bundled into the same ambulance and taken to hospital to be patched up. They shook hands on the way out and that was that, but Mac lost his foreman position as a result and Big Jim asked him to come over to Woolloomooloo and work with him knowing he was a tiger for work and had the respect of the men. He was certainly the best end to any argument and useful to have around the wharves where men were often riled and sometimes desperate. Mac hailed Sean from the wharf as he was guiding the next sling down the hatch.

"Gonna' be a dark'un, mate," his deep voice carried across the deck of the ship and from the groans below him Sean knew the team had also heard. "Smoko after the next sling". Mac adjusted his hat and walked along the wharf to yell the same at the crew loading the aft hatch. A dark'un meant overtime working into the night and sometimes through to rising of the sun, which was not popular with tired men. But these days, working the wharf meant doing whatever the ship owners required or not working at the wharf at all. The depression had seen commercial shipping slow dramatically with plenty of ships laid up so you took any work you could get on the once busy Sydney waterfront and you didn't complain. Even the gun workers with the best connections rarely managed to find more than a couple of days work in a week anymore and the many hundreds of casual wharfies, the Sussex Street men, never got a look in although they haunted the pick-ups each morning in the vain hope of a few hours paid work. They were a sorry sight and reminded you to be grateful for a wage at all, even a wage cut back to the bone.

"At least that will bring us some tea money," Joe Barker, an athletic young bloke friendly with Sean muttered bitterly as he accompanied him down the gangway. "The bastards want their ship out tonight and we just cop it. It's over the bloody fence making us work through. The blasted Union's gone to the pack now the work has dried up. They were supposed to have the ban on the overtime but … here we go again. And no gravy on our wage for doing it. It's a sorry picnic!"

"Better than no work, mate," Sean tried to lighten his mood.

"See, that's exactly what makes me maggoty!" Joe swung to face Sean. "They're using this bloody depression to squeeze us back into the hole we were just peeping out of." As they approached the rest of the gang of twenty odd wharfies taking tea on the slings looking out over the blue glamour of the harbour Joe ceased his talking. He was as smart as a whip and had an interest in politics, that is, Jack Lang's politics and the Waterside Workers Federation politics. Sean had known him since he was a kid and they got on like a bushfire but Joe's loud politics could get them in trouble and Big Jim always had his eye out. There would be no politics in his gang! Big Jim had been through the disastrous strike of 1917 where he had walked off with the rest of them disgusted to be loading wheat on ships bound for Europe when there was hardly enough food for Australians. He then saw the unions crushed and many good wharf workers put out of work and their families starved for principles. Work beats principles, he would say.

Sean understood, as Joe did not, that his father had seen the punitive realities of failed collective action at close range and feared for his own family should there be trouble at the wharf especially as he was almost 'past it' as he would say. Joe's hero, and the hero of the waterfront, the Big Fella', New South Wales' Premier Jack Lang, had re-instated those striking workers from 1917 but did not go as far as supporting the Communists. To Sean, Lang represented the possibility of legislating for a fairer society without fighting in the streets and without radical politics. This had already begun with Lang's widows' pensions, child endowments and worker's compensation. Like many of the wharf workers losing work, income and self-respect in the tightening economy, Sean longed for a fairer world where he would not have to slog his life away by the water for unscrupulous profiteers and for no fair return. Being a gentle soul, he believed this could be achieved without violence. Ironically, that view had so far earned him a number of black eyes. Street Labour meetings, Unemployed Workers and Anti-eviction rallies seemed only reasonable expressions of the despair many were suffering, yet they were frequently broken up with police batons or the crude weapons of the militant New Guard whose young recruits drove their trucks into peaceful Labour meetings and started shoving people around. For these reasons, he and Joe had joined the Australian Labour Army and attended Labour events with lead-filled sticks by their sides to ensure the speakers got a hearing. Sydney had never been so tense. It was as if the electricity recently installed across much of the city had got into the arteries of its citizens and the air was explosive.

As Sean and his gang sweated through the night, Guy and Nick Pace lounged in the smoky back room of Diamond Kate's Palmer Street brothel drinking the grog she sold at double mark-up after the 6pm closing and talking to Willy Lee. Willy was a Chinaman whose family had come out looking for gold in the '90s and never left. They had eventually settled in Surry Hills where Willy grew up and learned to speak like a local unless of course he was talking to the cops at which point he spoke strictly Chinese only. It was the first time Nick had met Willy and he couldn't take his eyes off him trying to reconcile the Chinese face with the broad Australian lingo coming out of Willy's mouth.

"No skiting, mate. This bloke's got the skills and the tools and I know the drum on getting the stuff into the country. Top quality job too. Been done before. The Netherlands. Made a motza. Of course, we need something up front to get us there. And then there's the wait. You know, the old slow boat to China!" Willy's small, black eyes remained focused on the tabletop stained with beer and cigarette burns.

Guy drained the remnants from his glass and rubbed the stubble on his chin as he did some calculations in his head. "So, what are we lookin' at, Will? Keeping it small, just the five of us remember."

"Well," Will screwed his eyes up so you could barely see them, "There's the cost of the passage and production and then there is agreeing the share in the profits. Big risks involved for me and my mate in Canton."

"Yeah, yeah, understood. Leave the distribution to us. You just get it here and we'll take over. We can give you the passage fare and the production costs but we have to make it worthwhile for our backer as well so the profit share has gotta' be reasonable." Willy looked up.

"And what's reasonable?" he asked Guy. His eyes were now wide open.

"Twenty per cent all round, mate. After cost recovery. Nice and easy arithmetic. This way everyone gets an equal cut: you, your mate with the coin-machine, our man with the funds and me and Nick who will be sprinkling new shillings all over Sydney. We're all taking risks here." Willy looked evenly at Guy and then Nick.

"Distribution has gotta' be careful. Gotta' be here and there not unloaded in a heap but it's gotta' be gone before they're awake to it. "

"There's more ways to skin a cat than suckin' its guts out through it's arsehole, mate." Willy looked blankly at Nick suspended on the two rear legs of his chair grinning at his own artfulness.

"Gotta' way with words your little brother," Willy offered.

"Don't you worry about a thing, mate," said Guy. "He's just sayin' we know our business."

The three men agreed a meeting place to arrange for Willy's passage and funds for the counterfeit shillings they were planning to manufacture and import and shook hands. Guy knew that Willy knew enough about the Pace brothers to make good on the deal. He may be Chinese but he had a family to lose just like anyone else. They made their way through the front room of the brothel where a skinny bloke was banging on the keys of an old, out of tune piano and a couple of Kate's molls were dancing a frenetic, squealing quickstep for two coves smoking on the plush sofa in the dim kerosene light. Guy didn't recognize them but understood from the quality of the coats hanging on the wall that they were not locals. He pushed Nick past the girls and the coats into the busy Woolloomooloo night where he handed the door girl a brown envelope. The men parted under the lamp.

"You sure he's dinkum, mate?" Nick grimaced as they walked up Bourke Street. "Not sure about doing business with a Chink." He tipped his hat vaguely at Johnno and his mates who were sitting on a wall outside a dilapidated boarding house.

"Occabot etam?" Johnno hailed them.

"All out, mate." Nick snickered at the old backwards speak still circulating Woolloomooloo. The street kids spoke in codes thinking the coppers wouldn't understand. Kept 'em busy anyhow.

"Don't you worry, Willy's as sharp as a shithouse rat with a gold tooth. He owes me one and I know he's done this before *and* pulled it off. He knows not to mess me around. We can make a motza on this. Spending on the horses, spreading it around, a bit here a bit there. It's eighty percent profit once you put the lousy bit of silver in a shilling." Guy paused and stopped walking as they approached a pile of broken down furniture on the side of the road covered with a few rags and attended by a deeply scarred, malnourished man in his forties. He wore a tattered shirt and stained duds with no shoes on his feet but on his chest were three medals and a Gallipolli Star.

"What's goin' on, mate?" Guy looked over the sorry heap of belongings.

"Evicted again." Behind him stood the dark, dilapidated cottage with boarded up windows and a lonely rat sniffing around an empty garbage tin. Guy reached into his pocket and pulled out a few coins.

"Bastards!" he declared as he passed the coins to the bloke and walked on. Nick doffed his hat.

"Good luck, mate."

"Can't earn an honest living these days, even if you want to. It's a bloody disgrace! The bloke's a bloody veteran" Guy spat. Nick shook his head and they walked in silence each reflecting on their brief and dishonorable war service. They had been quickly discharged for various offences generally to do with offending officers but not before they had the chance to observe better men putting their lives on the line. And for what? To stand like a shag on a rock, motherless broke with only the tin on your chest to comfort you.

The woman that Mrs Bradshaw, Section Manager for Ladieswear at David Jones, saw enter the employment office for interview was not the same woman who in fact walked through the door. Sybil Pace looked the picture of elegant and decorous femininity as she seated herself before the forensic glare of her future employer. She had the dancer's grace and had dressed in her best skirt and jacket with the white cotton shirt she had cut and sewn up herself from a tablecloth. Her unruly hair was plastered down under a fashionable dove-grey cloche hat and she removed her gloves to be sure her wedding ring was displayed. The ring was not lost on Mrs Bradshaw who also noted Sybil's fuller figure with some pleasure. She was looking for someone who could fill a corset for lingerie and married women were a much safer option than single girls who might start illicit 'romantics' with the staff or, worse still, the customers. Sybil's unusual height also gave the impression of physical competence which was more important than most people imagined for a DJs employee standing on their feet all day, up and down ladders, stacking and sorting.

The fact that Sybil was creating an illusion (being both coarser and poorer than she projected) did not in any way detract from her capacity to be a David Jones shopgirl at the splendid new Elizabeth Street store. The illusions of comfort, beauty, wealth and grace were the *raison d'etre* of the department store experience and a fuller figure indicated plentitude at a time when most people were half-starved, even if it were most likely a glandular condition rather than meat and potatoes behind the extra flesh. Sybil, with her cheerful nature and plump smile was an instant hit and, to her surprise, was hired for start the following day to replace a young girl taken gravely and suddenly ill. Her friend Edith Sacks who lived in Woolloomooloo and worked in the haberdashery section had put her forward for the interview as she knew Mrs Bradshaw was caught short for staff. Sybil shook hands lightly with Mrs Bradshaw and strode calmly out of the employment office past the sumptuous furnishings displayed against elegantly draped windows into the mechanical marvel of the caged elevator. She nodded at the uniformed attendant as the doors slid together and they rode in silence to the ground floor. Her heels barely touched the polished marble floor as she floated through the gilt doorways onto busy Elizabeth Street where she could no longer contain herself.

"You bloody beauty!" she exclaimed through gritted teeth, her hands clenched and her eyes wet with tears of relief. As she crossed into Hyde Park she couldn't help but pull her hat from her head and break into a run with her hair streaming after her like a hedge, laughing to herself and attracting curious stares from passers-by. She knew she looked like she had a shingle loose but it didn't matter. She had a job at David Jones! She would have an income after almost six months in Sydney with no work and not a penny to spare. Not much of an income, only one quid and two shillings a week but that was a lot more than she had ever had before, and with every second person in Sydney seemingly unemployed, it meant she was better off than most. She could contribute now and give Maggie half her salary. She knew Tom wasn't doing the right thing, he had never earned regularly as a musician anyhow. Now she could make it right at home and build a life for her and the kids. She slowed to a walk as she approached the centre of the park.

It was late spring in Sydney and the struggling, patchy lawns were a reminder of the unusually dry autumn and winter they had now lived through with the Paces. At the western end of the park work on the ANZAC memorial continued with hammer falls and the shouts of workmen ringing in the wind. At the fountain, two young men sitting in the sun with their slim legs crossed as only girls do watched her pass by and she smiled at them unwilling to imagine how their day might end. She followed the eastern avenue lined with heavy-limbed Moreton Bay figs towards Woolloomooloo passing the statue of Governor Lachlan Macquarie with his right arm aloft symbolizing the expanse of his powers no doubt, but always suggesting to Sybil that he was ready for a round of the Pride of Erin.

It was still early as her interview had taken place at 8 o'clock before the store opened to customers and a flow of people, mainly men in suits, emerged from St James train station as she reached College Street heading for the Domain. Usually, they would disperse for their offices but this morning there was unusual excitement and vigorous discussion as people huddled together over newspapers.

"The bank's buggered!" she heard. "They can't pay out deposits."

There were curses flying about as newspapers swapped hands and she moved next to a middle-aged woman in a smart red dress who was reading intently. The look of panic in her watery blue eyes as she pushed the newspaper at Sybil was frightening. The front page claimed the Government Savings Bank of NSW was insolvent and blamed Lang, just newly elected as Premier for the economic collapse.

"I'm gonna' get me money!"

"Too right!"

Several men headed off at an angry pace towards Martin Place. Only recently completed, the monolithic head office of the Savings Bank of NSW was the pride of Sydney with its four towering columns of flesh-pink granite encasing a marbled hall secured by a forbidding bronze door. The idea that this grand institution was in fact vulnerable shook the nerves of a community already shaken by relentless bad news. Sybil had never had enough money to start a bank account; she kept anything extra in a sock stuck in a shoe but she didn't know if Jim and Maggie would be affected so she quickened her pace home.

The panic set off by this story and ongoing informal reports and rumours encouraged by the anti-Lang conservatives was contagious. Jim had held his ground and refused to withdraw his modest savings convinced by Sean that the bank was as solvent as any and it was a run on the Lang government more than anything. It turned out that the deposited savings of the people of New South Wales were in fact safe but forcing the bank to peremptorily call in loans and recover investments meant its demise. Those who panicked and sold their savings books, often for half of what they were truly worth, took financial blows they could ill afford in the early years of what was to be a long and hard depression.

"Done like a dinner," Sean shook his head as he and Joe Barker stood by speaker's corner on a Sunday and listened to a Labour member recount tales of malicious misinformation put about by conservative forces to dupe the people of New South Wales and to cause the run on the bank.

"They won't stop," said Joe. "Lang's got them scared. He won't pay the Poms their bloodsucking interest and he won't cut wages. Fair enough too, I say. Here, I'll have a turn, mate!" With that Joe was up on the speaker's ladder explaining to the hungry crowd the principles behind Jack Lang's struggle with the federal government.

"They want to cut your wages, they want to increase your working hours, they want to hand Australian money over to the British while we starve. They will balance their blasted budgets over your dead bodies. Lang is the only one with the guts to stop 'em. "

They were lean and anxious faces staring back at Joe. Some of the men had swags at their feet or slung over their arms, itinerant and homeless but enjoying some free entertainment.

"And what makes you so sure, eh? The pollies are all out for themselves!" A bearded man with fierce eyes wearing shoes without socks yelled from the centre of the crowd.

"Who introduced the family benefits? Who speaks out against evictions of families? It's Lang and only him that has the interests of the working men and women at heart. Resist these mooching industrialists and conservatives, the capitalists who are bringing us to our knees!" Joe's face was burning and the crowd was split between hecklers and supporters but he appeared to have run out of steam and made way for another speaker from the Trades Hall.

"What's the point?" he hung his head and Sean followed him as he marched down the hill towards the bay.

"You will find salvation in the Lord, son," the neatly dressed, frail woman with white hair pulled into a hair net crossed herself as they passed.

"Oh for Christ's sake, Ada," Joe flung over his shoulder. "Give it a rest."

George was discovering his inherent flair for music in the Plunkett School percussion band but he had the most fun dancing with his mother and her David Jones' friends in the Pace living room on a Saturday night. For their first Christmas in Sydney, Tom sent them a box gramophone along with several recordings by Duke Ellington, Count Basie, Bennie Goodman and Artie Shaw. They had picked it up at Central Railway station and lugged it home on the tram.

"I can think of better things to do with the money," Sybil had huffed when George helped his little sister open the package on the kitchen table and the one-armed black mechanism emerged. But the children's excitement was irresistible and when they had got it going the rollicking joy of Goodman's rhythms had George swinging his legs and arms in wild abandon. Sybil took up his hand.

"Let me show you how it's done, son."

George followed his mother's lead and was startled to see her legs move at angles he had never anticipated. She pulled him back and forth and he was swept up in the organized chaos of swing and hop. Despite her heavy build, his mother seemed to fly above the floorboards, her spinning skirts unable to keep up with the rotations one way and then the other so that they wrapped her in a moment of inertia at every turn. To see his mother beat gravity and twirl herself into joyous abandon was a vision George would never forget and jazz became forever for him a symbol of freedom.

Mr Jones, who taught the senior year at Plunkett Street School, was so impressed with George's percussion performances that he had offered to teach him the clarinet and George had spent many lunch hours in the cramped 'music room', which was really just an oversized cupboard stuffed with sports gear and stationery, finding his way around the keys and pegs of the clarinet. He accompanied Mr Jones at school concerts once he had the basics mastered and was allowed to take the instrument home on occasion when he would try and play along with Goodman and could only marvel at the fluid wizardry of the great man. Mr Jones had granted George a loan of the instrument for the entire summer holidays and he learned to play *He's Not Worth Your Tears,* his mother's favourite, from start to finish. She would tap her hand on her knee and sing the chorus, "That's why I don't wanna' be told, he's not worth your tears." The sentiment of this song captured the blend of anger and determined resolve George could read in his mother's eyes whenever the topic of his father was raised. The clarinet transformed his anger and his mother's pain into something strong and beautiful and they shared an unspoken pleasure in this song.

George was equally as fascinated by the mechanical aspects of the gramophone as he was by the magical music flowing from its internal horn. He habitually followed the stylus with his eye as it moved almost imperceptibly within the grooves of the 78rpm records transfixed by the capacity of steel and mica to release music from a black disc. It seemed a modern marvel was discovered every day in the new decade with the endlessly faster motorcars, the wonders of electrification, the spread of radio, and now telephone cabling but it was the Harbour Bridge that was Sydney's alone.

At the start of the new school year in 1931, when the arch on the Bridge had finally closed, Mr Grant took George's class on a school excursion to Mrs Macquarie's Chair by way of a lesson in applied geometry. They walked two abreast to the Bay then up the long grassed hill to Mrs Macquarie's Road passing the downhill sweep of the Botanical Gardens on their left and the Domain Baths on their right where Maggie sometimes took George and his sister for a dip on warm weekends. As they passed the Baths the boys craned their necks to view the vertiginous five-story diving tower which the older boys threw themselves from as a mark of manhood. The class was quiet as they reached the tip of the promontory and took in the sweep of blue water and sky interrupted by the gargantuan steel protractor that drew Sydney's two shores together. Still adorned with cranes and cables with ant-like creatures scurrying along its awesome limbs, the Bridge was breathtaking.

"Arithmetic is a wondrous thing, children," Mr Grant's spectacles glowed in the sunshine reflecting off the water. "Geometry built this bridge."

"There's men building it, Sir," Edward 'the Lump' observed.

"Ah yes indeed, Edward. Men working to the laws of geometry. We are looking at the product of ten years of toil, six million rivets and nine lives lost." Mr Grant paused in somber reflection. "But it's a mathematical marvel!"

That evening Sybil listened to George's excited account of his visit to the harbour to see the bridge as she hung up her hat and coat and slipped her feet out of her smart leather heels into her broken down slippers with a sigh of deep appreciation. She had got used to standing around all day smiling at customers, dusting and re-arranging displays, sorting and folding columns of corsets, brassieres, petticoats and other unmentionables so that they could be retrieved and fitted to the widely varying shapes and sizes of women's private bits. She was pleased that her son was so interested in the mechanics of things. It meant he was less interested in music.

"That you, Syb?" Maggie called from the kitchen.

"Ma!" Little Anne came hurtling into the living room and threw herself at her mother. She was now three years old and large boned like her mother and brother. Sybil struggled to fit her onto her hip.

The delicious aroma of rabbit stew emanated from the kitchen and she headed towards it.

"'Lo', Maggie. The rabbitoh's been, has he?"

"Yes, he knocked on the door this morning just when I was thinking we would be having the mutton again. The poor man had come in from Bankstown to sell them… walking all that way! I hope he'll be able to afford the train back tonight."

"Has she been a good girl for you today?" Sybil sat heavily on the kitchen chair with Anne on her lap and began plaiting the fine, dark-blond hair so like her father's.

"She has. She's helped me with the washing and swept up for me, haven't you love?" Anne jumped from her mother's lap and hugged Maggie's legs as she did a lot. Sybil watched and swallowed the urge to call her back. Was it any wonder the child adored Maggie; they spent all week together since she had been working.

"Jim will be home in a bit, he is just across the lane helping with the Radcliffe's roof again. It's a terrible state of affairs in that house with the weather coming in all the time and the three little ones all trying to survive on the susso! You can hear the kids coughing across the Bay! Especially poor Bernard! He's never been well since the diphtheria."

Sybil sighed. "And Sean?"

"'Another one of those 'meetings'," Maggie shook her head disapprovingly as she passed cutlery across the table. "How was the shop today?"

"Oh, the usual," Sybil arranged the knives and forks and pulled George's earlobe as he sat at the table. "Wealthy ladies worrying about how they will fit their big bellies into their fine dresses." She made a face and mimicked the pulling and squeezing and breath holding required to fit a tight corset and they all had a laugh.

"What's so funny?" Jim entered the kitchen. "You having trouble with your unmentionables again, Syb?" George guffawed and Sybil blushed. Maggie's smile faded.

"How did you go love?"

"I dunno'," said Jim removing his cap. "We've patched that blasted roof so many times, there's more patch than roof! I hope it holds for them but there is no keeping out the wet. Bob's been given relief work out at Petersham on the road works. Poor bugger is not fit for that sort of work. But he's got no choice if he wants to keep on the susso. It's a crime the state of that house but they're behind in the rent so they can't ask for repairs. They're too scared."

The adults exchanged looks aware that George was keenly interested in this conversation pertaining to his friend Bernard's family. He and Bernard had become close mates and Bernard spent as much time at the Pace house as he did at home. Maggie and Sybil were always slipping food into the young boy's mouth knowing he got little at home and feeling the need to fatten his thin arms and try to get some weight on him so he was not so vulnerable to bullies and germs. But there was so little to spare.

"Now tell me about this miraculous bridge," Jim sat at the table next to George and took his pipe from his pocket. "It' d wanna' be good with what we're paying for it!" Jim was in a good mood despite the Radcliffe's because it was a Friday night and the horses ran on Saturdays. He had enough change in his pocket for a beer and a flutter at *the Anchor*.

The Firm Anchor was the nearest pub to the Pace home and conveniently situated between the wharf and the house, so it was almost unavoidable that Jim and Sean would stop in for a glass of neck oil after a hard day's slog. Unlike the bigger pubs on the waterfront frequented by sailors, ship's crews as well as passengers from cruise ships, *The Firm Anchor* was strictly for locals offering two modest rooms adjoined by a timber bar. Only Tooth's Ale was on tap and aside from rum, whisky and gin, there were sodas stored in the ice-box in case of the rare occasion a lady dropped in for refreshment in the 'lounge' which was distinguished from the public bar by a picture of the King, a table and four padded chairs.

Mr and Mrs Henry O'Brien lived above the bar and shared the duties of serving thirsty men until the six o'clock cut off. The floorboards were laid with fresh sawdust every morning and by end of day were littered with butt ends, spilled grog and worse, if Henry were too slow to see a patron about to throw a seven. As the rule was you had to be standing to get a drink, Henry had obligingly installed a railing running along the bar at waist height for the unsteady to tie their belts to. Jim and Sean habitually stopped in for refreshment and a yarn with Henry or his patrons but only on days they had work. 'No work, no grog' was a shared understanding between them and these drinking days were fewer each week as the depression ground on. Except, of course, on Saturdays. Saturdays were for drinking and horses and *The Firm Anchor* was always packed.

Roy Davies was the SP bookmaker at the *The Firm Anchor* each Saturday and he held court in the rear corner of the public bar near the door spilling into 'piss alley' as it was locally known where he could take tickets from his runner lads who brought him bets from local households, usually women who wouldn't be seen dead at the pub. Roy was a compact, well-groomed man always in a suit and tie but particularly well kitted-out on the Saturday with his button down waistcoat, braces, cuffs and highly polished shoes one of which he could prop on his knee in order to observe the goings on behind him, he claimed. Although he was a hairdresser by trade, he earned more from his Saturday ledger. Starting Prices were published in the *Herald* and Roy took bets and distributed tickets on the basis of these prices. If the prices changed at the course, it was next to impossible for the bookmaker to know unless he had a man on the track and a method for communicating the odds across the miles. Some bookers had a system of flag waving and a motorcar running to and fro but Roy just followed form. He only took bets he thought he had a chance on and he was usually right.

Harry watched out for Roy on the street corner most Saturdays to earn a few bob to supplement what he made with his horse and cart. He was never really sure what he was watching out for since the only cops that ventured to *the Anchor* seemed to be placing bets with Roy. Anyway, he watched. Two less likely cobbers were difficult to imagine with Roy done up like a sore toe and Harry rough as bags in his old woolen duds that seemed to have an extra pair of knees, darned shirt and workman's boots. They always shared an ale after the day was done before closure and talked horses. It was an interest that spanned all the distinctions that breeding and opportunity imposed between them and it pleased Roy to know the small change he paid Harry each Saturday filled his horse's feedbag.

"Been a good day then?" Harry accepted the beer Roy passed him gratefully. There was still an hour before closing time and Roy looked happy but then his expression never changed. He had a wry smile imprinted on his face like it had been ironed on. It made him hard to read which was an advantage in his trade but it made Harry nervy sometimes.

"Not really sure I'm any use to ya', Roy," Harry sipped on the cool beer. "Seems like the coppers are on your side." Roy responded to his wheezy, uncertain laugh with a slight inclination of his head. In truth it had been an ordinary day with no particular swing in his favour but he had more than covered his costs and he always enjoyed being the centre of attention at least for a day.

"Everything's Jake as long as they're winning, mate." Roy leaned closer to Harry as they stood propped up against the bar. "If they don't win, the party's over in a flash." Roy's smile firmed, the hardened white flecks of saliva in the corners of his lips indicated the day had been long. He drained his glass. "Been meaning to have a chat about that. If the bastards go me, I'll need a ring-in."

Harry scratched his neck. "You mean me?"

"You won't get bagged, mate. It'll be a fine, that's all. I'll cover it. And I'll make it worth your while. Whaddya' reckon?"

"I dunno', Roy," Harry screwed his face in confusion. "Why can't you just make sure they win?"

"'Cos' they wouldn't know a good horse from a bar of soap and I can't read the stars so, sooner or later, they are going to lose and then they might get snaky. Have a think about it. You could earn yourself a bit each week for the risk. Help keep that fine mare of yours goin'." Roy ordered two more beers. "You're draggin' the chain mate, it's half past five." Harry skulled the remnants of his glass and focused with everyone else in the pub on downing as much grog as possible before Henry rang his bell.

. . .

When the eviction notice was served on Bernard's family in the winter of 1931, they were given seven days to vacate their crumbling cottage across the rear lane from the Pace residence. Bernard Radcliffe, member and wicketkeeper of the Plunko Coves, George's best mate and nearest neighbor was to be put out on the street because the family had fallen behind with the rent trying to make ends meet on the princely sum of nine shillings a week, three shillings per child, provided as sustenance relief. The roof of their weatherboard house was so disintegrated over the living room that the family had erected a tarpaulin to keep out the weather but Sydney delivered fearsome winter storms and rain settled like a blanket over the city for seven days. Great Pacific rollers lunged bad-temperedly at the beaches reclaiming great swathes of sand otherwise hurled by a maddened wind through the arched colonnade of the new Bathing Pavilion at Bondi Beach. The weather kept everyone indoors except the homeless who huddled in caves along the beach cliffs while others found doorways and bridges. Eventually, many headed out for the shanty-town at La Perouse seeking to live in a tent or under a piece of iron sheeting rather than in the rain. For a third of the population now without jobs, despair was becoming a way of life and the city was awash with the implications.

"That's why rich people live on hills," Jim noted as a dirty river ran down William Street and flushed the streets and lanes of Woolloomooloo.

"I declare this meeting closed!" The Party Secretary was a portly bloke with a pair of reading specs that he would wave around, prop on various items of clothing, then mislay and occasionally, with great emphasis, place on his nose to read from some document pertaining to the business of the Communist Party of NSW. He had just chaired a meeting of the Unemployed Worker's Movement in Wolloomooloo. Most of the business of the evening had been organising the associated Anti-eviction Committee to attend a series of scheduled evictions in the area over the next few weeks.

Joe and Sean edged their way out of the crowded, smoke-choked hall into the glistening night. Joe was in a good mood.

"See what I mean? This is more than a few radicals like me mate. This is a movement of workers with no work. What is a worker with no work, Sean? What does he mean? This is a chance to change the meaning of work, who works for who, who gets a fair share." Joe was almost skipping along the pavement with his hands in his pockets and his narrow shoulders hunched against the cold night. Sean could not remember seeing Joe so happy and it struck him as strange that from all the trouble and strife that people were suffering as a consequence of this depression there should emanate this kind of ideological glee.

"I'm on for the anti-eviction team, mate. I can't stand by and watch people thrown into the street anymore but Communism is not up my street. I'm not political."

"You will be," Joe smirked.

"Even Lang is against the Communists, Joe!" Sean stopped. "I thought he was your hero." He watched Joe's smirk harden.

"He's stopped too short," Joe looked up at the yellow moon sailing between the clouds over St Comicals as the local church was known. "He's part of a broken system. One man can't fix that." They had reached the house on Palmer Street where Joe was boarding along with several other men and a family of four who were crushed into the front room. Even the sorry looking kitchen had a boarder in it and residents cooked what food they could in their rooms on small gas rings like campers in their own lives which had become uncertain and tenuous.

Jim was still up when Sean let himself in the front door sitting in the living room in the dark with his pipe glowing orange.

"'Lo, Dad," Sean placed his cap on the hook in the hall. "You're up late."

"Waiting for you."

"Oh yes?" Sean sat on the sofa. "Are we out of kero?"

"No, but I can see in the dark," Jim chuckled and reached for the bottle on the table in front of him. "I saved you a beer."

"Cheers," Sean could smell that his father had already had a few and braced himself as he sipped on the froth.

"Been out with the Marxists again?"

"I'm not a communist, Dad."

"I'm glad to hear it."

"And why? Why are you glad? A lot of what they say is only fair. There's no work, Dad. People are losing their homes. Why, if it weren't for Sybil earning too, we might ourselves be close to eviction. Maybe they're right. Maybe it's the whole bloody system that has to change." Sean hung his head and stared at the furniture taking shape around him as his eyes adjusted to the darkness.

"It will change, it's changing all the time. Not always for the better but eventually, even misery changes. A depression has an end, you know. I grew up in one. When the wheat prices bottomed out and the drought killed everything anyway, people were destitute. The nineties were bad, very bad, son."

"And it's happening again! Doesn't that say that there's a bigger problem? That the system's broken"

"Flawed, yes," said Jim. "Badly flawed, but the system we have is open to change. Communism... is like religion. It knows everything. Has all the answers." Jim waved his pipe dismissively. "My father was a religious man. He couldn't help it but it blinded him to things. There were things he couldn't even think about and one of those was me marrying outside his church." He paused searching for the right words to share with his favourite son in the darkness. "I don't like a system that rules out all other possibilities. Communism has tickets on itself, that's all I'm sayin'. It's a Furphy. And it will do you no good." Sean could make out Jim's shape now and slapped his knee affectionately.

"It's all right, Dad. I'm only supporting the Anti-eviction Committee. I'm not going to Moscow."

"Hmmphh," Jim drew long on his pipe. "Never trust a man with all the answers son. And that goes for an ideology too." Sean kicked his boots off and leaned heavily back into the sofa. "Now, if you need a hand at an eviction, I'm still tidy with the gloves." Sean smiled quietly to himself.

"Well as a matter of fact, the Radcliffe's are to be out on Friday."

The rain had stopped by the end of August but clothes still smelt musty and the drains flowed reluctantly in Woolloomooloo. The storm water had carried refuse from streets and yards into the bay and bottles, branches and worse bobbed against the idle wharf. Raucous cries of squabbling seagulls substituted for the rattling chains and hails of men working absent ships. At the back of the Pace home, twenty odd people stood about in the morning sun watching the two bailiffs carry out the Radcliffe's sorry furniture and place it in the laneway while two police officers observed. Sean and Jim stood by Bob Radcliffe and his wife and children as their frayed mattress landed with a dusty gasp on the pavement. Mrs Radcliffe was holding Bernard's hand crying quietly and still wearing her apron which now seemed presumptuous inferring there was a house to care for. Bob and several others had tried reasoning with the bailiffs who repeated that they were only following court orders. The coppers explained their presence as 'merely precautionary'.

The bailiffs struggled with a large, unsteady timber cabinet that was so oversized it had been left in the house by the previous tenants but they insisted it had to go anyway. It had to be angled out of the front door on its side and as it weighed a ton the bailiffs were sweating rivers trying to get it into the street. Not a man would lift a finger to help, not even the coppers, and so having tied a rope around the cabinet, the bailiffs gave one almighty heave and the cabinet creaked and collapsed into a pile. Even Bob Radcliffe had to laugh.

"Wouldn't it?" he asked.

The red-faced bailiffs collected the pieces of cabinet from the doorway and silently continued to empty the house. Once they had completed the job and were conferring with the coppers on the far side of the laneway from the Radcliffe's house, the crowd moved. An apparently idle and purposeless gathering of men and women, young and old, suddenly took up a piece of furniture each or a large piece between them and carried it all right back inside. They crowded the front hall and the rear doorway saying nothing, going nowhere. The bailiffs watched on helplessly, turned their backs for a quick chat with the coppers and then drove away in their empty truck. The coppers walked off towards Darlinghurst with grim faces. Inside the house sudden cheer broke out and a stunned Mrs Radcliffe sat precariously on her kitchen chair and wept.

That was not the end of trouble for the Radcliffe family as all three boys developed terrible coughs which did not improve even as the spring weather softened the bite from the wind blowing from the south and through the Radcliffe's bare sitting room with its gaping roof. The Radcliffe boys shared a mattress infested with lice and ate only what Mrs Radcliffe could put together from the scraps she could buy with a few pence a day. Mr Radcliffe had gone south to Woollongong looking for a bit of factory work when Bernard collapsed at his school desk after a violent coughing fit and was taken to hospital in an ambulance.

As Bernard remained in hospital for several weeks, Mr Grant offered to take George and his mates to visit him . It was after school when they walked across the Domain to Sydney Hospital on a bleak and blowy day in October. George, Bluey, Edward and Tony, who carried an orange for Bernard from his dad's shop, accompanied Mr Grant through the stone arches into the long dormitory heavy with the sweet, chemical stench of iodoform. A lady dressed like a white nun lead them past the rows of beds until they stopped at a bed under a window where Bernard lay heaving with pneumonia like a broken toy smiling nevertheless in his gummy fashion.

"G'day," he moved his pale hand but did not sit up. The bed was too high for the boys to sit on but they leant on the blankets and prompted by Mr Grant, they told Bernard about the Bridge and the big opening ceremony that was coming up in the new year and that they hoped he would be well enough to come with them as there would be cakes and fireworks and brass bands and soldiers. Bernard smiled but said little. George observed that his friend's skinny frame made little impression on the blankets pulled over him. He could not help but recall Bernard's fascination with magic tricks, particularly the game he loved to play in which he made a marble disappear by pushing upturned cups around a table. And here he was, performing the ultimate trick and disappearing before their eyes.

As they were leaving, George grasped Bernard's spidery little hand with both of his and pressed it to his forehead for a silent moment leaning his face into the bedclothes and blinking back the hot tears. Each of the boys swallowed hard and stared at the antiseptic white-tiled floor. When George raised his head, he looked steadily at his friend and said, "Be seein' yer', Bernie. Maybe the next meeting, eh?" But George knew without knowing how he knew that Bernard would no longer be a member of the Plunko Coves. He knew that his kind little friend had been swallowed by a giant stone building, taken by mysterious white nuns, by strange enemies named diphtheria and pneumonia, by a leaking house. George felt angry but he did not know where his anger should be directed. Angry because Bernard was the weakest of their gang, the easiest to bully or snatch away with his skinny, uneven legs and his pitiful ribs. George had often protected Bernard from other, bigger boys by simply standing in front of him but he was powerless against these conspiring and ruthless forces of man and nature that made Bernard's family dirt poor and squeezed the life from his wheezing chest. The group of boys and their teacher walked home in silence down the grassy hill as the light waned and thousands of flying foxes departed the trees in the Botanical Gardens forming a northerly trail across the gloaming like a giant cameo necklace.

They got the news of Bernard's death on Melbourne Cup day and it was his anger that kept George from crying. He was unresponsive as his Grandma hugged him after her conversation with poor Mrs Radcliffe. His sister, Anne, stared at him with her huge, apprehensive eyes, fearful of what he might do but he did nothing. She could always tell when her brother was angry and made sure to keep out of his way but this was a cold anger that she did not recognize.

"How about you go and get your Grandad from the pub, son?" Maggie asked. "The race will be done by now and if he doesn't come home soon, he will be rolling down the blasted hill."

Every man and his dog had bet Phar Lap for the Melbourne Cup in 1931. The horse of humble origins that had torn home at every race for three years was a sure thing and you couldn't get decent odds anywhere except at *The Firm Anchor,* that is. Roy offered worthwhile odds for the champion on the basis that the horse's luck was running out and he was handicapped out of sight.

"He's dodged a bullet this year already, I reckon he's on the slide. I'm not sayin' he's not a marvel. It's just a matter of form." The nation sat in stunned silence as Phar Lap came home in eighth place and Roy shook his head sadly as he collected winnings from every man in the crowded pub. "It's a crying shame."

It was Jim who staggered home with tears in his eyes once George told him about Bernard on the pavement at the door of the pub as the deflated crowd spilled out at 6 o'clock. George held his Grandad's heavy hand, comforted by the roughened stumps of fingers and the familiar smell of the hops. "Poor soul," Jim sniffed as he rubbed George's hand compulsively. "Poor bloody soul."

The Ceremony for the opening of the Sydney Harbour Bridge on Saturday March 19, 1932 was the most exciting day of George's short life. Finally, after a decade of construction, the grey marvel was ready to go. Tested with the weight of many hundred vehicles, it only required a blessing from the Premier Jack Lang himself before it was open for traffic. The whole city threw off its depression for a day and over a hundred thousand Sydney siders made their way from both the north and the south of Sydney to be able to come together as one city on the 320 000 tons of steel now linking its two shores. The family made a day of it and took George and Anne early to Dawes' Point to get a good spot along the approach to the bridge. There they could see the parades of marching and mounted infantry, as well as the motorcade of officials, some in dark business suits and others dressed in elaborate military uniforms with feathered helmets and golden sashes across their chests.

"Is that the Kaiser?" asked George when the Governor General passed by. Sean bleated with laughter.

The amplified announcements of the King's message were passed along from spectator to spectator as the ceremony at the centre of the bridge got underway.

"I am pleased, blah blah…, the people of Sydney, blah, blah…" Sean was repeating what he overheard when suddenly there was a commotion on the bridge as one of the NSW mounted infantry's horses broke ranks. At first, everyone thought the horse had got a fright but then the officer in the saddle drew his sword, dug his heels into his mount and charged the white ribbon meant for the Premier to cut. He yelled something about the decent citizens of NSW as he slashed the ribbon before a gaggle of police rushed at his rearing horse and pulled the officer to the ground.

"Well, I never," said Maggie. "What a kerfuffle!" For a moment, the large crowd of people stood silent and stunned. The offender who turned out to be an ex-military and member of Sydney's brutal New Guard, was arrested and taken from the scene in a motorcar. The crowd jeered as he passed.

"Off to the giggle house for him, I expect," said Jim. "Mad as a meat axe!"

The ceremony resumed after someone retied the ribbon and Lang snipped it with a wry glance at his nemesis, the Governor of NSW, Sir Philip Game, who stared determinedly into the spaces between the riveted girders for the remainder of the speeches. Once the formalities were over, the bridge was cleared of the outraged official party and the real parade of colourful floats, marching bands and costumed dancers began. The clouds parted as people flowed after the parade crawling like ants across their new bridge onto the rail and tram tracks along its edge and down around its giant pylons on either side then back again, enjoying the marvel of crossing the harbour in less than an hour on your own two feet. Below the bridge boats of all shapes and sizes sailed to and fro, waving flags and scarves in delight at the spectacle. George sipped on lemonade and chewed cheese and tomato sandwiches as his head rolled about on his shoulders taking in the gargantuan girders that seemed to move as he did in dizzying overlays of angles. Everything was moving, the bridge seemed to shift above them in the harsh sunlight, the crowds weaved in and out of the bridge supports and the harbour itself was swollen with tossing craft. Sybil held his forehead a little later on as he vomited into Jim's hanky. As he clutched his mother's hand, all he could think about was Bernard's gummy smile.

Willy Lee had been similarly unwell, gripping the ship's side as they lurched their way home through the heads earlier on that memorable day. He was accompanying his Canton cargo of brown paper rolls stored below deck in a locked crate that he had visited with nervous frequency over the two weeks of the passage. He had been away for almost three months orchestrating the production of the gleaming Australian shillings each marked 1930 and as close to the real thing as you could get. The only imperfection Willy could spot was a slightly accentuated bend in the standing leg of the emu holding one side of the Australian coat of arms. It was so slight a difference he wasn't sure that he wasn't imagining it. In any case, he was confident that he had done his end of the deal and looked forward to delivering the stock and receiving his remuneration. As the ship pitched its way into the relative calm of the harbour lit orange by the rising sun, Willy wiped his pale and wet face and promised himself he would never make the trip again. He cursed the Pace twins as another wave of nausea forced his head into the bucket at his feet.

Two days after Willy Lee had chundered his way through the heads, the Pace twins were tailing a bad debt on behalf of Roy Davies. Roy had sent for them on collection day once his debtor failed to show.

"He's into me for a full pony and I can't carry that so I want you to get it back. The bastard was supposed to be here this morning with ten quid down payment. He's done his dash with me!" Roy's fixed smile seemed more menacing when he had money troubles and a Monday often brought trouble. Most punters were small time placing bets of a few pence and occasionally lashing out with a shilling. These debts or winnings were almost always resolved on the day or else by Monday morning if a credit agreement was not in place. Like all bookies, Roy encountered a runner every now and then and that's when the Pace twins were required.

They were sitting in the small kitchen of Roy's flat in Kings Cross set above his cupboard-sized barber's shop opening onto Darlinghurst Road. As he was a small man, the cramped dimensions of his work and living spaces were adequate for him but challenging for the burley twins who squeezed their legs together under the kitchen table as they waited for Roy to pour the tea. Through the open window they could hear the tram rattling through the Cross and the spiel of the grocer spruiking apples to passersby. Roy turned between the ice-box, the kitchen dresser and the table arranging his tea implements without lifting his feet so constricted was the space. As usual he wore a neatly ironed shirt buttoned to his neck with his clipped hair oiled to perfection. Nick noted his trim nails and feminine hands as he poured from an enamel pot with a green horseshoe imprinted on the side.

"He's not a big bloke, about average size so I don't expect he'll be much trouble for you. He's about forty and a bit taller than me with dark curly hair. Always wears a black cap. I can give you the address he gave me but that's all the drum I have on him other than his name." Roy watched his dainty teacups disappear into the fleshy, battle-scarred hands of the Pace brothers who drained the contents in two slurps. "Yeah, you boys'll be right."

"Twenty-five quid's worth a stroll to Surry Hills, eh Nick? We'll get our usual commission?"

"When I get my money, you'll get yours', boys." And so the twins walked to Surry Hills on a cloudy Monday afternoon to stand over a Bill Stevens of 27 Forster Street.

"Ya' reckon Roy's a horse's hoof?" Nick looked sideways at Guy as they made their way down William Street.

"Nah, do you?"

"Well he hasn't got a missus and his shirts are always ironed so something's out of kilter in my book."

"Just so long as he pays up, it's not our business who irons his shirts. You've got a missus and she's never ironed anything!" Nick nodded in acknowledgement and walked in contemplative silence for a few minutes.

"Just so long as he doesn't put the hard word on me, that's all. I'll job him one no questions asked if he does!" Guy laughed and shook his head.

"It's all right, princess. You'll be safe with me around to look out for your pretty arse." They jostled each other along the footpath of Palmer Street heading up the hill towards the Foster Street address. When they arrived, they found a narrow, cream-coloured terrace house with peeling paint and a broken iron-lace balcony. A blind was drawn over the front window with the solid timber door shut to the street. They walked nonchalantly past the house and stepped into the nearest laneway.

"He's got to go in or come out sooner or later. We'll do the usual routine ok?" Guy looked up and down the sorry laneway with a couple of stone cottages on one side and badly patched iron fencing on the other. The lane was bare of life and littered with broken glass, fence palings, window frames, all broken. These laneways were essential to allow the night man to take away the human waste from the outhouses of these simple homes but were otherwise generally inhabited only by children or criminals.

"I'll wait here."

Nick returned the way they had come and leant against a wall a couple of doors from the target taking in the brief shafts of sunlight peering between rolling grey clouds. So, the brothers held positions either side of the house, one in view, the other hidden, as was their usual technique. Within an hour the front door opened and a bloke in a black cap stepped briskly into the street heading towards Guy who was smoking in the laneway. Nick skipped quickly after him and called out as he approached.

"Hey, Bill!" Once the bloke turned his head, it was on. He ran as they knew he would straight into the arms of Guy Pace as he stepped out of the laneway and into his prey.

"Hello sunshine," Guy beamed. "Roy asked us to drop in on ya'.'" Guy hauled Bill Stevens back into the laneway where Nick joined them ready for a parly.

"I'm getting his money! I'm gettin' it now." Guy landed a blow right in his guts just to shut him up. "Too bloody late. Where were you this morning, eh?" Bill Stevens was bent over clutching his guts and panting so that Guy didn't see his upper hook until it had already made contact with his jaw. As he staggered backwards, Stevens turned on Nick who was staring stupidly at Guy and got him in a headlock. As he was slamming Nick's head into the stone wall, Guy recovered and grabbed him around the throat from behind with a furious roar. He tore him off his brother and tried to stranglehold him but Stevens twisted and freed himself turning on Guy with his fists in front of his face.

"Come on then, you bastard. Let's see what you've got." As he skipped on the pavement Nick kicked his legs out from under him and then they held him between them while Guy smashed his teeth with the knuckleduster he had pulled from his coat.

"You fucking bastard!" Guy's face was flushed purple with rage as he bashed Stevens' skull until Nick intervened.

"That's enough, mate," Nick pulled Guy off the moaning Stevens whose mouth was now a bloody and ill-defined mess. Nick reached into Steven's jacket and pulled a worn brown wallet from the inside pocket. He turned it inside out and collected the few coins that fell from it before dropping it in the gutter in disgust.

"That's just a taste," Guy spat at the prostrate Stevens. "I'll be back tomorrow if Roy hasn't got his money and next time I won't be so gentle." A curtain relaxed in the window of one of the cottages in the laneway.

"Let's go," Nick grabbed Guy's coat and pulled him out of the laneway. Guy was rubbing his chin as they walked briskly down the hill. "The bastard got me one."

Nick felt the top of his throbbing head gingerly checking for blood. "There's gotta' be an easier way to make a crust."

Jim and Harry were turning soil in the morning sun in the patch of dirt across from the stables where they were trying to cultivate vegetables. Mainly spinach, beans, carrots and the odd tomato that managed to grow in the poor piece of earth that Harry dug with horse manure when he could remember to. Neither was much of a gardener which had surprised Jim as Harry had once had a bit of land down Camden way which he had tried to farm. He had left it behind many years before when his missus died but the land he claimed had been useless. Too much clay in it for digging and not enough feed for sheep. Still, with his talent for growing vegetables, Jim doubted Harry would ever have made a farmer and wondered why he had even tried.

Suddenly, Sean came hurtling through the back door of the Pace home nearly pulling it from its hinges.

"Dad!"

"What is it?" Jim stood up and shaded his eyes from the sun leaving a smudge of dirt across his brow.

Sean was waving a newspaper at him. "Take a look. Take a bloody look!"

Jim read the giant black letters plastered over page one of the *Daily News*: "Lang Dismissed."

"Stone the flamin' crows!" He continued reading the article accompanying the headline rubbing his chin and his head as he read, steadily smudging himself black.

"What's up?" Harry stood by waiting for Jim to explain.

"Lang's gone," Sean offered. "The Governor dismissed him from office yesterday."

"He can't do that! Can he?" Harry looked from Jim to Sean bewildered and outraged but uncertain exactly what part of it so outraged him.

"He's the King's man, mate. I reckon that means he can do what he bloomin' well likes! And now we will have another bloody election!"

"Strike a light!" Harry shook his head. Nobody liked an election. Too much yakking and always trouble.

"It's a bloody insult to all Australians!" Sean was fuming and unable to stand still in his agitation. He paced up and down with his hands thrust in his trouser pockets.

"You mean News South Welshmen, don't you? Can't see how anyone else would care much about Jack Lang." The derision in Jim's voice expressed the disillusionment of many who had once supported the Big Fella, or the Red Wrecker, as he was know by the other side of the political spectrum. The Lang Plan had not created jobs or stopped the evictions and now his own party had split in two over his policies.

"Just the same," Sean's head was vibrating left and right with disbelief, "you don't dismiss a Premier elected by the people because it suits the bloody King!" He turned abruptly and headed down the yard for the laneway. "I'm gonna' find Joe."

Jim and Harry shared a worried glance, "Oh, well." Jim bent back to the dirt and unearthed a carrot that was bent like a boomerang. They stared silently at it.

"What are we doing wrong?"

As it turned out, Joe was busy getting his face kicked in by the size ten boot of Constable Samuel Long at the battle of Union Street, Redfern on the day that Lang was dismissed. While Australia was not formally at war in 1932, domestic violence had broken out between the state, represented by police supporting the rights of landlords, and the growing unemployed represented by themselves and organized by the Unemployed Workers Movement. At first, the UWM had organized passive resistance to the increasing forced evictions of unemployed families with their members picketing the offices of the agents representing the landlords. Joe and Sean had done plenty of that along William Street, even enjoying the name calling, sloganeering and relaying with other members who were now calling each other comrades and ensuring that there was no peace for the agents as they went about their business harassing the jobless. In the evenings, the windows of these same offices were not so passively smashed by rocks hurled from the darkness. The police, too had held a calm vigil over evictions unwilling to interfere in what had seemed a civic matter, until the civic got organized, that is. As the numbers in the UWM and the affiliated Communist Party swelled, propelled by long-term joblessness, poverty and the dismal failure of Lang's 'moderate solution', the government, the newspapers, the landowners and the Colonial Secretary lost their nerve and their patience. The result was uglier than anyone had envisaged.

On the day of Lang's dismissal, Joe was one of twenty-three men of the UWM occupying 43 Union St, Redfern, home of Mr Ian MacGregor, returned serviceman, his wife and five children. The family themselves were sheltering with neighbours as the bailiffs and the police were expected any minute and the two-storey terrace brick house had been barricaded so that it was almost as difficult to get out as it was to get in. Not that Mrs McGregor really wanted to get back in with all those burly men having settled in for weeks now. It was no longer a home so much as symbol of the rights of the poor. A red rag had been tied to the end of a broomstick and lashed to the railings of the first floor balcony that had been piled with barbed wire. The makeshift flag moved reluctantly in the light breeze and a gang of Magpies picked over the overflowing rubbish bin in the front yard as the men shared tobacco, drank tea and waited.

Sean's rage at the dismissal of the Premier drove him like a spinning top through the streets of Woolloomooloo, Darlinghurst and Surry Hills. He needed to see Joe. He went directly to the Palmer Street boarding house and knocked on the door to Joe's room. As he was staring dumbly at the familiar scarlet letters painted across the door …*according to need,* one of Joe's neighbours called across the hallway.

"He's not here. Hasn't been home for a couple of days."

"Do you know where he is?"

"He said he was going to Redfern. Protesting!"

It was then that Sean remembered the McGregor family eviction and he started running. He crossed busy William Street, dodging between the smart black motorcars, old carts and bicycles, skipping over the dusty pit of the road works where they were re-laying the tram tracks now it was the widest road in Sydney. Joe had told him about Jim McGregor a returned serviceman with a wife and five children who had been unemployed for almost a year and well behind on the rent. The family had been served and were to be evicted any day.

Daytime drunks spilled from the door of the 50/50 Club in Forbes Street to the strains of a tinkling piano and Sean dodged around them as they blinked and swayed like grotesque tilting dolls in the morning light. He slowed his pace as he climbed the hill past the school aware of the clattering voices of girls taking morning break and headed on past the green gates of the old Gaol. Now Sydney Tech, the once formidable Gaol was overlooked by Darlinghurst Police Station squatting like a square-eyed witch with its brick roundhouse and pointy slate hat. He resisted the impulse to spit on the stone steps out the front and hurried across the intersecting roadways of Taylor Square. He took a turn to the right and headed up Crown Street unwilling to approach Riley where even in the mornings, the girls were hanging in doorways like pretty spiders with their sulky minders tracking the streets for trouble or prey.

Sean worked his way through the back streets of Strawberry Hills with its odd wooden cottages built rough and leaning up against each other like broken down drunks. As he hurtled across Redfern Park, he heard the unmistakable sound of distant gunfire and picked up his pace although his legs were losing their will and his lungs groaned. He knew the Anti-eviction Committee were barricading the McGregor house and expected Joe was in the thick of it.

When Sean finally reached Union Street the gunshots were quiet and the still hissing crowd over two hundred strong had parted to let the procession of ambulances make their way to and from the front yard of the embattled home. Police motorcars were lined up either side of the property dripping with eggs, scratched with knives or rocks with one vehicle sporting a pile of fresh horse manure on the bonnet. It was clear whose side the locals were on.

Sean pushed his way to the front of the crowd, his lungs still aching with the exhaustion of the long run. The terrace house was in ruins with the doors and windows smashed in and split sandbags intended as barricades spilling onto bloodied floors strewn with rocks, bullet shells, crude weaponry and broken crockery. A policeman was slashing at the rope that fixed the broomstick to the side railing of the first-floor balcony from which hung the limp, red cloth. Plumes of smoke rose from inside the first floor and the fire truck could be heard approaching. A line of police officers stood between the crowd and the property ensuring no one entered as the clean up proceeded. They wore disheveled uniforms and bore the cuts, bruises and bad tempers of those recently embroiled in a violent struggle. A young Constable shoved Sean back as he tried to pass into the house.

"Get out of it!" he growled as Sean stumbled backwards, exhausted.

The crowd continued to taunt the police officers but it was clear who had won the day. Sean watched in furious impotence as a colleague that he recognised from of the Anti-eviction Committee, Eugene Peters, was stretchered out of what remained of the front door. He was dead or unconscious with a bloody bandage around his bare chest and a face barely recognisable. Sean struggled to breath as his fists clenched and his head shook uncontrollably in a paralysis of rage and exhaustion. Another fellow who Sean didn't recognise was marched past him in handcuffs, bleeding from the mouth, cut across one eye and limping badly.

"Have you seen Joe Barker, mate?" He called but the fellow didn't hear him.

"Where are they taking them?" He demanded of the young Constable.

"Back to bloody Moscow, I hope," answered the Constable.

"Are there many left inside?" The Constable ignored him.

"These bastards won't tell you nothing, mate. They're up to their armpits in blood and guts. Been shooting away like there's no tomorrow at blokes just trying to keep a family's roof over their head."

The old bloke next to Sean was clearly riled, rubbing his long chin ferociously. "You oughta' be ashamed of yourself, ya blasted mongrel!" He shook his finger and the crowd responded with more of the same.

"Ya' blasted dogs! Doing the dirty work of the blasted landlords, shame on you."

Women as well as men hurled abuse at the silent Officers. Sean backed out of the crowd to speak with the driver of a nearby ambulance as he started the engine and prepared to depart the scene.

"Where are you going, mate? I'm looking for my cobber."

The driver looked evenly at Sean's still breathless state.

"Going to Camperdown."

Sean hung his head staring with dismay at his sore feet.

"Get in the back, quick as a flash, mate." The driver glanced anxiously at the coppers but the crowd had closed on them again.

In the back of the ambulance Sean stared bleakly at Eugene's still body. The officer sitting next to him was trying to clean him up.

"How is he?" asked Sean.

"He's been shot in the chest, mate. And his leg. He's not good. You know him?"

"Yeah." They sat in silence for the remainder of the short journey to Prince Alfred's. Sean staggered from the ambulance as the rear doors opened and entered the scene at casualty where a dozen or more men were being treated and admitted. All were bloodied and many were seriously wounded sitting upright in chairs or lying prostrate on the floorboards waiting for assistance. He saw Joe slumped in a chair in one corner behind a police officer and his heart raced.

"Joe, you're alive!" Joe lifted his head from his chest at the familiar voice and Sean saw that one of his eyes had slipped down his face somehow. He was nursing an arm and a piece of bloody metal protruded from his torn pants, clearly embedded somewhere in his thigh. "Christ, Joe!" Sean sank to his haunches next to his friend who said nothing but shivered convulsively on occasion until a doctor helped him away with Sean's assistance. Then the doctor asked Sean to leave.

Sean couldn't remember walking home that evening. He was numb. He didn't feel the wintery cold nor the blisters that had formed on his heels and his toes when he entered the Pace home near midnight also unaware of Joe's blood on his shirt. Sybil was lying awake in her bed in the front room listening to Anne's steady breathing when she heard the front door and the familiar step of Sean in the hallway. She crept from the bed and slipped out of the door into the dark hall where Sean stood motionless with his back to her and his head buried in the coats hanging from a row of hooks on the wall.

"Sean," she whispered and touched his shoulder so that he turned to face her. Even in the gloom of the hall, Sybil could see the blood on his shirt but it was the wretched pain and turmoil in his eyes that caused her to take his head in her hands. He let out an involuntary cry.

"Those bastards!"

"It's all right. Shhhh. It's all right," she pulled him to her and rocked him gently in the dark as she rocked her children, knowing it was not all right. But saying it anyway. For less than a minute they were locked together in silence in the hall until Sean lifted his head.

"I'm sorry, Syb. I'll go to bed." He smiled tiredly.

As they parted, George silently closed the door to his bedroom at the top of the stairs and lay awake practicing the raised eyebrow look he had been working on and which he planned to show his mother in the morning. It was inspired by a newspaper photograph he had seen of Groucho Marx, the famous comedian, and he felt it would be a telling expression to accompany his burning curiosity about what had made his Uncle Sean cry.

Sean continued picketing on William Street the days he could not find work as he felt that at least he was doing something useful carrying a sign and marching up and down and yelling. Joe was now blind in one eye and although his other wounds would repair, he would always limp. This meant he would be hard put getting work at the wharves, even if there were work to be had.

"Picketing is better than fighting…. and better than doing nothing," Sean told Sybil as they shared a bottle of Jim's home brew on the back step watching the sun sink in the west beyond the crumbling skyline of Woolloomooloo.

"I don't want to see you get in trouble, Sean," Sybil didn't dare look at him. She had become strangely shy of him as if he had grown up suddenly and was not the boyish brother she had known. He reminded her more these days of Tom. She was distracted by the sun-blonde hairs on his strong forearms and found a new depth in his laughing eyes. She was keenly aware that he was a man now and so she feared for him. "Your mother worries herself sick over your brothers and now she frets over you." Sean was silent for a few moments digesting this along with the rough grog that smelt like a damp church hall but was warming his guts. He watched little Anne drawing daisies on the brick pathway at the front of the stables with a piece of yellow stone. She was kneeling on her shins with her shoes sticking out from the back of her faded red dress and you could see the cardboard stuffed into the soles to cover the holes that were worn through them. Sybil was contributing all her wages to the household now, he knew and it made him angry and ashamed that neither he nor his father were able to bring enough home to support the family. Tom hardly contacted them at all and had stopped sending money which was only further cause for shame for all of them. There was nothing to do but drink and fret.

"He's shook on you," Edith Sacks arched her penciled eyebrow as she leaned over the mannequin's shoulder to whisper knowingly in Sybil's ear. Sybil blushed and focused on fitting the elastic girdle to the rigidly small waist of the plaster mannequin they had named Shorty.

"The last person on Earth who needs a blasted girdle is Shorty," she muttered through the pins she held between her teeth. Although the girdle was fully elasticated, Shorty's pinched waist could not fill it and Sybil had to pin it. "How does it look?" She peeped at Edith over Shorty's gleaming, yellow finger waves.

Edith pursed her bright red lips and took a step back appraising the fit. "Looks like she could use a feed." Shorty continued to gaze with fixed admiration across the shop floor at millinery. "Why are you ignoring me?" Edith poked her face closer to Sybil's. "It's as clear as day! He's always smoodging up to you and shouting you drinks. I reckon he'll make a move on you any minute." She squealed and jumped back as Sybil flicked a pin at her.

"Stop yabbering! You'll have the whole place talking about me. I'm still a married woman, even if he is a toe-rag of a husband. And anyway, Ted's a nice bloke and all that but," her forehead wrinkled, "... he's got a face like a dropped pie!" They both laughed and Edith dipped her head and shuffled back to haberdashery as Mrs Bradshaw approached the lingerie counter on her usual morning round.

"Morning, Mrs Bradshaw."

Sybil pulled mercilessly on the elastic girdle fixing one last pin at the back of Shorty's waist. She smiled broadly at her manager who wore her usual string of pearls over the compulsory black. Mrs Bradshaw examined the corset with an approving nod.

"Another elastic miracle."

"I think our Mrs White will like this new contraption," Sybil offered. Mrs White was a rotund customer in her forties who was determined to be slim and was prepared to do anything to achieve it as long as it didn't interfere with her dinner.

"Hmmm, will she be wearing anything else by opening time?" Mrs Bradshaw blinked at Shorty's tough white breasts and glanced at the clock overhanging the grand staircase leading down to the ground floor from where customers would soon emerge.

"Oh yes, of course!" Sybil grasped the elastic brassiere from the counter and threaded Shorty's arm through one strap and then the other ensuring her modest breasts were out of sight as she fiddled with the fit. "Nearly there," she assured Mrs Bradshaw who nodded and made her way towards hosiery. It was an expectation that all mannequins were dressed out of sight of the customers who were to be protected from nakedness, even false nakedness, at any cost. Those staff working in lingerie had to be extra-careful not to offend the fine sensibilities of the David Jones' customer by displaying or referring to sensitive body parts in any direct or crude manner. Sybil had learned to speak discreetly of bosoms, bodices, hips and derrieres, rather than the tits, bellies and arses she was more familiar with, as well as to note the 'warm curves' of customers who no longer craved the flat, boyish lines of the flapper. Her own significant curves made her fashionable when ten years earlier she had seemed ungainly. Indeed, Ted Jeffries, the publican at the Fitzroy where she and Edith would take a quiet beer in the Ladies Parlour now and then frequently complimented her on her womanly shape. She bit down on her lip as she considered Ted with his large head, patchy hair and gap-toothed smile. He was a good friend but that was it.

As she counted her cash float in the drawer of the cash register, she watched Mrs Bradshaw make her way from millinery to the staircase, her eyes scanning the floor like searchlights on a ship. She was a slim, dark-haired widow not yet forty who had been married only three years when the war took her husband at the Battle of Fromelles. Sybil often wondered how she had coped over all that time with the loss of love. She was beginning to find it hard herself. Now and then, when a handsome gentleman felt delicately between his capable fingers the quality of silk in a chamois intended for a sweetheart, she felt her throat tighten with desire and her pulse quicken in response. The intensity of her longing shocked her and when she had a few beers, she sometimes shed a tear or two from self-pity. She was particularly sensitive to the mellow pain of the trombone as it brought back that evening in Moore Park when Tom had approached her on the lawn out the front of the Dance Hall playing a soft, metallic serenade just for her. How did Mrs Bradshaw manage for so long without love? She admired her even as she dreaded becoming her for she could see no further opportunity for love as a working mother living with her in-laws. She couldn't divorce Tom as that would be a disgrace and any alternative a bigger disgrace, yet she longed to be touched as he had touched her. Before she died.

For his ninth birthday, George's twin Uncles gave him a shilling. A whole shilling to do what he pleased with. It didn't take George more than a second to make up his mind.

"King Kong!" His eyes shone like a maniac and he jumped up and down on the spot with his fists tightly clenched.

"King Who?" laughed Jim.

At Sybil's request, Sean accompanied George and Bluey on their excursion to the State Theatre in Market Street on a Saturday afternoon to see the greatest moving picture ever made. It was the first picture any one of them had seen so there wasn't much competition as far as they were concerned. It was also the first time they had been inside a building like the State Theatre. George's heart was beating so fast and his boyish shyness so intense that he remained silent out of fear he would make a fool of himself as they entered the glowing glamour of the theatre's foyer. Grand balustrade staircases swept up either side of the marble walls and a throng of people dressed in their best clothes cooed in wonder at the rich mosaics along the floors and walls of this building that reminded George of the crystal glow of a bowl of sugar in the sun. The only place he had seen that sparkled so vastly was David Jones but even the opulence of the seventh-floor restaurant which his mum had shown him on a Saturday outing seemed reserved compared to the eclectic richness of the Theatre. They lined up at the box office behind a dozen others. George and Bluey ignored with obvious contempt the fearful squeals of a group of teenaged girls waiting in trepidation to see the king of the apes.

Once they had secured their tickets, Sean suggested a tour of the building and they climbed the staircase to tread along the voluptuous, curving corridors of the dress circle. George and Bluey exchanged wide-eyed glances at the sight of so many near-naked ladies smiling in their paintings or cast in stone trying to hold things up while their gowns slipped off. They were to take their seats in the stalls so they made their way back down the stairway to join the throng of people passing through the hallway of mirrors between the golden doors to take their seats in the Palace of Dreams. The overture built as they shuffled politely past people's knees to seat themselves and then engage in several minutes of head rolling taking in the huge auditorium, the murmuring circle of spectators above them and the monstrous Koh-i-Nor chandelier that hung like a merry go round from the domed ceiling. As George was counting the arches along the sides of the auditorium, the lights went down and they entered the crackling, flickering world of the big screen.

None of them were quite comfortable ensconced in all this glory. Sean was keenly aware that the price of the entry tickets could feed a family but tried to remind himself that it was George's birthday treat. Despite himself, the theatre made him strangely proud. Proud that an Australian had built this magical theatre and proud to be part of a species prepared to spend vast sums of money on nothing but beauty. The same species that were prepared to belt the living Hell out of each other over almost nothing. It was awkward timing, he reflected, building the 'Palace of Dreams' when the city had been cast into an impoverished and violent nightmare.

"'Twas beauty killed the beast," read the introductory script on the screen as the orchestra swelled with anxiety. Sean glanced sideways at George and Bluey's faces lit up like deathly lanterns with their mouths hung open and eyes glued to the unfolding drama. The picture started commonly enough for a Woolloomooloo mob with a wharf-side meeting of a ship's crew, a city soup line and a shabby girl trying to steal an apple. Fay Wray had eyes like planets and Sean watched her with some appreciation until the on-deck film tests in which she wore a sheer gown that revealed her scrawny frame. He couldn't help but think they she should have got a Sheila with a bit more meat on her. A real woman, someone like Sybil. Especially as she were about to grapple with a giant ape. Wray's rehearsal scream startled him from his reflections. There was nothing wrong with her lungs! George and he shared a wincing glance.

"Girls!" groaned George.

From the moment Kong ripped through the forest and the great gates beneath Skull Mountain all three of them were rapt in the adventure. The monster's scale, his gleaming teeth were terrifying but his protruding eyebrows moved in gentle waves and his eyes softened despite the frantic screaming of the bound starlet and immediately George was on his side. He was not sorry when a crew member was eaten by the brontosaurus. He couldn't remember a time when it had been so difficult not to cry at the end of the picture when the giant ape climbed the Empire State Building to escape his cruel captors only to be gunned down by planes that circled him like mosquitos on a hot summer night. Bluey's nose was running too when they left the theatre too stunned to say anything for a while, their eyes adjusting to the afternoon sunlight as they made their way down Market Street. As it was a Saturday afternoon, the shops were shut and it was just the dazed theatre crowd moving across the city, like sleepwalkers.

"Why didn't she love him?" George was the first to speak. Sean laughed.

"He's a gorilla, mate!"

"Well? He was the best bloke in the picture!" exclaimed George.

"Too right!" Bluey agreed. "He should've eaten all them people in the first place!"

With what remained of the birthday shilling, Jim bought George a broken-down bicycle from his cousin Paul who had a shiny new black bicycle even though it wasn't his birthday. Uncle Guy had said George could have it but Jim insisted on him paying for it, even it were only a few pennies.

"It means you own it," he explained. "And it cannot be taken back."

They worked on it together in the back yard over the school holidays pulling it apart and cleaning and oiling and putting it back together. Jim kept coming home with bits and pieces from the wharf where he said there were plenty of old bike carcasses until George's bike was restored and complete with sprung leather seat, a horn and tyres that still had most of their tread.

Bluey whistled, "She's a beauty!" He had been inspired to repair his own old bike but had to make do with the worn, patched tyres and go easy on the corners being as the takings at his parents' pub were down and his dad was doing the relief at Concord.

Sybil looked at the bicycle from under hooded eyes as she farewelled them from the back steps on her way to work.

"You're not goin' on the roads, mind you!" George looked at his Grandfather in consternation. Bluey stared fixedly at his bare feet.

"There isn't anywhere else to go," George pointed out staring evenly at his Mother.

"Never on William Street and no further than the wharves," Sybil relented fixing her hat down over her curls and twirling back into the house. "And stop lookin' at me like that!" George was growing so fast, she could feel the child slipping from her reach and in its place a calm, young man who had his own ideas was emerging. She was not yet comfortable with *him*.

"You listen to your Ma now, mate. No good stirring the possum." Jim smiled and wheeled the bike along the yard. "Let's give it a burl in the back lane."

Sybil hurried through the cold wind blowing winter into Sydney from the south. In Hyde Park it swept the remaining few leaves from the trees and they streamed across Elizabeth Street carrying Sybil with them up to the grand doors of the store. She was out of breath but hurried up the stairs to find Mrs Bradshaw and tell her about Edith before the store opened. Poor, broken Edith who had been to see the 'nurse' and was not fit to stand. She had ruminated all morning about what she should tell Mrs Bradshaw that Edith was suffering from. Being an incompetent liar, she had decided to say as little as possible. She knocked gently on Mrs Bradshaw's office door and entered. Mrs Bradshaw was poring over sales reports and looked up over her reading spectacles.

"Good morning, Mrs Pace."

"Good morning, Mrs Bradshaw. I have come to tell you that Edith is unwell and can't come to work today. She's very sorry for the short notice. I can work through my breaks today, if that's any help."

"Oh," Mrs Bradshaw removed her spectacles. "I hope it isn't anything too serious?" She clearly expected an answer.

"They've sent for the doctor and I expect we'll know more tomorrow. She's very poorly." Sybil shook her head and left it at that. Mrs Bradshaw sighed and rose from her desk.

"Very well, I shall have to adjust some schedules." As she passed

Sybil, she added, "I should be grateful for an update and a note from the doctor tomorrow, Sybil."

"Yes, M'am." Sybil made a face. Crikey! Why had she mentioned the blasted doctor? What was wrong with Edith was past a doctor. She had guessed Edith's condition before Edith was sure herself. Breasts bursting from her shirt and sickly every morning. She was seeing a couple of fellas, one who was married and another who was not the marrying sort by any means being in jail as much as he was out. Sybil had tried to caution her but she insisted she was using protection.

"What will you do?" They were sharing a sorry lunch of stale bread and butter in the basement where a staff area was set up.

"I'll get rid of it." Edith's face was still. Sybil sat with her in silence. There was nothing to say. She knew what that meant. "Have you got the money?" She knew from the local gossip, Mrs Mills who ran the corner shop, that it was not cheap to 'see the nurse' in the dingy terrace on Bourke Street.

"Charlie's gonna' pay for it." Edith put aside her half-eaten sandwich. "I told him it was his."

"Is it?" asked Sybil.

"Does it matter?" Edith laughed in an ugly kind of way and Sybil put her arm around her while she had a little cry. Benjamin from menswear was looking at them over a newspaper. Sybil stuck her tongue out and he returned to reading.

Sybil had felt obliged to accompany her friend to the 'nurse' as there was no one else Edith could turn to. Edith had the ten quid, a princely sum, tucked in her purse and was waiting in the gathering darkness on the front step of her family's home in Nicholson Street at half past six the next evening. She had explained to her mum that she was going out with Sybil for a stroll and wore her shabby green overcoat and black hat pulled low.

"You ready, then?" Sybil asked pulling her own coat tighter against the cold night air.

"Well, I'm not here for a haircut," answered Edith.

They walked the few blocks in silence. The sky was alive with stars and a crescent moon was rising shedding little light on the quiet streets. As they turned into Bourke Street, they passed a gang of young men smoking under the gaslight at the corner.

"Evening ladies," a cocky young bloke lifted his oversized cap as they passed. "Looking for love, are we?"

"That'll be the day! You're Eric, aren't you?" Asked Sybil. "You're at Judge Lane, yes? Your Ma cleans at the school? I'm one of the Paces. Give Dulcie my regards"

"Ah, regards to Sean." The young man stepped hastily back among his friends as Sybil and Edith proceeded. "She knows more than her prayers," he offered to his mates as they howled with laughter.

"Little buggers think they run the place," Sybil snorted. Edith pulled her hat down lower on her head.

"Keep quiet, Syb. I'll be in the blasted newspapers tomorrow!"

As they approached the peeling terrace in Bourke Street, Sybil gave Edith a hug. "Be over in no time now, love."

A woman edged the front door open when Edith knocked.

"Miss Sacks?"

"Yes," Edith whispered and the door opened wide enough to let her in. Sybil pushed it wider to follow Edith inside.

"Have you got the ten quid?"

The smell of stale lard emanated from the rear of the house. The woman seemed annoyed that Edith had come with a friend and told Sybil that she would have to wait outside as there was no room for her to sit in the house. Edith looked panicky and turned to Sybil. "I'm sorry, Syb. You just go home. I'll be right."

"I'm not goin' anywhere," Sybil folded her arms aware that she towered over the slight woman in her dirty apron by a good foot. "I'll be fine here in the hall, if you need me. Don't worry, I won't be sayin' anything." She spoke directly to the nurse who clicked her dentures in disapproval and led Edith into the front room.

"If she's a nurse, I'm the Queen of Egypt," Sybil muttered to herself as she closed her eyes and leant on the floral wallpaper. She didn't want to remember this place or what was happening here. She crossed her fingers behind her back for Edith as she waited. Sybil did not believe in God. She might have wanted to but she had never had instruction and wouldn't know how. In any case, she felt this world was too unlucky to have a God. For she did believe in luck. Luck that could happen to anyone, all of a sudden, bad or good, from out of the blue and she hoped that a little bit of luck, the good sort, was waiting around a nearby corner for Edith. During the procedure Edith never made a sound. When the nurse came out after a short while and signaled to Sybil she could go inside, she was carrying a parcel of rags and heading for the stove in the kitchen.

"She'll be all right. She needs to stay in bed for a day or two. She'll need plenty of padding. "

"Righto." She knocked once on the door to the front room and entered. Edith was sitting on the edge of a long table in the centre of the sparsely furnished room trying to put her coat on and crying quietly. She looked smaller.

"You all right, love?" Sybil asked as she helped her with the coat and that started a rush of tears.

"All right, all right, it's done now. Let's get you out of here and home to bed." She, stuck Edith's hat on her head and led her through the hall into the cold night. Edith was doubling in pain and leaning on her as they made their way back.

"God forgive me," she moaned.

"God's too bloody busy to mind your business," said Sybil. "Now when we get to your house, you just tell them you've eaten something awful and you've been chucking up, okay? I'll deal with Mrs Bradshaw in the morning and you stay in bed, all right?" Sybil's tone was not to be argued with. Edith nodded and wiped her nose on the sleeve of her coat as they approached her home.

"Thank you, Syb. You're a good friend." She clutched Sybil's plump hand with her own cold fingers. Her pale face, free from the make-up she was so fond of looked like someone familiar, but not Edith. Maybe one of those black and white photographs of Edith; a monochrome of the bright and pretty girl Sybil knew.

"I *am* your friend, and I'm telling you now, I don't want you within a bee's dick of that Charlie, nor the other one. No more. You got worse taste in men than me!"

When Edith didn't show for work on the second day, Mrs Bradshaw visited Sybil in lingerie. "Has the doctor discovered the problem?" she asked evenly. Sybil was caught short of a word and licked her lips hoping something sensible would come out. Mrs Bradshaw cocked her head to one side and lowered her voice. "You know, Mrs Pace, I didn't come down in the last shower. I had my concerns about Edith." Sybil stared at Mrs Bradshaw as if she were an apparition. "I just hope she is all right and will be back at work tomorrow. I can't keep covering for her with no doctor's note." With that Mrs Bradshaw slipped quietly away leaving Sybil wondering if she knew anything about human nature at all.

Nick was lying in the dark on the floorboards of his room in Barcom Avenue with a folded blanket under his buttocks so that his testicles, still sore and enlarged with gonorrhea, were exposed as closely as possible to the fire without actually frying. The quack up at Kings Cross had been injecting him with mercurochrome which he said could cure him in time but had recommended heat therapy as well and setting fire to scraps of wood in the small hearth of his room was the best heat Nick could arrange. The flickering on the wall lit the dark room containing a single cot with a thin mattress and a few pieces of clothing hung on hooks hammered into the walls. A table stood against one wall with a piece of mirror and shaving brush, razor and wooden bowl. In the corner, lay a pile of rubbish made up of food wrappers, bottles and newspapers. He was swigging on a bottle of beer to help ease the discomfort when he heard his brother calling him up the stairs.

"What?"

"Come down," yelled Guy. "Need to talk."

"I'm busy cooking me balls," Nick laughed at himself. Guy opened the door and grimaced, taking a full step back.

"Gor'struth! That's a sight you don't see every day!"

"They're some marvel, ain't they?" Nick gestured for Gus to come in. "Don't mind me hanging me goolies out. I'm not wasting this fire. The Quack says it'll cure me."

"Thought you were getting jabs for that."

"Jabs and heat," Nick responded. "Whatever it takes. Can't stand the pain and I need a root like you wouldn't believe." He offered Guy a swig from his bottle.

"Well, we got other problems," Guy declined a swig, sat on the edge of Nick's bed and tried to avoid looking at him. "They've bagged Willy Lee."

"What for?" Nick looked sideways at his brother.

"Dunno'. Got the word on the street down the Cross just now. Just gotta' hope he keeps his mouth shut."

"The shillings are all gone, mate."

"Yeah, gone where? They might be gone from you and me but they're still out there and we don't want any connections made." Guy was clearly fractious. They had distributed the shillings slowly over a year cashed in at various banks and paid to an unsuspecting public in the form of winnings through Roy's bookmaking with a significant kickback for Roy, of course. Roy, had in turn been betting with the shillings himself with other bookies; not uncommon in the trade. If a bookie took too much money on a horse, he would often bet the other way with another bookie to safeguard himself against ruination or a mobbing.

"I thought you said Willy was tight?" Nick winced as he delicately returned his testicles to his underpants. "It's probably all the snow you've been shoving up your nose that's making you toey." Guy had been trading shillings for cocaine and sly grog with some of the Darlinghurst mob. His growing fondness for the drug was evident in the pockmarks on his face and the wild vacuity of his eyes. "I'd rather get bagged by the cops than the Riley Street mob mate. They won't muck around if they sniff you've been feeding them fake deeners."

Guy remained silent for a few moments. "I'm just sayin' Willy's been bagged. Could be something else. Could be just because of his ugly mug. In any case, we'll find out soon enough."

It was just the following afternoon that the shooting occurred. Misters Joseph Fields and Horace Dowd, residents of Albion Street, Surry Hills, stared in disbelief as a bloodied and groaning Guy Pace hauled himself up the final couple of steps out of the infamous Frog's Hollow with a bullet wound to the temple, blood caked through his hair and still flowing down his neck. After an initial moment or two of inert disbelief, Fields, who had some first aid training, quickly took stock of the situation and dragged Guy across the pavement to slump him against the base of a lamppost where he attempted to stem the flow of blood with a hanky and his belt. Guy appeared delirious as well as drunk and gestured repeatedly to the vacant block from which he had crawled rasping: "It's over there."

A couple of seamstresses from the clothing factory across the way were smoking in the street when they noticed the drama unfolding and they hurried inside to use the telephone to summon an ambulance. As they waited for the ambulance to arrive, Guy continued to moan and muttered, "I shot me'self. Tell me wife, Madge."

As it was a Monday, it was washing day at 107 Dowling Street and Maggie was wringing the last of the heavy, dripping bed sheets through the mangle grunting with the effort of turning the heavy handle when George and Bluey came tearing into the back yard on their bicycles.

"Grandma!" George dropped his bike even as the wheels were still turning and ran up the steps to the back door. "Where's Grandpa?" He panted.

"He's down the wharf," said Maggie shielding her eyes from the late sun with her hand and squinting at George. "Why? What's the matter?"

George swallowed and gulped in air before he spurted, "It's Uncle Guy. He's been shot. The ambulance is coming. He's in Surry Hills. Mrs Mills told me." As Mrs Mills had a telephone installed in her shop, she was always the first to hear of any drama. Maggie stood stunned like a garden statue holding a wrung sheet over one shoulder.

George stared at her for a moment and then noticed Harry's horse in the stable.

"Get your coat, Grandma." With that George was through the fence to the neighbour's yard yelling his lungs out at Harry's window.

"S'matter?" Harry stuck his balding head through the narrow window of his room. "What's all the din about?"

"We gotta' get to Surry Hills. Uncle Guy's been shot!" Harry saw Maggie running up the steps into her house wearing a wet sheet and knew from the very fact that Maggie was running, a sight he had never seen before, that there was trouble.

"I'm coming down," he said. "Get Winnie's bridle."

They were quite a spectacle pulling up at the side of Frog Hollow on Harry's cart. Maggie was riding up the front next to Harry while George and Bluey sat in the back of the cart with little Anne jammed between them. Anne was too young to understand the drama and was thrilled at her ride in a horse cart making whooping sounds and giggling with joy as they turned corners as fast as Harry dared take them. Guy was being stretchered feet first into the ambulance as they arrived with a crowd gathered around murmuring their understandings of what had happened.

"He says he shot himself."

"Oh Yeah? Not much of a shot then, is he?"

"Where's the gun?"

"That's what the coppers are asking."

Maggie dismounted the cart as quickly as she could and raced to the ambulance.

"Is he alive? Is he breathin'?" She looked from one ambulance officer to the other, afraid to look at the body on the stretcher.

"I'm alive, Ma," the body on the stretcher gasped from in the ambulance. "It's all right." Maggie shrieked and stepped onto the ramp to take his hand.

"What happened, son? Who shot you?" She pumped his hand gently as if that would help him stay alive.

"No-one. I shot me'self" Guy moaned. Maggie digested this in silence and dropped his hand as the ambulance officers secured the stretcher and prepared to close the back of the wagon.

"Where are you taking him?" she asked.

"St Vincent's, Missus. Will you come with him?" Maggie looked back at Harry holding his horse and his hat at the kerbside. He waved her along.

"I'll take the kids back and watch 'em, Mags." He called out. "You go along and I'll make sure Jim gets the word."

"No," Maggie quietly shook her head. "Your father will be along." She called into the ambulance noticing for the first time that Guy's hair was thinning on the top of his bloody scalp. She turned and walked back to the cart with her head hanging on her chest and her eyes open but somewhere else. Anne broke away from her brother's grasp and ran to Maggie throwing herself around her middle and Maggie absentmindedly pulled her ponytail but said nothing. They rode back to Dowling Street in a thick silence broken by the horse's hooves against the gravel of the road and the chuckling engines of motorcars as they rushed past. The maniacal laugh of a single kookaburra high in the spindly limbs of the gum tree straddling Palmer street heralded their return to Woolloomooloo.

Jim and Sean attended the hospital that evening once they had washed away a day's work in the yard and heard Harry and Maggie's account of Guy's incident in Surry Hills. Jim merely shook his head and rolled his dentures around his mouth like a cow chewing its cud. Sean ran his hands through his wet hair as he put his coat on and repeated after Harry.

"So, he shot himself, did he?"

"That's what he says," Harry leant his head to the side as an affirmation and sipped heavily on the cup of tea Maggie had put in his large, sun-worn hand.

"In the head?" Sean continued.

"Yep," Harry stared at his tea.

"He was bleeding all over the place, Uncle Sean," George was bemused by how calm everyone seemed. Sean nodded and lifted an eyebrow at his father.

"Ya' right?"

"Yeah, let's get on with it." Jim pulled his wife's earlobe gently and winked at her before they left through the rear door. "He'll be right, love."

"He's never been right," she muttered as she dug her darning needle into the worn elbow of George's school jumper.

Guy did mostly recover over a period of months but his hair never grew back around the right side of his head and so he wore it shaved close. When he removed his hat, he was now even more intimidating with his shot off ear and scarred skull exposed to the world. Despite the cynical looks he received, he never wavered from his confession and refused to discuss it further with anyone, including Nick, but there were plenty of rumors around providing alternative accounts of what happened that afternoon in Surry Hills. As no weapon was ever found, the police accepted Guy's story of self-harm concluding that a local must have found the gun and swiped it before they arrived on the scene. A cartridge belt with thirty .22 bullets and a jack knife were found between the steps Guy had been crawling up and a concrete wall. As the police did not expect Guy to recover, they had made little effort to enquire further as shootings and thrashings were almost daily occurrences in the troubled ghetto of Frog Hollow. Nick heard more, however, about Guy's behavior in the Hollow that day. About a drunken prostitute cut across the chest and thrown down a set of stairs and her pimp rammed into a wall until he collapsed unconscious.

"You're a tin-arsed bastard," Nick had observed as he had accompanied his brother home from the hospital. "No doubt about it. Better pull your head in mate ... what's left of it." Nick laughed at Guy's thunderous glare. "That's Tilly's mob you've stirred up. All I'm sayin'." They continued in silence up Barcom Street to Guy's home where he kicked the garden gate and yelled.

"I'm home."

The front door opened and his youngest son tore out and grabbed his father around the middle. Guy ruffled his dark curls. "You need a haircut son." Guy's wife could be seen at the far end of the dark entrance hall with her arms folded over her apron. "'Lo, love," Guy sighed weakly and closed the gate.

"So much to live for," Nick winked. "Mornin', Madge." He chuckled as Guy's wife tossed her head and turned on her heel. "Stay home for a bit mate."

Guy watched his brother walk on up the avenue with the peculiar chimp-like stride he had developed to accommodate his swollen goolies and smiled to himself before hauling his squealing son over his shoulder and entering the house.

Over the long summer holidays George's confidence in the saddle developed along with the scabs and scars on his knees and elbows. George, Bluey and Tony each had bikes and the boys took turns doubling Edward 'the Lump' as his mum was too poor to get him a bike. Sybil had drawn a line between William Street and the wharf across which George was not allowed to ride but she had omitted to rule on the Domain and so the boys charged up the green hill, their thighs burning with the effort, almost every day of the holidays. Once they had cleared the hill and reached the Art Gallery and Speakers' Corner they could roll down the roadway to the pool or Mrs Macqaurie's chair, or their preferred option, ride top speed along the meandering lawns and pathways of the botanical gardens to the spectacle of the waterfront and gaze in wonder and longing at the mad, unblinking mask of the brand new Luna Park gates across the harbour. As the summer afternoons cooled into evening, the Park lit up like a fairy's palace and the boys sometimes heard the squeals from the roller coaster in the salty harbour breeze.

"I gotta' ride that roller coaster," Bluey would say and let out a lovesick sigh as they turned their bikes to race for home and be in the house before dark as was their curfew.

Over the long summer their noses and lips peeled, they lost the tips of their big toes and their hair turned almost white, except for Tony's Italian mop which gleamed purple and black like a crow was perched on his head. They spent their days climbing the giant

Moreton Bay Figs in the Domain like pale stick insects with their skinny legs and arms clinging to the wide, dark branches splayed out from trunks draped with a forest of trailing roots. As they were unable to afford the entry fee for the pool at the Domain, they swam off the rocky ledges of Woolloomooloo Bay and often dropped a fishing line baited with a grub to catch a kingfish or a flathead which they let Lumpy take home to his mother, if it was big enough. They played marbles, chased goannas or just baked on the warm rocks by the water until hunger usually drove them home before darkness fell.

The autonomy of a bicycle also introduced George to the intricacies of urban squalor, the street life of families, merchants, sailors and the local gangs of Woolloomooloo. He saw children walloped by their mothers, learned to distinguish the street women from the regular women by their clothes and their demeanor, watched sailors bash each other into the pavements outside the pubs shouting unknown curses from foreign lands and came to know some of the street folk of the area. Dirty Larry was a favourite, a longhaired, bearded man of indeterminable age with brown skin and a high-pitched, soft voice like a film star. Larry carried a dirty canvas bag of 'laundry' up and down Cathedral Street and always greeted the boys stopping to yarn before he headed off 'to do his washing'. They yearned to know what really lay in the bag. It did not seem possible that anyone could have that much washing, especially if they didn't actually have anywhere to live but slept rough.

"Body parts," Bluey liked to propose pulling a ghoulish face.

"There isn't any blood," George would point out.

"That's 'cos he knows how to dry them," said Bluey. "Drain the blood out, so they keep."

The boys had learned where Frank Green 'the little gunman' lived from the older boys who hung around in gangs around the wharves. Everyone knew Frank worked as a strong-arm man for the fancy lady of Darlinghurst, Mrs Tilly Devine, and that he fixed any problems she might have with his razor or his pistol. George and his mates dared each other to ride past the gunman's doorway as penance for losing a bet. If Green's scar running from his right lip to his right ear were not enough to give you the willies, the fact that he carried a gun and was in and out of jail for using it, meant that he was to be avoided where possible. As the front door of his cottage in Charles Street opened directly onto the pavement with no verandah, you had to be game as a pebble to ride past his house where he might step in front of you at any moment. He was the meanest character in Woolloomooloo and as the ragged curtain on the front window was never opened, the boys competed at guessing what gruesome secrets lay within, scaring each other half to death.

"My big sisters told me that any girl that doesn't do what Tilly says, gets taken by Frank Green and is never heard of again," Bluey declared.

As they rode their bicycles around the streets of Woolloomooloo, George and his mates became well-known to the local street gangs of teenaged boys who sometimes asked them to run a message, initially in return for not bashing them but increasingly in return for a smoke or a durry as they called them. Although none of the boys smoked, they would run these errands, usually messages between the boys and their donnahs and then pass on the smokes to blokes they befriended on the streets and in the Domain. Particularly Dirty Larry and Terry.

The first time the boys met Terry he had scared the living daylights out of them when he popped his curly, black head around a tree next to the rocks they were spread out on and asked:

"What you fellas doin'?" He giggled when they jumped out of their skins. Tony let go of the fishing line and had to jump in to recover the bobbing cork around which the line was gathered.

"Fishing," said George staring openly at Terry's long, black feet with yellow undersides.

"Catch any?" Terry asked as he moved to the edge of the rock and glared into the lapping water from which Tony was hauling himself.

"Nah," said Bluey. "Not today. What you got there, Mister?" Bluey nodded at the long basket contraption Terry was holding by his side.

"Ah," said Terry holding his basket before him. "This is for catchin' eels."

"Eeeew!" Lump declared. "Yuck!"

"You ever eaten an eel?" Terry studied Lump with his large brown and yellow eyes.

"No!" Lump looked at him in horror.

"Taste good," said Terry. "Wanna' help me catch one?"

"Too right!" said George.

Many out-of-work blokes slept rough in the Domain under newspapers and bits of tarpaulin; the locals referred to them with some distrust as the Domainiacs. Terry slept there too but he was different because he was an aborigine and they were supposed to sleep out and wander. He spent his time between Redfern and the harbour and sometimes worked the railway yards at Everleigh. He came and went as he liked and it seemed to George he had an idyllic life with nothing to worry him and a hundred tricks to find food and water and keep himself going. He loved to smoke however, and he was willing to yarn and teach the boys some fishing and fire-building tricks in return for a smoke or two. Terry was a master of birdcalls too and could mimic just about any bird you could think of. He could give you the whip-like melodies of the butcherbird, or the morning calls of the magpies. He made them laugh with his disappointed crow calls, the larrikin screech of the cockatoos or the mournful lament of the tawny frogmouth which he produced with his head dropped to one side and a look of abject misery on his wide face. George practiced manipulating his tongue and his lips as Terry did but only achieved a satisfactory rendering of the simpler calls of the cockatoo and the kookaburra.

"Can't catch these in the harbour!" Terry would comment as streams of ghostly smoke poured from his wide nostrils and he kept the boys enthralled with tales of the hundreds of dead bodies lying buried under Town Hall and cursing the city and all within it.

The Sunday evening before the first day of term in George's final year of junior school, Sybil made sure to run a hot bath and scrub the boy from head to foot despite his protestations that he was almost eleven and old enough to do it himself. She had boiled the copper and sloshed cold water with the hot in the outdoor washhouse determined that he should be presentable after weeks of roaming free.

"You're hurting my ears, ma," he tried to duck his head from her.

"Don't be a sook," she laughed. "I'll be shaving your head after this too, if you don't let me get this hair clean." Anne, who was now ready to start her first year at Plunkett Street School, was washed and combed sitting in the living room on Maggie's knee glowing with soap and excitement as her grandmother read to her from a library book about a Magic Pudding. George soon joined his sister and his grandmother to allow his mother to take her own Sunday night bath.

The washhouse in the yard was basically an extension to the stables with walls made from the same wooden planks and a door that was more a gate with a loose hook holding it closed to provide privacy. Within there was the tin hipbath and an old sack on the dirt floor to drip on. Now Sybil had bathed the children, it was time for her to enjoy the greatest luxury of her week and top up the bath water with the boiling kettle from the kitchen stove. She was careful to keep some aside for the bucket of water she kept for rinsing her long and complicated hair. As she sank into the warm water she sighed and lay still watching the last light fade from the rectangle of sky she could see through the hole in the wall which was meant to serve as a window. She stayed in the soapy water as long as she could still feel some warmth and then stood in the bath pouring the bucket of clean water over her soapy hair, her pink body steaming in the dusky light. It was just then that Sean returned home entering the yard from the rear laneway where he stood transfixed, staring at his sister-in-law's naked body, knowing it was wrong but unable to move forward or back and smiling like a shot fox.

DECEMBER 1934

On a mercifully cool Saturday afternoon, Harry was sitting on the pavement and leaning into the red brick wall of the shipping warehouse on Dowling Street near the corner of busy William Street. He was watching the light Saturday traffic, mostly women returning from a shopping trip to town lugging their string bags up the hill or clambering from trams. Harry knew the tram timetable like the back of his hand and once the 4:05 pulled up outside Miller's fish and chip shop he knew it would be time to relax his watch and head up to *the Anchor* for a cool one with Roy. They would talk over the day – which horses were the standouts and those that were donkey-licked – while knocking back the good, cold grog that warmed their lonely hearts against the Saturday night.

On his Saturday watch Harry generally stood at the corner of Dowling and William Streets across from Mrs Mills' corner shop or else at the corner of Forbes and William Streets across from the 50/50 club where there was always free entertainment watching the grogged up patrons trying to walk out of the heavy doors. From either corner, he had the wood on the coppers who would be heading down from Darlinghurst. Harry would be at *the Anchor* spreading the word and burning tickets before they were even in the 'Loo.

He was rarely alone for long on his Saturday vigil as he was known to all the locals from his fruit and vegetable delivery rounds. In the warmer months, the residents of Woolloomooloo liked to wander the streets for a natter and a smoke on a Saturday and Harry was good for either, no matter who you were. Harry was friends with everyone, publicans, shopkeepers, wharfies, washer women, the working girls and the vagrants like Dirty Larry who wore his bag of 'washing' on his back like an oversized turtle. It was the softly-spoken Larry who Harry was yacking with when he first noticed the two men coming down the hill. They were not the uniformed constables he was usually looking for but it was clear as day that they were narks in their clean shirts and ties with their hats pulled down low and their purposeful strides.

"S'cuse me, mate. Gotta' see a man about a dog." Harry turned from Larry and trotted down Dowling Street for *the Anchor*.

By the time the two plain clothes coppers entered the front door of the pub, Roy had scarpered out the back lane and was half-way up the hundred odd stairs cut into the cliff face up to Potts Point. He had to stop halfway and loosen his tie to recover his breath. Harry was sitting in front of a fresh beer chewing betting tickets with some difficulty as he had so few teeth left to chew with. As the coppers approached him, he dipped his head and winked good-naturedly at them. They lifted him from his stool and slammed him into the rear wall of the pub. Half-eaten betting tickets spewed from his mouth and one started reading him his rights while the other kicked him in the guts.

"S'only a few bets on the nags, fellas," Harry gasped trying to gather himself up from the floor. The cops turned to face the group of patrons of *the Anchor* who were starting to protest. Chief among them was Big Jim.

"Leave the old boy alone, ya buggers!" Jim's jaw was set on the angle. Never a good sign. He had been drinking lightly, enjoying his Saturday flutter when Harry had suddenly breezed in and Roy had just as suddenly tore off.

"Mind your business," said the copper nearest to Jim.

"I am," replied Jim as he sank his solid right hook into the clean-shaven chin of Detective Gregory Madden. By the time the uniformed coppers arrived in their motorcars, there were few patrons left at *the Anchor* but plenty of onlookers who had 'no idea' what had started the brawl. The two detectives were lying soundly beaten and groaning on the dusty floor of the pub among the stub ends, spills and torn tickets. Jim sat quietly with blood pouring from above his swollen left eye nursing his badly bruised fist waiting to be arrested next to Harry who stared at his shaking hands. Next to them were Teary James, Fatty Coulis and the Gong, all mates from down the wharf. They had all got a fist in once the coppers showed their colours and sat bleakly now, large, bleeding men sitting in a row calm and well-mannered waiting for justice.

"Sorry, Jim," Harry offered.

"Not your fault, mate. They shouldn't have booted you. Bastards!" He paused for a moment and added, "Maggie's gonna' be ropeable though." He couldn't help but chuckle at this and Harry couldn't help but join him. It was amusing to each of them that they were more frightened of a woman than they would ever be of the coppers. Each cooperated quietly as they were handcuffed and loaded into the motorcars to be taken to the Station. The charges of affray, assault and illegal gambling were no surprise but both Jim and Harry protested when the coppers included distribution of counterfeit currency against Harry.

"Yer' off yer' rockers!" exclaimed Jim. ""He's got nothing to do with any counterfeit! He delivers fruit and veg, for cryin' out loud!"

"Shut up and get in," Jim's head disappeared into the back of the wagon and he remained silent during the short journey to Darlinghurst police station. As neither Jim nor his wharf mates had prior convictions, they were eventually offered police bail which was met by the publican, Mr Henry Davies. Henry lobbed into the Station early that evening with a wad of cash provided to him by Roy who remained scarce fretting in his apartment and cursing the Pace twins. Jim and his mates were to appear in court at a later date to answer the charges of assault but the police wouldn't let Harry go as he was charged with counterfeit as well as assaulting an officer of the law and illegal gambling and was to be held until his court hearing. Police expected to provide evidence in court of the counterfeit coinage distributed through the bookmaking syndicate operating out of *The Anchor*.

Jim walked from the Police Station with his wharf mates as far as the Cross under a burning, orange sky as the sun sank behind the Blue Mountains. As the elongated shadows of the group of men turned down the hill at William Street, Jim farewelled them and continued along Darlinghurst Road skipping among the Saturday night traffic of trams, motorcars and pedestrians competing for passage across the broad intersection. He passed the Kings Cross Theatre lit up for the evening with excited patrons gathering at the doors to the box office smoking cigarettes and listening to the oratory of a group of young women banging saucepans and taking turns yelling from the steps out the front of the tobacconist at the corner of Bayswater Road across from the Theatre. They held a large banner declaring "Women Textiles Workers Unite" and a speaker with a young child at her side yelled at the crowd:

"We gotta' work faster, longer, into the dark of night for ten percent less pay. How can we survive this? How can we feed out children? In Victoria, Tasmania and now New South Wales the employers are cutting our wages. Stop them! Help us resist the brutal mill owners!"

Two young women were handing out leaflets and one crossed the road and jumped before Jim shoving a leaflet in his hand. He read the title and intended to throw it on the ground but the anxiety in the young eyes of the woman before him stopped him. He folded the paper and placed it in his hip pocket.

"Blasted Unions! Even the women are at it!" He muttered to himself.

He continued along Darlinghurst Road past the bustling cafes beginning a busy Saturday night trade spewing jazz riffs, tobacco smoke and chatter onto the pavement. When he arrived at Roy's barbershop he banged on the dark door until Roy popped his neatly oiled head out of the window of the apartment above.

"You coming down? Or am I coming up?"

Once Jim learned the origin of the counterfeit coinage, he sat silently at Roy's kitchen table with his head in his hands.

"I thought you were smart," he finally said looking up at Roy who worried his lip as he studied Jim. "And those boys of mine,... they think they're pretty sharp too, eh? Well now the three of you can put your ugly mugs together and work out how to get Harry out of the lock-up. If you don't, I'll dob the lot of you in to the coppers. I give you a week."

When the lifeless body of Willy Lee turned up in the gutter outside the police station several days later, there was no longer any evidence of any counterfeit. The charge was dropped and Harry returned to Woolloomooloo. Harry no longer watched for Roy on a Saturday and it was a long while before Roy returned to the back room at *the Anchor*. The lawyer who Roy hired to represent Harry produced two witnesses who swore that the coppers had failed to identify themselves as policemen and had started the violence which then became a public brawl. The court dismissed the charges of assault of officers and the entire matter faded into the forgotten annals of Woolloomooloo. There was almost nothing that couldn't be forgotten if the right palms were pressed in Woolloomooloo. But Jim didn't forget and he collected Nick on his way to Guy's home the day after Harry came home to make it clear to the twins that they were no longer welcome at the house.

"That's three of us down," said Guy with a brutal laugh as they stood in the street out the front of his house. "I don't know why you even had a family, old man! Only Sean left,... for now. When will yer' throw him out?"

"He's different," snapped Jim. "He doesn't shy from a hard day's work. He's not like you and your brothers. He's got goodness in 'im."

"From Mum," Nick nodded his head with his arms folded protectively around his broad chest as if compensating for the love of a family which he had lost. Jim looked sideways at Nick and wondered, not for the first time, if he was all there.

"I won't have your mother fretting over you anymore. There's a dead Chinaman to account for," Jim sighed. "And you know what follows from killin' a Chinaman!"

He left the twins, who he had loved as roguish boys but who he despised as roguish men, standing among the weeds in Guy's front yard and made his way back down the hill.

George was lying on the grass of the upper Domain watching the blue sky turn and feeling under him the busy earth alive with ants and bugs. The heat of the full noon sun meant he could feel his heart throbbing in his eyeballs. He closed his eyes and tried to follow the orange and purple spirals of light inside the crackling, electric darkness of his eyelids. Sometimes he felt the Earth moving so intensely that he feared he might slip off its surface and fly into the air like a lost balloon bumping along the lawn of the Domain out over the harbour wall. He could imagine looking down at the white topped, waves of the sprawling harbour reaching into the land like the tentacles of an octopus grasping Sydney to itself.

Nearby, Bluey lay asleep on his stomach in the patchy shade of a eucalypt. Dried spittle had collected in the corners of his lips. They had ridden for hours over the morning between various addresses in Woolloomoloo, Kings Cross and Darlinghurst gathering bets for Roy and delivering them to him at his barber's shop which was officially closed on a Saturday but which was in fact a buzz with the ringing telephone that Roy had recently installed. Strictly speaking they were not supposed to be helping Roy out with the race bets but as the topic had not come up directly at home and as Roy paid them well and shouted them an ice-cream when he was having a good day, George took care not to mention Roy's errands in front of this mother or his Grandmother. He was sure his Grandfather, Sean and Harry would turn a blind eye as he was passing almost all his messenger boy earnings over to his Grandma and every bit helped in these hard times. Now he was finished with his junior schooling, he was always looking out for a way to earn a few pence and frequently rode messages for the wharf management, the post office and Mrs Mills who was also making money out of relaying messages she received for locals on her telephone in the shop. He and Bluey were faster and cheaper than most of the other local boys and they were building a good list of customers. They were planning to make a motza over the summer now the school year was finally over.

George started thinking about his father, that barely familiar visitor who he had met with his Uncle Sean and his grandma at Harry's Café de Wheels two days before. He had shaken his father's long, soft hand and Anne had kissed her father warily on his cheek recalling something in his fragrance perhaps that made her squint and look at him more closely as she held her Grandma's hand and waited for her beef pie sunk into a steaming pile of sloppy peas.

George remembered more than he let on as he listened to the familiar rhythm of his father's voice as he chatted with Grandma. He remembered a lively, purposeful man surrounded by other men always arriving from somewhere and then leaving for somewhere; a man in perpetual motion smelling of aftershave. Whereas, he remembered his mother sitting, cooking or sulking on the outskirts of this circle of masculine energy and musical equipment that sometimes forged itself into the disorderly order of a jazz tune. His mother would often be shouting for quiet so the children could sleep. His father would be shouting too.

"All grown up," Tom commented as he took in his son, now a stripling, bare-foot and tanned with an awkward shyness about him so typical of a boy not quite a man. It had been over five years since he had clapped eyes on him and he was taken aback at the size of him.

"He's a good lad," Maggie observed. "Doing well at his school and earning some of his keep already with running messages for the wharves. So, how have you been, son?" She perched herself a little awkwardly on the low wall of the wharf next to Sean who had lit a cigarette and held his head to one side silently observing his older brother.

"Good, Ma. I'm good. How's Dad?"

George studied his father from his seat on the wall as he pulled his pie apart a little to release the fragrant steam. His mouth flushed with saliva but he waited for the pie to cool so that he could savour the rich gravy that glistened in the sun. His father was not a giant as he had remembered him but a slightly built man with large, intense eyes and long eyelashes like a girl. His father had the same straight, light-blonde hair as his sister Anne but combed into a fashionable peak over his forehead and his mouth shared Maggie's pouting innocence but was shadowed by a fine line of moustache. There was no denying his father's resemblance to the women in the family, George thought. But how did he himself resemble his father, he wondered? He was almost as tall as him already but his unruly, thick curls and dimpled chin belonged to his mother. As he bit into the hot wet heart of the pie, he watched for signs of himself in the man standing uncertainly before them casting glances at each of his children, smiling and raising his eyebrows hopefully when he caught their eyes.

"Same as ever," Maggie nodded. "Been finding it hard going to get the work down the wharf, of course." Tom nodded grimly then playfully kicked Sean's shaking leg. George observed his father's brown leather shoes with a complex pattern of little holes punched across the toes and thought about the holes in his own shoes which were much bigger and formed under his big toe. Fancy putting holes in the top of your shoes.

"Still shaking that thing, eh?"

"Your son's got it worse," Sean responded gruffly. "So, how's the band going? You making a living?"

"Not much of one," Tom confessed. "These are hard times. Not a lot of spare change for a night out at the orchestra." It was true that the pockets of his grey, tailored trousers were frayed and his white shirt although it had a fresh collar bore stains from another day.

"I s'pose not," said Sean. Tom squinted at his younger brother examining his face once so familiar and now older, harder but with the same freckled nose.

"You still getting work, mate?"

Sean shrugged and crushed the butt of his smoke underfoot. "When I can."

Suddenly, Maggie shifted her weight so that she could look directly at Tom. "It's nice to see you, lad, but …your father is not ready, Tom. Sybil has made a good life down here with her job. The children are healthy and happy; you needn't worry. But you can't come home." With her usual calm, Maggie fished from the air the unspoken words that had been swirling like a cloud of seagulls around the little party at the wharf perched on the wall consuming hot pies.

Tom shifted his weight from one foot to the other and nodded. "It's all right, Ma'."

He turned to his son. "I hear you're pretty sharp on the clarinet, mate. What are you playing these days?"

"I'm okay," George shrugged. "My best tune is *He's Not Worth Your Tears*. Do you know that one? That's Mum's favourite."

"That sounds about right," Tom laughed quietly.

When the pies were gone and they had discussed the weather and the cricket, there seemed no more to be said and so Tom farewelled them giving George and Anne a coin from his pocket and a stroke on the head like they were dogs, George thought. He watched his father make his way on foot along the Cowper Wharf Road towards the city and it was then that he finally saw himself in Tom's rhythmic, bouncing swagger, the way he moved his head back and forth a little as he walked in step to some music playing in his head. As his father receded into the world that they were not a part of, George's throat suddenly closed and he ran. He ran down to the wharf, ignoring Maggie's calls, looking to be again among men he understood.

Suddenly Bluey was stirring and shaking his red head. "What time is it?"

"Time for a swim!" George leapt suddenly from the grass onto his bike and pedaled madly across the grass. Bluey shook himself awake and fumbled into his saddle yelling after him.

"Wait! Wait, yer' bastard!" Bluey's cracked adolescent call carried with the crow calls across the Domain.

"Race yer!" George flung back.

When they reached the Domain Baths, they leant their bikes against the outer wall and approached the gates panting and laughing. They paid the entry fee from their morning earnings which they kept in the buttoned pockets of their shorts and pushed through the turnstile into the noise and movement of the Domain Baths in high summer. The balconies of the dark red and cream timber grandstand were awash with children dressed in various heavy bathing outfits put together from whatever oddments they possessed in their meager wardrobes. George and Bluey simply removed their shirts and flew into the air dropping into the water like heavy, flightless birds.

George floated on his back in the cool, billowing water below the diving tower that reared into the spinning sky above him like the Empire State Building. Five tiers high built from a strong timber frame and steel rivets, he had long meant to climb it and fling himself from it. Jack Darling from Darlinghurst held the record for the youngest boy to dive from the tall tower and it would be only a few months before George reached twelve and he would lose his chance at the record. He was tall enough now and he decided that today was as good a day as any.

"Where ya' goin?'" Bluey clung to the wooden ladder against the concrete siding of the pool as George pulled himself out of the water. George simply looked up at the diving tower and beat his chest running like an ape across the hot concrete to the staircase at the back of the tower. Bluey slapped his hand into the swirling water. "Crikey Moses! He's gonna' do it!" He watched George with his breath held as he started the climb.

Once George reached the top tier of the diving tower he allowed himself to look about him from the platform. His knees almost collapsed as he took in the view of Sydney from this giddy height sweeping Macquarie Street and the upper Domain to the north, across the sparkling harbour to Garden Island at the south. Over his shoulder lay the Finger wharf and the curved road of pubs and shops of Woolloomooloo Bay. But George was imagining another scene; black and white and flecked with the noisy buzz of tiger moths and flashes of fire as they shot their spiteful guns into the King of the

Apes. He didn't expect to survive his fall but he ran into the sky, placed his palms together and lifted his legs.

"As dives go, it was not flash," grimaced Bluey as he hauled a breathless George up the wooden ladder from the water. "A God-awful slap! But yer' *did* it." Bluey glanced up at the group of teenaged girls sunning themselves on the stepped grandstand above them. "Got a nice audience, too!" He smiled at the giggling girls, increasingly aware that he no longer hated girls but was, suddenly and inexplicably, fascinated by them. The red weal on George's belly would fade but the record would stand. George's wet smile was stuck on his face despite the stinging pain of his belly. He had conquered himself. That meant he had conquered everything and that there was nothing he couldn't do. He felt like he felt when he was dancing to a great jazz song. Free from worry about his estranged father, his lonely mother, their endless poverty and his own powerlessness. His fear had not stopped him diving into the sky. He had wings.

Sean leant against the side of the ship in the glaring sun of a warm March day on the wharf. The rest of his gang also lay around the deck, idle but jumpy as they smoked and waited. Mac the Stack had gone to get Jim on account of the gang's refusing to stow a load of wheat. The gang had downed tools and called for Joe Walsh who had been employed as Vigilant Officer for the Waterside Workers' Union since he had been blinded in his right eye in the battle of Union Street, Redfern. Sean watched his old mate approach the ship's gangplank with his unmistakable limp and his battered straw brimmed hat which he wore low on his head to help disguise the worst effort at a glass eye Sean could remember seeing. The eye sat half way down his cheek where his eye socket had ended up and stared straight ahead while the other eye moved here and there giving anyone talking to Joe the impression that he was looking two ways at once. This was not an entirely bad thing for a Vigilant Officer. Joe hailed the gang and they drew together on the foredeck of the tanker. Alongside on the wharf stood two fully loaded lighters brimming expectantly with sacks of wheat.

"All right," Joe started. "What's going on?"

"How many men do you see standing before you, mate?" Cled Stewart offered lazily.

"Where are the other two?" Joe knew his stuff and he knew the ruling that there had to be ten men to haul a wheat load. This had been established as one of the few rules protecting the rights of the workers on the Sydney waterside for decades now and there were only eight men standing grimly in front of him.

"That's what we keep asking." Mac and Big Jim were stamping up the gangplank as Cled continued. "Seems like the bosses are having another go at breaking us down. We're not havin' it!" There were murmurs of agreement as Jim approached the huddle on the deck.

"What's keeping yer'? It's only a hundred ton. And a nice tidy hatch. You could be through this lot in no time."

"They're two short, Jim," Joe turned to face his old boss. "You know the rules."

"That's all the labour we're getting' for yer'. I've had my instructions." Jim appealed to the group. "I know the ruling but on this occasion, you don't need ten men."

"This occasion becomes every occasion, Jim. The load stays where it is until they have a full wheat gang. It's only reasonable." Joe looked evenly at Big Jim with his good eye while his glass eye stared menacingly at Macca who moved awkwardly out of its line of sight. Big Jim merely sighed and turned his back heading down the gangplank muttering.

"They're gonna' be in more strife than Ned Kelly over this, you watch!"

Jim was still unused to talking on the telephone in the wharf office overlooking the dock and gingerly lifted the handset from its cradle and placed it near his head. He liked to look a person in the eye when he spoke with them and had a habit of removing the headset from his ear to look at it when he wanted to make a point. His telephone conversations were invariably short. He got through to head office in

Macquarie Street and the ship-owner's representative, Harold Dawson.

"Well?" Dawson was clearly not about to waste much time on this matter.

"They won't work without the full gang. Joe Walsh is here and carrying on. He's calling for a Board of Reference." Jim pulled the earpiece further from him as Dawson let loose with a stream of expletives. He didn't catch a good part it but there was no mistaking the insinuations of his final comment.

"You losing control down there, Jim?"

George, Bluey, Tony and Lump were all attending the Darlinghurst comprehensive high school and coming to terms with being junior again after their senior year at Plunkett Street. George was no longer the biggest boy in school but his solid build and promising height gave Mr Parson great hope that he might join the rugby team. Mr Parson was the physical education teacher and a great enthusiast of rugby having played for the state in his youth. He remained a strong and stocky man although he was almost entirely bald and rarely smiled giving an impression of a sour temperament when in fact he was only embarrassed by his lost teeth and kept his lips firmly met. As he considered himself a man of action rather than words, this was a habit he found rather easy to adopt. In time, his reluctance to speak encouraged others to afford great weight to the little he said. And so, Mr Parson enjoyed the respect of all, including the senior boys, even Billy Mcfaddon.

George had first noticed Billy McFadden in the school yard, the tallest of a group of other older boys sneaking a cigarette under the willow that draped the far edge of the grey yard where the rest of the school took their lunch and played ball games and jump rope. Billy seemed a god-like presence with the other boys always looking to him for direction or else watching him for fear he may turn on them for he had a reputation as a scrap fighter and a bully. He was a solidly built boy with bristling blonde hair and oversized hands and wrists which had outgrown his jacket. His demeanor encouraged George to avoid him until Mr Parson introduced them as team members on the school rugby side. Billy snarled at George.

"Our new junior," he folded his giant arms over his chest and looked George up and down. "Can 'e kick?"

"Course he can," Mr Parson's chuckled. "And he's on your side, so …friendly, Billy."

"Friendly?" Billy murmured as Mr Parson strode away and blew his whistle to gather the rest of the boys into the centre of the field at Rushcutter's Bay. "Bit too pretty for rugby," Billy smirked. "Maybe I'll rearrange yer' face for yer'. Then yer' might do. Friendly enough?"

George sighed as Billy ran after Mr Parson. He wasn't sure that a rugby jumper would be worth the trouble. He knew he would have to fight. That's what boys did in high school but he had no stomach for it. He had learned some boxing from his Grandpa and his Uncle Sean. But his grandmother and his mother were always banging on about the evils of fighting and he tended to agree with them. It never made anything better in his experience. His uncles had been street brawlers with a fearsome reputation among the locals but he could see, even as a boy, that their predilection for violence had brought nothing but trouble into their lives. His size had meant that so far, George had been required to break up fights rather than start them and he hoped to keep it that way.

George joined the front row as a loose forward due to his speed and intelligence which Mr Parson was quick to observe. He had to play closely with Billy and learned to turn a blind eye to the fact that Billy never passed him the ball and shoved him with his arse when they were trying to settle the scrum. When he nicknamed him 'arse-rag', George simply shrugged and walked away.

"How can yer' let that Bastard call yer' that?" Bluey wailed at George as they strode home down the hill from Darlinghurst after school.

"He wants me to fight him and I don't want to do what he wants," George shrugged.

"He's got a nerve," Tony chimed in. "Thinks he runs the blasted school! Everyone's scared of him. He takes lunches from smaller kids all the time." Tony clutched his lunch tin to his generous belly and frowned.

"Well, he'll get a blasted shock if he gets hold of your lunch!" Lump had them all chuckling at the prospect of Billy scoffing great lumps of the garlic-laden salamis and cold, green spaghetti that Tony's Italian mother sent him to school with.

That afternoon, as most afternoons, George deposited his schoolbag on the kitchen table, scoffed a slice of bread and butter and jumped on his bicycle to call in to Mrs Mills shop to see if he could run a message.

"Back before dark," Maggie's familiar refrain called after him.

Bluey was waiting at the corner on his bike and ready to go. They both groaned when they learned the messages that afternoon were to be delivered to the grocer at King's Cross. That meant riding up Darlinghurst hill. This, they had learned from much practice, was best done flat chat and sticking to the pavement hoping that the momentum gained at the start of the hill would get you to the top before your heart burst. They both made it to the fire station where they hopped off for a breather.

"God, I hate that bloody hill," panted Bluey as they wheeled their bikes across the busy road.

"But now we get to ride down it," George smiled.

They turned into a lane way off Darlinghurst Road where a couple of boys from their school were sitting on a low wall in front of a vacant and crumbling weatherboard house. Several other boys were gathered at the doorway looking over one another's shoulders at some commotion happening inside. The laneway was otherwise bare of people and they nodded at the boys on the wall as they passed by.

One of the boys hissed anxiously at them, "It's Billy." He gestured inside the house and they heard Billy yelling something from the front room.

"What's he doing?" Bluey asked.

"Take a look," the boy pointed at the cracked window to the house and Billy and George leant their bikes against the wall and peered in the window.

The room was mostly full of boys and it was difficult to see at first what was happening against the far wall of the house but George never forgot the sight of the young, skinny boy from his class held at each wrist by a couple of bigger boys, friends of Billy's, as Billy shoved dirt into his mouth and screamed in his face. The boy had been stripped of his shorts and had filth smeared over him. It was clear he was having trouble breathing as tears streamed from his eyes. The many onlookers were mesmerized, some were red faced from a kind of feverish excitement but many looked on with growing uncertainty. None intervened. Billy was in a rage and clearly enjoying the humiliation of this defenseless boy.

George hated him. He looked at the strutting and cruel boy and experienced a flood of rage like he had never known before. He did not remember making the decision to enter the room.

George and Bluey had never torn down Darlinghurst hill so fast as that afternoon. They dodged traffic and pedestrians as they pedaled furiously homewards ignoring the curses of an old man who they almost toppled in their dash down the pavement. They heard the wail of the ambulance as they squealed to a halt outside Mrs Mills' shop.

"All done?" she asked as she counted pennies from her apron pocket.

George nodded silently and took half the money, handing the rest to Bluey who looked at him intently.

"It was his own fault," Billy avoided George's gaze as they wheeled their bikes down Dowling Street.

"What if he's dead?" George whispered. He could not shake the sight of Billy lying still on the filthy floor of the vacant house with blood trickling from a gash to his skull. His head had made the sound of good smash at the cricket when it hit the stone wall. George felt ill with grief and guilt. Billy was a filthy bully but he didn't want him to die.

That evening George was very quiet at the dinner table and concentrated on his mashed potatoes as his Grandma reprimanded Jim and Sean.

"We will not have talk about the wharves at the table! It's bad enough you should be warring at work but you won't be doing it here."

The large men moved their chins from side to side and held their noses high but ceased arguing.

"Cat got your tongue?" Anne leaned in to George teasing him in her usual way. The ongoing debates between her Grandfather and Uncle about what was fair and what wasn't at the wharves was so familiar it was merely background noise to her. She was far more interested in her brother's oddly subdued behavior.

"Shut up," he responded and his mother glared at him from across the table as they heard a rap on the front door.

"I'll get it," Sybil offered and headed up the hall. Anne studied George harder as he squirmed in his seat. They heard some murmuring and then Sybil returned to the kitchen.

"George," she was pale and spoke quietly but she was blinking furiously and that meant trouble. "Mr Gordon, the School Principal is here and would like a word with you." George slid uncomfortably from his chair and accompanied his mother to the hall where Mr Gordon stood with his hat in his hand. The rest of the family approached from the kitchen.

Jim called, "Come in to the front room, Mr Gordon." So, they shuffled back down the hall into the light of the front room and George stood by the sofa with his legs suddenly trembling under him. At least he had finished a good dinner before they came to lock him up, he consoled himself and held his hands crossed in front of him imagining that any moment he would be wearing handcuffs. The room before him suddenly seemed a palace and his life in which he was free to do as he liked (other than attend school, of course) was a joyous luxury for he had no doubt that he would soon be behind bars for murder. What a hopeless criminal he was. His first offence and he would be bagged when he hadn't even meant it. Poor Mr Parson, with Billy dead and him in jail, he had ruined their chances in the competition this season. He realized himself that was an odd thought in the circumstances and he was having trouble trying to concentrate on the conversation in the room.

"So, he's recovering," Sean eyed Mr Gordon.

"Thankfully, yes," said Mr Gordon. "But we can't be sure he will fully recover for a while. He was heavily concussed."

"What have you got to say for yourself, George?" Sybil demanded through tight lips.

Billy was alive! It was music to George's ears. He wasn't a murderer. He was just bad, very bad perhaps, but not a murderer. He stared at the floorboards in the loud silence as all eyes watched him expectantly. He didn't care how they punished him. He had not killed Billy. He was so pleased that at that moment he could have kissed Billy McFadden.

"In George's defense," coughed Mr Gordon bowing his head slightly, "I am sufficiently convinced by other witnesses at the scene that he was acting to protect a younger boy who was being bullied by Billy. And as this is not the first occasion of bullying from that young man, I am inclined to reprimand George with a severe warning and a week of suspension from school. Violence is not tolerated at our school, for any reason young man! I shall expect an essay from you on what lessons you have learned from this episode by Monday morning 9am, on my desk." Mr Gordon turned his attention back to Sybil. "There will be no charges from the family, Mrs Pace. We have discussed the situation and they are content to have George suspended. They know Billy has something to answer for here as well."

Once Sybil had shown Mr Gordon out the front door and thanked him for going easy on her son, she whirled back into the front room like a ferry at full throttle and smacked George hard across his left ear.

"What have I told you about violence?" she yelled and stared at the boy as he rubbed his ear and ducked in fear of another one.

"Now, now, Syb," Sean offered and placed his hands gently on her shoulders.

"I always worried what Woolloomooloo might do to him," she cried. "All the larrikins and gangsters and molls in the streets. How can yer' hope to bring up a good son?" Sybil burst into tears and George felt as low as a snake's belly for making her cry.

"Let me and Dad have a talk to 'im, Syb," Sean steered her towards her room. You just have a lie down and Maggie will get you a cup of tea". Maggie started from the trancelike state she had been in since Mr Gordon arrived.

"Tea? Yes, tea," she said thankfully and headed for the kitchen flapping her slippers with purpose.

Jim and Sean stared at George and sat him on the sofa.

"What happened?" Jim started.

As George told them about what Billy was doing to the young boy and the rage he had experienced and how quickly it had happened they listened in silence. "That boy…," said George, "…he reminded me of Bernard,…. always gettin' picked on. I lost me mind."

Sean and Jim shared a long look.

"And where did you hit him?" asked Jim.

"Well, I didn't hit him. I just shoved him."

"From in front or behind?" asked Sean.

"From behind," confessed George. "I shoved him from behind and his head hit the wall, and that was it."

Jim nodded his head and looked sternly into George's eyes. "It's not all wrong, what yer' did. But it's not right to hit, or shove, from behind. A fair fight is when a man knows what's comin'. Yer' gotta introduce yer'self before yer' knock a man out. Yer' never want to kill a man by accident."

Sean nodded in agreement as Jim lectured George.

"I reckon he needs some solid instruction, Dad" Sean and Jim exchanged a sly look and pushed George out the back, down the steps from the kitchen into the dark yard. For a good half hour they boxed and wrestled, running through the routines for turning a man and hitting him and Jim landed George a solid smack in the jaw which he apologized for saying it was an accident but it didn't feel like an accident.

"You got worse from yer' mum!" Scoffed Jim. "Now get to bed and don't be getting in any more fights from behind."

Jim let out a sigh as George entered the back door. "He's not a bad lad."

"No," Sean replied. "And I like your point about a fair fight. Giving your opponent the chance to defend himself." Sean couldn't help but smile as he strolled back inside. "I thought that was just what the Union was doing."

Even Sybil was taken aback by the image she projected in the floor to ceiling mirror in the Ladies Department fitting rooms of David Jones. Instead of her usual, shapeless black work dress, she wore a shimmering, dark-red gown that hugged her curves and framed her bare neck and shoulders like the petals of a flower. It was a French label and cost the Earth. She had never worn a dress like it, nor had the sort of money you needed to ever own one. But she did have staff access to the store and when evening fell and everyone was gone home, who would be the wiser if a gown were missing from the rack for a few hours?

Those were Edith's words and it was Edith who had put her up to it. It wasn't every day you were asked by a handsome young man to a Ball and she had absolutely nothing she could wear to an event like the annual Artist's Ball at East Sydney Technical College. Edith's brother Larry was studying technical drawing there at night and he had won two tickets to the Ball in the College raffle. Larry was a tall, slender young man, whom everyone knew was as camp as a row of tents. As he couldn't take a bloke to the Ball and wouldn't be seen dead stepping out with his own sister, he had asked Sybil. Or rather, he had told Edith to ask Sybil.

At first, Sybil had thrown her head back and laughed – after all, she was now thirty-one years old where Larry was in his early twenties. But the more she thought about it over a dreary day spent serving customers, dusting shelves and counting stock, the more sense it made. Larry would be terrified to ask a real girl out to a dance in case she actually expected anything from him. And Larry loved to dance. He and Sybil had shared the front floor of the Pace house on many a Saturday night kicking their heels back to Duke Ellington's, *It Don't Mean a Thing, If It Ain't Got That Swing.* That was Larry's favourite and he was an excellent dance partner being both lithe and nimble without the wandering hands. She had decided she might even go to the Ball when she had remembered that she didn't have a gown.

"I've got more gowns at my fingertips than you could poke a stick at!" said Edith when Sybil explained her situation. Edith gestured towards the Ladies Evening Wear section in which she now worked. "'Bout time one of them had some fun!" She winked at Sybil's alarmed face. "Nothing to worry about! They sit on the rack all through the dark night. No one will be any the wiser if you take one out for a spin. So long as we get it back before shop opens in the morning, and so long as you look after it. I know just the gown that will do the job too. It's a ghost and ghouls theme and I've got the dress!" Edith's eyes, normally half shut with boredom at work, were shining with excitement as she grabbed Sybil's hand and rushed her across the polished floor to the evening section. They gazed silently at the blood-red, silk gown draped over its hanger by soft, wide straps that crossed at the back and rejoined the bodice under the arms. The bodice was pulled tight at the waist but draped generously around the bosom exposing the shoulders and neck as well as a good part of the back. It had no further adornment, its beauty resting in the artful cut and generous luxury of the fabric which fell to the floor in folds. This was a dress designed to flatter a womanly figure such as Sybil's.

"Oooh!" Sybil couldn't help exclaim. "It's beautiful." She crossed her legs and clenched her fists with the excitement.

"It's dangerous! It's blood red and it's perfect!" shrieked Edith. "I've gotta' see you in it." Sybil tried the dress on with Edith's help in the fitting room after the other staff and Mrs Bradshaw had gone home for the day. They stared in reverent silence at Sybil's reflection in the mirror. The shopgirl had been transformed into a glamorous vixen and when they caught each other's eye, they burst into laughter.

"God's trousers!" said Edith. "You look like a flamin' film star!"

"You really think I can go out like this?!" Sybil turned to inspect the rear of the dress in the mirror and blushed almost as deeply as the red of the dress. Her white back was exposed from the waist up except for where the straps crossed.

"Well, it's not a dress you would stay home in!" Edith exclaimed.

"I'll have to wear my hair down," Sybil decided. "That'll hide a bit of it."

"What are you hiding from?" asked Edith. "This is going to be a magic night for you, Sybil. You might meet your next husband – Larry won't be standing in your way."

"Not sure I want to meet the next love of my life at a ghoul's ball!" laughed Sybil as she manoeuvred her way out of the dress.

They planned that Edith would package the dress for Sybil to carry out of the store after work on the day of the Ball. Edith held her breath whenever a customer fingered the gown for the couple of weeks leading up to the Ball and subtly guided them to alternatives with more flattering necklines or a better price tag. The day before the Ball, the gown still hung full of promise on the evening rack in Ladies Wear but disaster had struck at the warehouse where Larry worked. He had been knocked unconscious by a crate of tinned pineapple that slipped from the towering storage shelves he was clearing. The doctor was called and he was revived but confined to bed for several days. While they expected him to make a full recovery, dancing was out of the question for the time being. Edith dragged herself over to Sybil's counter in lingerie to tell her the news feeling as disappointed as if it were her own Ball she couldn't go to.

"Never mind," said Sybil, hiding her disappointment. "I'm sorry about Larry. I hope he's okay."

"I can't believe it," said Edith. "The luck of it!"

"Murphy's law," Sybil let out a deep breath of regret as they each leant on the sparkling glass display cabinet with their chins propped on their hands. "Unless,…." Sybil cocked her head to glance sideways at Edith. "Has Larry still got the tickets?"

"Yeah, I think so…" Edith gazed quizzically at Sybil.

"Do yer' think he'd mind if I went with someone else?"

Sybil could hear the shouting as she approached the Pace home that evening. The days were getting shorter now summer was well and truly over and it was twilight by the time she approached Dowling Street. Lavender and gold coloured clouds held the last rays of the sun as it sank and the windows of the taller buildings on the eastern side of William Street shone like dusty jewels. She was vaguely aware of the smell of frying fish and the screeching of the trams groaning up the hill as she thought nervously over the idea she was formulating in her head dodging pedestrians making their way home from work. The single street lamp lit up as she turned the corner. Jim was doing his block.

"Stubborn bunch of bastards, the lot of yer!'"

Sybil bit her lip as she stepped warily into the front hall of the Pace home.

"'Lo," she called. "Anything wrong?"

Sean turned wearily to greet her from where he sat on the sofa while Jim stood over him.

"It's just a wharf matter," he offered.

"Oh," Sybil removed her hat and hung it next to her coat on the hook in the hallway. She stood immobile in the hall as the two men stared at her.

"You all right?" Sean asked.

"Yep," she nodded. "I'll go and help Maggie." As she passed behind Sean she said, "I need to ask yer' something. When you've finished discussing yer' wharf matter." She looked sideways at Jim who sighed and plonked himself in an armchair.

Maggie raised her eyebrows and rolled her eyes when Sybil entered the kitchen. It was her habit to maintain a quiet in the kitchen when there was shouting in the house and there had been plenty of that over the last thirty years. She rarely intervened unless there was violence started and then she had been known to pick up a kitchen knife. Sybil smiled quietly at Maggie and took an apron from the kitchen drawer. Anne sat with her head bowed over the kitchen table writing in a schoolbook with her tongue sticking like a small, pink salamander from the corner of her mouth. Sybil kissed Anne on the nape of her neck then picked up the wood tray and started out the back door for more kindling for the kitchen stove.

"Larry got knocked out for a seven yesterday."

Anne looked up from her book and Maggie turned from the stove squinting, "Isn't he taking you to the dance tomorrow night?"

"Don't see how he can," laughed Sybil.

"Aw, momma!" Anne slipped from her chair and hugged her mother around her hips. "That's not fair! You've gotta' go to the dance!"

"It's only a dance, love. I can't go without someone to take me."

Maggie looked steadily at Sybil and then her eyes moved meaningfully to the lounge room where Sean was talking quietly now to Jim. She looked back at Sybil and they each smiled conspiratorially.

"Do 'yer think?" Sybil lifted an eyebrow.

"'Course he will!" Maggie beamed. "Go and ask him! Jim!" She yelled. "Jim! Come 'ere, will you? I need some more wood." Maggie snatched the wood tray from Sybil and pushed her into the front room as Jim appeared in the kitchen.

Sean was lighting the kerosene lamp on the table. His sun-bleached hair was longer than most men wore it and fell in a straight line over his cheek obscuring his face from her. She was suddenly shy and flustered looking at his broad shoulders and watching him turn to her and smile as he always did when he saw her.

"Hey," she said, "Larry Johnson's been knocked for a seven."

"Is that right? I'm sorry to hear it. Will he be all right?" He sat heavily back onto the sofa lifting the newspaper from the table.

"Yeah, it was a box of pineapples." Sybil stood quietly for a moment then blurted: "So, will you to take me to the dance instead of Larry? It's tomorrow night at the Tech. Ghosts and Ghouls… and free beer."

"What, me?!" Sean dropped the newspaper and looked over his shoulder at her to check if she were serious. She had her hands on her hips now and so he knew that there was not really a choice. Nevertheless, he pursed his lips and looked at the ceiling for what seemed a long time before he smiled again.

"'Oright."

Sybil kissed his forehead. "We'll have so much fun, Sean! You're an angel!" She squealed.

"Try tellin' 'im that!" Sean grunted indicating the kitchen where Jim was bent over packing wood into the stove and muttering under his breath.

"Nice arse," commented Maggie with a wink at her granddaughter. Anne giggled hysterically and Jim stood up unable to resist a chuckle as George charged into the kitchen from the back yard as he usually did, like he was bowling in the cricket.

"Don't you walk anywhere, boy?" Jim demanded.

On the day of the Ball, Sybil could not concentrate at work returning the wrong change to a customer and mislaying a petticoat on order for a delivery.

"Are you well, Mrs Pace?" Mrs Bradshaw looked at her with some concern as Sybil hastily packaged the petticoat which she had finally discovered under the counter in the section where the pricing tickets were stored.

"Yes, yes, I am fine, Mrs Bradshaw. Just forgetful today." She smiled apologetically and hoped that Mrs Bradshaw would find something else to focus on.

"You're as toey as a Roman sandal!" Edith complained as they sat together at the staff table in the cool basement at lunchtime eating tomato sandwiches. At least, Edith was eating while Sybil chewed her lip and stared at the pink, damp bread around the sliced tomato with unseeing eyes and no appetite. "I'll stay behind a bit with you this arvo' and make sure your parcel is nicely wrapped," Edith assured her. "All you have to do is walk out the door with some shopping under yer' arm like you've done so many times. Then tomorrow, you get in here before eight o'clock with the parcel wrapped up again. All right?

I'll be here around then and we'll slip everything back in place before anyone's awake to it. Just like Cinderella," Edith quivered with excitement.

Sybil's cheeks flushed and her smile was complicated but grateful. She wanted to go to the Ball so badly. She wanted to wear the bewitching gown. She wanted to dance like she was young again and forget for one evening the monotony and the drudgery of her life as shop girl and mother. For one night she wanted to be just Sybil again. But another part of her told her that this evening was a false step. That her life was full and rich and that she had more than she deserved in her children and her family and her work. She felt that she was somehow doing her life an injustice but she could not resist it.

Edith looked into her friends' uncertain, brown eyes and took a hold of her shoulders: "For God's sake! You're only havin' a bit of fun. It won't kill yer! Now stop mulling on it and let's get on!"

Anne was allowed to sit with her mother in their bedroom that evening while Sybil prepared for the Ball. Sybil watched her daughter stroke the red gown hanging on the back of the door as if it were a kitten. Sybil had bathed and applied a dash of lavender water to her neckline. Other than to climb into the gown, there was little to do as she was wearing her hair down. She had taken care to wash and calm her mass of brown ringlets with a raw egg mixture the evening before and had tied her hair in a scarf for the day. When she undid the scarf, her hair spilt obligingly around her face and down her back concealing much of the bare skin exposed by the cut of the gown which Anne helped her button around her waist. She had the pair of gold drop earrings given to her by her mother on her wedding day as her only adornment. She removed her wedding ring and placed it on the chest of drawers and with that she felt some of her uncertainty subside. She applied a little powder to her face and painted her lips the same red as the dress with the rouge Edith had given her. She gazed at the glamorous woman in the mirror before her and noticed Anne also gazing shyly at this strange vision of her mother.

"Wadder yer' reckon?" Sybil placed her hands on her hips and twirled.

"You look beautiful, Ma," Anne whispered as if she were afraid to break a spell.

"I'm goin' as a vampire's victim," she laughed, "...so watch this." Sybil took up the rouge and carefully added two small red 'puncture' marks at her throat. "That's where Dracula got me!" She pulled a distressed face and Anne giggled anxiously.

"And your Uncle Sean is going as Dracula himself!" she added taking hold of the old sheet that she had died black. "Let's go and find him."

When Sean laid eyes on Sybil as he descended the stairs and she laid eyes on him from the hall, they were equally shocked. Sean was smiling broadly showing off the costume vampire fangs he had fashioned from almond nutshells which he had painted white and pinned to a rubber band that fitted around his top jaw. But he forgot all about them when he clapped eyes on Sybil.

"Crikey, is that you, Syb?" He remained half way down the stairs uncertain if he should approach this glamorous vision. "Yer' look like the Queen of England!" Both Anne and Sybil burst into uncontrollable laughter.

"Uncle Sean!" squealed Anne. "What have you done to your teeth?" Anne performed her favourite trick of 'fainting' over the back of the sofa and Sybil had to go and re-do her lipstick.

"Of course we're walkin!" Sybil scoffed at Sean's suggestion they may need to get a cab. "It's only up the road, and such a lovely night."

"Rightio'," Sean acquiesced. They headed off up Dowling Street as it was almost dark with Anne waving from the front step and George squinting after them. The tassells of Maggie's black, silk shawl swung joyously from Sybil's almost bare shoulders as she walked with Sean into the night. George watched them as they turned to look back from under the streetlamp, laughing with Sean supporting his mother's elbow and her gloved fingers resting comfortably on his forearm. He noticed for the first time that they were the same height. They were like a pair of something that would come in a box together.

"I wish Sean was our Dad," said Anne. George peered into his sister's impassive grey eyes.

"You're a lot like your Grandma, you know?" He said after a moment.

"Whadder' yer' mean?" she asked.

"Sayin' things other people won't say," offered George. "It's all right, Anne," he turned her shoulders and pushed her gently inside the house. "But Sean can't be our Dad. He's our Uncle."

Although Darlinghurst Gaol had been transformed into East Sydney Technical College several decades earlier, it retained a somber and oppressive air despite the fact that the prisoners had been marched away to the new Gaol at Long Bay many decades ago and the gates had been flung open to a wary public. The gallows, where so many executions had taken place, were no longer there but the chilling knowledge remained. Infamous rebels, Captain Moonlite and Jimmy Governor, along with plain murderers and cutthroats had met their demise inside the thick sandstone walls just a few yards from the busy commercial centre of Darlinghurst. It made Sybil shudder to think how close. To add to the ghoulishness of the evening a row of hangman's nooses were strung over the jamb above the infamous green gates so you had to part them to enter the grounds. Rows of burning lamps lit the pathway to the Women's Cell where the Ball was centred and from where light spilled along with the energy of music and laughter.

Darlinghurst Gaol had been designed as if it were a wheel laid flat on the Earth with the moral anchor of the circular Chapel at the centre and the long cell block buildings splaying out like the spokes. The grounds were pleasant enough nowadays with garden beds and graveled pathways around and between the buildings which now served as classrooms for art students. But the sandstone walls of these buildings that rose over thirty feet high were still relieved only by the regular rows of deep, barred cell windows less than a foot square.

"They look more like upright drains than windows," commented Sybil as they headed along the pathway towards the comparative merriment and light of the Women's Cell.

"Look, you can still see the marks of the convicts on some of the stone blocks." Sean drew Sybil off the path against a wall to show her.

"Isn't it strange to think of these men building their own prison? Working like dogs day in and day out only to build the cells in which they would be locked away." As they stood for a moment in quiet thought a sudden howl followed by the sound of a lashing whip and a curse emanated from a dark cell window above their heads. Sybil jumped and clutched Sean and then they laughed and ran back along the brightly lit path.

"That's the hall of horror behind you," said the young attendant who took their tickets. "You must go and visit it when you are quite brave! One of the men's cells. And it was there they held the prisoners ready for execution. It's terribly haunted. Enjoy yourselves!" Sybil and Sean shared a look of amusement as they entered the giddy light, noise and movement of the Ball. Sean pulled his cape over his face to fit his vampire teeth then lifted his cape above his shoulders like a bat and bared his almond fangs.

"Time for a bit of refreshment!" Sybil shrieked with laughter and pushed him before her.

Inside the glowing, yellow room were crowds of costumed men and women clustered around tables, drinking, chatting and admiring each other's outfits while a jazz band played some mid-paced melodies from a podium set deep into the room and draped with chains.

The towering ceilings had long cobwebs fashioned from flimsy ropes which hung upon the exposed timber beams that supported the roof. A waiter dressed as a mummy in torn bandages was ladling cupfuls of blood red punch from a barrel into small cups and Sean and Sybil took one each as they made their way around the room towards the dance floor.

Sean spotted Alf Craven who managed one of the warehouses in Woolloomooloo dressed as the Devil sitting at a table with his girl Bethwyn. He introduced Sybil who listened to Bethwyn tell about the domestic science classes she was taking at the Tech and which buildings were haunted the worst. The fact that she was dressed as a ghost in a roped sheet with blackened eyes and blue lips made her tales all the more unnerving.

Sybil couldn't remember when she had felt the blood pumping more keenly in her veins. Her eyes drank in the smiling faces, the exotic and bizarre costumes, the white-clothed serving tables laden with sandwiches, fruits and cakes and the beer flowing free from great barrels. It was like, just for one evening, the Depression had never happened. The dour and ceaseless working, pinching and scraping and making do. All the while hoping for something, something rich and beautiful to happen. It was happening. This was rich and beautiful.

Sean observed Sybil over Alf's shoulder as she watched the dancers now beginning to sway around the dance floor. Her face was alight and he savoured her happiness.

"Struth! She's a good lookin' sheila, your sister," Alf shouted above the music.

"She's my sister-in-law." Sean corrected him. Sybil was swaying in her seat to the music her reddened lips parted showing her small, even teeth. There was something about their smallness, the way her incisors were a little ahead of the rest, her pink gums and her habit of wrinkling her nose when she laughed that fascinated him. Her pretty mouth meant more to him than it should, he knew. She turned to catch his eye and she saw, he knew, his admiration for her before he had time to shield his emotion. She held his eyes for a long moment smiling gently and then winked at him.

"I need a beer," Sean glowered at the red liquid in the small cup in his hand and headed to the bar.

"That's a beautiful dress," Bethwyn said. "Where did you get it?"

"Borrowed it," Sybil smiled. "Excuse me." She followed Sean to the bar and pulled on his cape.

"'Eh! Count Dracula! Will you dance with me?" Sybil was warmed by the punch and the music and her hips swung into his. Sean swallowed the beer he was holding in several gulps and took her arm.

The evening was a whirl of colour and energy and Sybil danced with Sean, then with several ghosts, a pirate and an unraveling mummy until she was exhausted and had to stand to the side and recover sipping on a cordial. In their group was a bloke with a razor slash scar drawn from his lip to his ear and a shirt stained with globs of red dye. He and Sean were talking. Then, suddenly Sean was dragging him violently by his shirt collar out of the ballroom through the chattering, dancing ghosts into the cool air of the night where he shoved him onto the gravel.

"Take off your jacket," Sean was shrugging out of his vampire cape with some difficulty. "C'mon, you bastard!" He had his fists up and was swaying with beer and indignation by the time Sybil made it through the revelers into the courtyard at the front of the Women's Cell.

"For Christ's sake," the bloke on the ground was crawling to unsteady feet. "I was only jokin', mate!"

"Sean!" Sybil called out and rushed in front of him pushing him back and looking urgently into his angry eyes. "Sean, don't! Stop it!" It was then that she heard the unmistakable tear of the silk lining inside the skirt of the beautiful red gown as her foot caught and ripped it from the seam at the waist. She gasped in horror.

"Your brothers cause trouble when they're not even here, Sean Pace!" shouted the young blonde woman in a skeleton outfit who was leading her razor-slashed partner away from them out of the Gaol grounds. Sean stood on the gravel immobilised by competing concerns to pursue the smartarse who had insulted his family or to attend to a fretting Sybil who was bent over examining the inside of her gown and groaning.

"You'll keep, you bastard!" he spat and turned to Sybil. "You all right? What are you doing?"

"I've torn me gown," her utter dismay seemed disproportionate to a tear in a dress.

"He said we were a bunch of cutthroats," Sean explained to no one.

On the long and unsteady walk home Sean calmed down and Sybil became more wretched.

"I'm sorry, Syb," Sean offered aware that her heels were hitting the pavement with unusual force. "Have I ruined yer' night?"

She sighed. "What did yer' have to start a fight for?"

"He said we were cutthroats!" Sean declared. "The lot of us."

"He meant yer' brothers, you know that."

"Even so, that's not what he said," Sean hiccupped.

"I've wrecked this blasted dress," Sybil moaned. "I'm in for it."

"Why? Just sew it up, can't you?" Sean offered.

"It's not mine,… I took it."

"Where from?" Sean studied Sybil sideways.

"David Jones, Ladies Evening Wear," she replied. Sean was laughing so hard he had to pull up and hold his knees for support.

When Mrs Bradshaw drew aside the heavy curtain of the women's fitting room in Ladies Wear at seven-thirty the next morning, Sybil jumped out of her skin and thrust the needle she was using to darn the red gown deep into her thumb.

"Quick!" Mrs Bradshaw rushed to grab the gown from the stream of blood flowing down her wrist. Sybil sat speechless with the horror of it all. She was only halfway through mending the seam and had not expected the manager to be in for half an hour. The pain of her thumb was nothing to the moral torment she was going through in her head. She was done for. She was a thief and she would lose her job. The tears began to flow down her cheeks and would not stop.

Mrs Bradshaw stared at the silently weeping woman with the bleeding thumb seated on the bench before her. She sighed. "Go and wash your face and patch your hand, then finish darning this dress." She inspected the still torn seam. "Make sure you do a good job. And then come and see me." She shook her head and marched to her office.

"I'm sorry, Mrs Bradshaw," Sybil offered as she entered the Manager's Office a short while later with the gown laid like an exhausted dancer over her forearm. She wiped her eyes which were still flowing. "I just thought,.." she hiccupped and her mouth opened and shut but could not seem to form the words she wanted.

"Oh, stop it!" Mrs Bradshaw looked at the ceiling. She turned the newspaper she had open on her desk in Sybil's direction. "Did you really think this would go unnoticed?" To Sybil's horror, there she was standing in the now infamous gown between a pirate and Count Dracula in a photograph printed in the society column. Sybil merely hung her head and waited for her execution.

"Mrs Pace, I have hired many girls from Woolloomooloo and none of them are ever quite the clean potato. Is there something in the water down the hill there? Makes people take what isn't theirs?" Sybil started sobbing again.

"I just thought, for one night,… I just wanted for one night…," she was unable to continue. "I'm sorry, Mrs Bradshaw." The Manager continued to stare at Sybil and imagined how she might finish the sentence she was trying to articulate. She found it surprisingly easy: for one night she had wanted to be beautiful and glamorous and not poor and struggling and lonely. She knew Sybil worked hard without a husband to support her children. And she was always reliable and hardworking. Until now. Something in the bent head and the hopeless certainty that her life was ruined touched Mrs Bradshaw's heart.

"Go away," Mrs Bradshaw said quietly. She curled up the newspaper and placed it carefully in the waste paper basket. "Go back to lingerie and finish your day. I can't say what the outcome of this will be, Sybil. I am prepared to give you this chance but I am not the only person who may 'uncover' you. What you did was stealing. The gown is returned." Mrs Bradshaw took the gown from Sybil's arm and opened the skirt to inspect the neatly mended seam. "But it's still stealing."

Sybil's tears began to dry up. "Oh, thank you! Thank you! Will I keep my job, Mrs Bradshaw?"

Mrs Bradshaw shrugged. "Time will tell." She handed the gown roughly to Sybil and dismissed her from her office with a weary brush of her hand.

As Sybil was hanging the gown in its place on the rack in Ladies Wear, Edith arrived at work and removed her coat. "Well?" she asked with eyes sparkling. "Tell me all about it."

Sybil screwed up her eyes and ducked her head to the side as if Edith had swung a punch.

When Sybil had trodden a sorry path home that day unsure if she would soon be one of the shoeless vagrants she watched picking through the waste bins in the park, she found the family gathered around the table in the kitchen with the newspaper open at the photograph of her and Sean and the Pirate.

"What a lovely photo it is!" Maggie exclaimed when she saw her. "Society girl now!" Sybil managed a meek smile as her eyes met Sean's.

"How was work?" He stared at her and she felt the sting of tears but firmed her mouth.

"Made it through another day," she sat heavily in a kitchen chair.

"Your Ma was the belle of the Ball last night, Anne. The most beautiful woman in the room." Sean beamed. "And she's a Woolloomooloo girl too! Aren't yer' Syb?"

She glared at him.

"Was it fun? Did you dance? What did you eat? Tell me, tell me," Anne pleaded staring at the photograph in the paper and trying to imagine the rest of the magical room behind the photo.

"It was a bonzer night," declared Sean.

"Until someone lost his temper," Sybil muttered.

"Argh," Sean waved his hand dismissively. "There was no fighting, only a bit of push and shove. It's not a real Woolloomooloo party without a bit of push and shove!" Maggie looked from Sean to Sybil, pursed her lips and put the kettle on.

In the middle of that night, after tossing and turning while Anne lay next to her soundly sleeping, Sybil crept from her bed into the kitchen. She wanted to see the photograph again. To see it alone so she could really see it. She found the paper in the wood tray ready for the morning's fire and opened it at the society page only to find the photograph had been ripped out. She closed the paper and stared bleakly at the front page showing a photograph of Adolf Hitler at the opening of the Summer Olympic Games. He stood with other officers in the German uniform with the baggy duds and the braided, high helmet saluting from a concrete podium above the crowds. But it was the other photograph that was unsettling. That was the picture of twenty thousand adoring Germans saluting back at him.

She shivered and dropped the paper back in the wood tray and slipped back into her room and into bed hugging her warm daughter to her and finally finding sleep.

MARCH 1937

Jim watched Maggie darning the collar of his good shirt as they sat at either end of the scarred timber table top they had dragged in from the back lane on the back of Harry's cart so many years before. He watched his wife a lot now that he was out of work. He was fascinated with her constant, purposeful activity that seemed powered by some unseen force, possibly tea. She was active from the crack of dawn, building a fire in the stove, putting together modest meals from whatever groceries she could collect with her housekeepings now supplied from whatever Sybil, Sean and George brought home along with Jim's miserable new pension. There was a lot of porridge and a lot of stew at their table but they knew to be grateful for it as there were still plenty of folk who went without. Once the house was empty of the morning scramble of children and the two remaining workers, Maggie moved on to ironing, washing, darning, scrubbing, fetching wood and therefore never sat without some task in her hand. Her face was lined now but her sunbaked expression remained as untroubled as the day he met her over thirty years ago as she had passed him the warm bag of chips across the sweating glass counter of her father's fish shop at Manly wharf. Her hands were well worn and the wedding band cut into her plump finger as she moved her needle in and out of the thick cotton. She was getting old, he thought. They were both getting old. But it pleased him greatly that her untroubled expression remained after they had been married so long and been through so much. It was a kind of triumph both for her and himself.

The kitchen looked unfamiliar in this mid-morning light as he was used to being at work by now. He felt almost as if he had stepped through a portal into someone else's life, someone else's kitchen. He stared into the grain of the wood and found the horse's head that he always saw with the eye, passive and wise, perfectly captured in the swirl of the knot of pine staring back at him as if nothing had changed and he hadn't been sent packing from the wharf. He asked himself silently how he was feeling about it all but all he could feel was the idle shirt on his back. He began to whistle as he could think of nothing else to do.

"For Gord's sake," Maggie exclaimed. "Will yer' find something to do!?"

Jim's shocked expression and look of helplessness caused Maggie to soften her tone. "Will you go up to Mrs Mills and fetch some flour? We need some for the dinner and then I want to show you where we can have a new planting outside." She smiled at him and took his stubbled cheek in her hand. "Don't worry, love. I'll always find you something to keep you busy." She kissed him smartly on the lips and returned to squinting at her stitches.

When Jim returned minutes later from Mrs Mills shop it was without the flour but with George slung over his back and Bluey wheeling George's damaged bike behind them, Maggie panicked.

"What is it? What've yer' done?" She fluttered around them like a startled bird as Jim made his way into the hall and tried to pass her.

"Will yer' get out of the blasted way, woman?" Jim muttered straining under George's weight and making his way to the sofa where he cautiously lowered George onto his back. "He's not too bad. I think he's broken his leg." Indeed, the femur of George's left leg was at a sickening, new angle. Maggie stared in horror at the pale boy.

"Bluey, go and get the doctor," she urged.

"Righto," Bluey raced out the front door and tore up Dowling Street returning with the young Doctor Jason from the family clinic. George's leg was indeed broken and had to be set and immobilized in plaster. Bluey watched the agonizing process in fascination as Maggie turned in circles wringing her hands and moaning while Jim held George's hand.

"No more school for you for a while, son." The Doctor patted George's good leg once he had dressed his patient and George smiled weakly at him feeling the effects of the morphine the doctor had administered.

"That right?"

If George had known that his accident would have ended his schooling, he would have broken his leg himself. Now he was thirteen, he had only a year left at high school and although it was uncommon for the children of Woolloomooloo to complete, his mother had been adamant that he should attend to 'better himself'. So George had completed several reluctant weeks of his final year at school but as most of his mates including Bluey, Tony and the Lump were already working or apprenticed to a trade, he resented every moment of it and frequently rode the streets on his bicycle rather than sit in class and learn the history of Norman invasion. Now, school was out of the question and the doctor himself had said so.

"He didn't say forever," a despairing Sybil pointed out when she got home from work and had digested the day's events. She sat on the sofa with George's head in her lap listening to his steady breathing as he slept off the morphine.

"It's going to be hard for him to keep up, if he's stuck on the sofa for weeks on end," pointed out Jim.

"I'll get him books from the library, Sybil," Maggie suggested.

For six weeks George sat immobile on the sofa studying those around him and reading while his bones knitted themselves back together. Maggie asked the local librarian to recommend books and she brought home novels by Charles Dickens, Rudyard Kipling and Jack London. His Uncle Sean insisted he read some Australian writers and brought him colonial tales by Rolf Bolderwood and Marcus

Clarke. He read everything he could get his hands on, including the daily paper and in this he learned of the raging Spanish Civil War which he had heard Sean speaking about in pained tones. He saw photographs of Adolf Hitler and the German Reich and followed Mussolini's invasion of Ethiopia and Stalin's purge of the Red Army. He asked Maggie for an atlas and began to study where these far away countries were. In the evenings he talked with his Uncle.

"Stalin's killin' off his Generals," he watched Sean's face as he knew that Stalin was a communist and Grandpa often called Sean a communist.

"Yeah," Sean looked tired as he sat across from George reading the paper with his brows crossed.

"Why?" asked George.

Sean sighed. "Power, I suppose."

"Hmmm," George nodded his head. "Are you a communist, Uncle Sean?"

"Nah," Sean laughed bitterly. "I'm not anything, mate. Don't like joining causes."

"But Grandpa says you are because you're in the Union and you read too much and you fight with the police."

Sean guffawed. "That's not all it takes to be a communist, mate. Do you know what communism means, George?"

"Yes, it means that everyone works as much as they can and everyone gets enough money and everything to live. So, no rich people."

"That's not bad," acknowledged Sean sitting up straighter in the armchair and looking intently at his nephew who he realized was almost a man.

"What's wrong with it?" George screwed his face up in genuine consternation. "I don't understand why Grandpa hates it."

"It's radical change, George. Older people don't like too much change. But it's more than that..." Sean ran his hand through his hair. "People are corrupt, George. There is nothing surer than that. The politicians..." He didn't know how to finish what he was saying and studied his nephew's anxious face. He realized with horror that in four or five years George would be old enough to enlist. He would make a grand soldier too with his solid build and his calm manner. He glared at the floorboards and watched the particles of dust shimmer in the shaft of afternoon light shining through the narrow window of the lounge looking into the back yard.

"Do you remember the war?" asked George.

"I was a nipper!" laughed Sean. "So was your father. Your Grandpa was too old to go to war. We were lucky, I s'pose. Your twin Uncles went … for a bit," Sean snorted. "Might be part of what's wrong with them," he added. "War never does any good for anyone, mate. The thing I remember most was the dancing in the street when it was all over."

"Do you think there will be another war, Uncle Sean?" George held his head to one side considering his own question and Sean was taken aback at the evident thoughtfulness of his nephew.

"There's always a war, George. Somewhere."

"Like in Spain," George offered.

"Yes, like in Spain. But there won't be a war like the Great War. Not again." Sean delivered the reassurance that he had rapidly eroding faith in. He had read about Stalin's purge of the Red Guard and the starvation tactics he had employed in the Ukraine against the Kulaks. Now he was turning on the old Bolsheviks and reports of forced confessions, torture and imprisonment in the newspapers seemed to echo the private war Hitler was unleashing on the Jews. The ideological distance between fascism and communism, once expansive, seemed to Sean to be shrinking and the utopian possibilities that had always been part of Sean's notion of communism were rapidly lost. Now that the worst of the depression was easing and evictions were not such a frequent reminder of the inequalities rife in Australia, he was less attracted to the notion of a social revolution. Stalin was transforming communism into yet another version of oppression. Perhaps his father was right after all.

"If there is, and Australia goes to war, I will fight." George's eyes flashed and Sean swiveled his head around checking their perimeter.

"Don't let your mother hear you say that! Ever!"

George smiled knowingly to himself. He had had plenty of time to observe his mother and Sean. He saw how they spoke to each other even when they were speaking to other people. How each held the other in the corner of their eye partly from fascination but also as if to keep a careful distance. They were like orbiting planets irresistibly drawn to each other but ever wary of a collision. For years now they had been linked as a platonic couple by others, thrown together relentlessly, partnered in social invitations, seated together at every event, pushed together so that it was no longer possible to establish if it were their natural affiliation or the magnetism of constant closeness that gave them feelings for each other which they each resisted as something unfitting and shameful. So, George watched his mother and his Uncle step warily around the forcefield that drew them together and was evident to everyone except themselves.

Despite everything he had read, adults remained a mystery to George. Novels had themes he had been told by his English form teacher and these themes helped explain human nature. He wondered how many blasted novels you had to read. As far as he could make out, adults seemed to spend most of their lives doing things they didn't really want to do, like working or going to war or not loving someone, and not doing things that they yearned to do. He wasn't looking forward to growing up for that sort of caper. He was learning to be ever more cautious in following his heart. At least, he thought he was until he met Gracie Jenkins, little sister to Bluey's girlfriend, Clara.

Bluey's longstanding dislike for the fairer sex had undertaken a radical revision as he matured into a solidly built teenager whose lush red hair now pushed through above his upper lip and patterned his broad chin. Bluey's mum worked with Clara's mum at the local Day Nursery and when he met Clara at the annual Nursery picnic, he made sure he loaded the picnic baskets as high as he could balance them when he carried them from truck to table and even played a game of cricket with the older children smiling broadly when he caught Clara's eye. When she agreed to visit the Baths with him that Saturday, he thought all his Christmases had come at once. As a fourteen-year old Bluey had finished his schooling and was working down the wharf trucking and loading now that the depression was easing and the shipping was picking up again, he had a wage and whatever he didn't give his mum, he was happy to spend on a pretty girl.

Bluey and Clara often played board games with George as he lay recovering on the sofa in the Pace front room. Gracie was always along as Clara had to watch her and so Gracie and George were often partners in cards left alone when Bluey and Clara wanted to smooch and bump foreheads like two brumbies out the back lane. Although Gracie was a year George's junior she was as tall as her sister and as game as a pebble so their friendship developed quickly. George came to admire the lights in her dark-blonde hair and her straight nose with the delicate nostrils that flared when she laughed. And she laughed a lot. She wasn't afraid to tease him and he liked that for some reason he could not fathom.

"I heard about yer' jump from the high diving tower at the Baths," Gracie commented as they played a game of Gin Rummy in the Pace's front room on a weekday afternoon. She casually placed three Kings on the sofa. "Made quite a splash!" She laughed. "How many people did ya' say saw ya' jump?"

"I didn't say," George guarded his cards from her quick green eyes, one slightly larger than the other.

"Bluey says it was thousands," she continued.

"Bluey can't count very well," George snorted.

"Did it hurt?" She looked at him evenly.

"Like buggery!" They laughed.

"Will you do it again? When your leg's better?" The excitement in her eyes stimulated a feeling in George that he was unfamiliar with. It felt like euphoric fear. The only experience he could compare it with were those few moments he had spent on the high dive platform before launching himself into the air.

"No worries."

So, as luck would have it, George found himself, in a very short space of time, in the same cautious orbit that his mother and his

Uncle inhabited, only he was circling young Gracie Jenkins and was shorter with her at times than he wanted to be in order to hide this strange new vulnerability.

After several weeks on the couch and more weeks hobbling around clumsily on crutches, George was at last able to walk unaided. The moment he had gained his balance, his mother marched him across Darlinghurst to East Sydney Technical College housed in the old Gaol where she had danced at the Artist's Ball two years previously. It was there that he was offered the choice of studying sheet metalwork, steam engines or mechanical drawing at the night school. As he had an offer of a job at a building supplies and construction company in Surry Hills, George chose metalworking.

In the daytime, George worked with skilled metal workers carrying, holding and loading various metals for forming and cutting and pressing into pipes and gutters and occasionally he watched his boss, Jonesy, patiently mold a custom piece with a dolly and a mallet until the metal took a precise and smooth form to fit an obscure space in a machine or a rooftop. At his night school, he studied the various metals, their gauge and allowances and practiced precision measuring and drawing with a caliper and a protractor. He marveled at how the arithmetic he had learned from chalk markings on a blackboard and from words in books transformed through practice to build things. As George progressed from building a pipe, to a funnel, to a bucket, the rules of geometry suddenly made sense and he recalled the mathematics instruction he had received at Plunketts with renewed appreciation.

The workshop was a high-ceilinged, simple brick building situated off Commonwealth Street among other industrial and warehousing offices in the busy back lanes of Surry Hills. A garage door was flung open onto the laneway at the side of the workshop in order to provide some ventilation to the work space which rang from seven o'clock in the morning with the sound of machinery and hammers and smelt of burning pennies. In the workshop it was always warm because of the ceaseless glow of the furnace, almost unbearable in summer when men wiped rivers of sweat from their brows and cursed the metal into shape.

George enjoyed walking to work through the lower end of Darlinghurst across Oxford Street into Surry Hills. The only trouble was, it brought him into frequent contact with the enemy. Since before he could remember, there had been trouble between the Darlinghurst mob and the Woolloomooloo mob. Street fights were regular between groups of boys from these neighbouring districts, usually erupting when one gang visited another gang's territory and George found himself the subject of taunts from Grunty Taylor and his gang who walked Riley Street or hung around Taylor Square after work as George made his way home. He had been in street scuffles with Grunty's mob before, the outcomes of these battles were never cut and dried as it was usually the case that individuals on either side copped a bloody nose, or a black eye and the fight would end up as a chase which would end up with a backslapping and laughing retreat by either side to the streets to which they laid claim. It became clear to George that as he had to walk to Surry Hills each day, he would have to either suffer continued humiliation or take a stand against Grunty.

He worked after hours on the slim bar of solid metal, rounded to sit nicely in a palm and light enough to swing adeptly. It fitted inside the sleeve of his jacket and tucked into the seam of the cuff where he made a small hole to hold it in place.

"Yer' a bit scared around here without yer' mates?" Grunty Taylor stepped behind George as he entered the alley off Oxford Street in the darkening light of a Thursday evening. "Bit toey?" Grunty leered in his face and shoved George into the wall. "Yer' orter be! Yer' out of your territory, mate!" As Grunty threw the first punch George moved his right arm in front of his face and shoved the steel bar into Grunty's throat with all his weight. He pinned Grunty to the wall behind him as Grunty gasped for breath like a gurgling drain. One of Grunty's mates tried to leverage his arm from Grunty's throat but George collapsed him with a sidekick to the knee from his giant work boot.

"I'll fuckin' kill him, if you blokes don't back off." He pushed the bar harder and harder and watched Grunty's face turn redder. "You got me mate?" He hissed in Grunty's face.

"I'll be walking these streets anytime I like and I'm a metal worker now. Feel that rod at your throat? Well, you'll be wearing it in yer' skull next time you make an arse of yer'self." He released Grunty who clasped at his neck trying to remember how to breath.

"You've smashed me throat," he wheezed taking a seat on a factory step.

"Next time, I'll smash your teeth in," George stared in his even way at Grunty recovering his breath before heading down the hill. It was this incident that encouraged his cousin Paul 'the Rats' Pace to approach him a few days later. As his cousin was a Darlo' boy himself, he had quickly learned of George's encounter.

"Heard you can handle yer'self in a scuffle," he commented to George when they met in passing on William Street on the Sunday afternoon. As the twins were still on the outer in the Pace family home, George barely knew his cousin, who went by the street name Rats, but he knew *of* him. He was several years older than George and worked with Guy 'helping out' bookies and the like and working on bar doors up at the Cross. "Grunty's still talking like a girl," Rats laughed. "I might have some extra work for yer', if yer' interested."

"I'm working like a dog as it is, mate" George observed the loud, red neckerchief his cousin wore and the slim moustache lining his upper lip which relentlessly worked a fag as he talked. "It's not running messages, mate and it pays well. Mainly weekend work. There's a bit of rough and tumble now and then." He smirked as he observed George from top to toe through clouds of blue smoke. "But yer' look like yer' could kick the arse off an emu! Why don't yer' pop by the house tonight? I know the old boy doesn't want our mob around Dowling Street but there's nothing to stop you calling in on family."

It was curiosity mixed with a misbegotten sense of duty that took George to the ramshackle house in Barcom Avenue on a Sunday evening. He had spent a quiet afternoon with Gracie wandering the Domain seeking patches of spring sun in which to sit and strolling up to Speakers' Corner listening with good-humoured disinterest to a woman writer calling for a revolution against capitalism and quoting Karl Marx. She stepped down from the ladder and was replaced by a well-dressed aboriginal man who introduced himself as Jack Patten. He described the poor conditions aboriginal people were living in around Sydney and New South Wales, how aboriginal families were having their children taken from them and he tried to explain all that his people had lost in the one hundred and fifty years of white man's settlement. Sydney was getting ready for a party to celebrate the anniversary of the first fleet while aboriginal people roamed the city without home or work, without a decent education or a sense of themselves and most importantly without full citizenship in their own country. He was understandably angry and he spoke well with members of the crowd murmuring assent now and then. Quite a few of the crowd were black fellas and George recognized Terry from the eel basket tied across his back. He edged over to him.

"Caught any lately, mate?"

"Na," Terry flashed his brilliant teeth and hung his head. "Been a bit crook."

"Sorry to hear it," George noticed Terry's hands were shaking and his pants were filthy.

"Yeah, been out of luck. No work." Terry shuffled and smiled and nodded at Gracie. "Got yer'self a sweetheart? That's why I'm not seein' yer down here so often, eh?"

George and Gracie blushed red in unison and fidgeted awkwardly in their coats.

"Na, I broke me leg. And now I'm working at a metal yard."

"Pretty good speech that fella' made," Terry nodded towards the speaker . "Whaddya' reckon?"

"Can't see why aborigines aren't citizens anyway," said Gracie. "Never really thought about it." She blushed again. "I mean, I should have thought of it..."

"S'all right," said Terry. "Can't say I thought about it much me'self before today." He chuckled. "I'm off to try me luck with the eels." He shook George's hand with his long papery fingers and winked at

Gracie before heading up the hill towards the Baths where the fishing was good.

"Poor old Terry, he's so thin he wouldn't cast a shadow," George sighed as he watched Terry grow smaller. "I hope he catches a rip snorting eel to roast tonight." He nudged Gracie. "Better head back, eh?"

As they walked in silence past the Art Gallery and down the hill towards Woolloomooloo, George was thinking about Terry and wondering how it could be so hard for an aboriginal man to survive in his own country. If he were honest with himself, he had to admit that he too had never really thought about the injustices done to aborigines even though he had seen with his own eyes the homelessness and sickness that characterised the sad groups of blackfellas that sat around Hyde Park or the Domain like creatures from a dream. It was as if they were invisible.

Gracie ventured, "Are we sweethearts?" George avoided her eye and stared out across the bay now heavy with transport ships and cargo ships docked in grey water that reflected the sky, creating the impression that they floated in the clouds. Gracie's question created the same kind of disorientation in George's mind.

"Yer' too young." George quickened his pace and Gracie hid her chin in her coat collar and smiled to herself. He hadn't said no.

On approaching his Uncle's home later that evening, he heard the loud chatter and laughter of men warmed by alcohol and their own company from several doors down. Rats opened the front door and roared.

"Here he is, the man from iron bar!"

He ushered George along the narrow hall into the rear room where seven men and five women sat around a low table strewn with empty beer bottles and smoking ashtrays. George's Aunt Madge, who he had met only two or three times in his life, looked a lot happier than he recalled ever seeing her. She had heavily hooded eyes and slouched on an armchair next to a struggling coal fire in the small grate. Although she smiled at him he knew she didn't recognize him. His Uncle Gus approached him unsteadily.

"It was an alloy actually, mate," George commented quietly to Rats as he shook his Uncle's large, scarred hand.

"Here he is, young George!" bellowed Guy. "Come and meet the mob." George nodded at the other men and shook hands with his Uncle Nick who sat between two women on the scruffy couch with his right leg extended over the lap of the blonde woman on his right. She was rubbing his shin and giggling, her low-cut blouse struggling to contain her large, rolling breasts. George accepted the small glass of reeking whisky from Rats and sat on the arm of the sofa realizing quickly that he was the only sober person in the smoke-filled room.

"I'm Pam," the dark-haired woman next to him yelled above the music blaring from the radio behind them.

"G'day," George gulped the rough liquor and allowed Pam to refill his glass. She was a good-looking sort with curled dark hair arranged in unraveling rows across her head. She wore a red and white, polka dot dress with the fashionable tall shoulders and a pair of black high-heeled slippers that she propped on the low table around which they all sat exposing her sturdy, stocking clad calves.

George guessed she was at least ten years his senior and struggled to avoid leering at her legs.

"Get that into yer'" yelled Nick approvingly. "I hear you're working in a metal shop, mate."

"Yeah," George sipped more cautiously at his second glass of the burning brown liquid.

"Good man! And what pittance are they payin' yer?" Gus yelled across the table patting Madge's knee in an apparent effort to keep her from nodding into sleep.

George laughed. "I get by."

"A bloke with a real job!" exclaimed Pam. "Don't see many of them around here." She placed her hand on George's thigh and beamed at him and he noticed her chipped front tooth and sweet scent.

After another couple of drinks and an enthusiastic conversation about the blasted All Blacks and the straight run thrashing they had delivered to Australia in their recent rugby tour, Rats tapped George on the shoulder and gestured for him to follow into the back kitchen where he had pushed aside saucepans and dirty plates to make a space on the kitchen table for a large mirror patterned with neat rows of white powder. George lifted his head from the table and felt his eyes watering as the acrid powder made its way through his nasal membranes into his bloodstream. He felt no obvious affect from the cocaine but experienced a sudden and overwhelming urge to dance. With a confidence he knew as strange, he took Pam's hand and they cleared furniture to the side of the room and turned up the radio.

It was well past midnight when George tiptoed through the front door of the Pace home in Dowling Street. His ears rang with mad jazz and he still felt the warmth of Pam's body against his as they flew together around his Uncle's living room. He knew that he had established friendships that evening that were going to take him places that he would best avoid but there was no questioning the thrill the evening had given him. Like no other experience, he felt the evening had heralded his crossing into manhood and marked his life as his own. Not his mother's or his family's or Gracie's or Jonesy's Metal Works' but his own. He smiled naïvely as he slept fully clothed on his single bed in the back room at the top of the stairs with one hand gripping a steel bucket.

The months passed by with George gaining confidence in his job and learning to use the mallet in combination with dollys and pegs and various metals to shape objects for increasingly specialist fittings. For his mother's birthday George spent many hours shaping a small mixed-metal bowl on the underside of which he engraved her name and birthdate. For Gracie, he made a simple silver brooch engraved with the tram number of the Bondi toast rack they caught almost every weekend down to the surf in the warmer months.

In the summer of early 1938, the city was alive with people visiting for the Empire Games held at the Sydney Cricket Ground. On a calm and sunny Sunday George, Gracie, Bluey and Clara took the crowded tram in the late morning to Bondi Beach with their swimming gear and a picnic lunch in a duffle bag. The ride itself was always fun, if you could get a seat, of course. The tram groaned up the hill and then picked up speed as they hurtled down past Rushcutters Bay and then dragged itself uphill again through the eastern suburbs until they turned the bend from Bondi Road from where they glided towards the magnificent panorama of Bondi Beach. Sundays were always crowded at Bondi but the foursome had found a barren ledge along the northern arm of the rocky bay that they made their own. It took a bit of effort to climb up to it but it was flat enough to lay on and had broad views of the ocean and beach. From the ledge you could see the rollers coming in and sunbake in peace between refreshing plunges off the rocks when it was calm or from the sands when the waves were pounding.

Being February in Sydney, the weather was hot and close, the air heavy and reluctant. By eleven o'clock in the morning they had each worked up a sweat and were groaning as they climbed the rocks to their ledge.

"I gotta' get in the drink," declared Bluey throwing the worn towel he carried onto the rocky ground. He squinted through his yellow eyelashes out to sea. "Looks like a big day down here."

Along the beach, the surf lifesavers were setting up their rescue lines and dragging the long wooden surfboats to the shore ready for action. Lines of brightly coloured carnival flags were being pegged around the white tents they had pitched and groups of tanned children were lined up for running races between the flagged markers. People flowed like ants down the steps of the Promenade onto the beach where they erected umbrellas, set down blankets and stripped down self-consciously to their swimwear. Bluey looked impatiently at Clara who was manipulating a towel around her as she removed her dress from over her swimsuit.

"What are yer' doin?" he asked. "Yer' wrigglin' like a snake in a sack!"

"Don't look, I'm getting changed," declared Clara clutching the towel tighter to her breast.

"I dunno' what you're hiding. We'll all be looking at yer' swimsuit in a minute," Bluey pointed out.

"That will be the minute that *I* decide," answered Clara sitting sulkily on the ledge and holding her towel to her as tightly as ever.

"Well, are yer' comin in?" asked Bluey impatient with the heat.

"Not yet. I have to get hot first."

"Hot!?" Bluey shook his head in exasperation.

George had helped Gracie up the ledge and was staring out to sea. It was a clear and calm day on the water with regular waves no more than a foot or two high rolling benignly over a giant sandbar that had formed across the mouth of the Bay. The twinkling blue of the water was broken by brief white caps of foam and the mingling squeals of children and seagulls interrupted the regular dull pounding of waves breaking on the sand. The smell of salt water and seaweed was invigorating and people crowded along the sand bar enjoying the gentle shallow waters. Several surfboard riders sat astride their long boards at the south end of the bay which was free from the sand bar and where the waves were gathering momentum.

Bluey and George stood looking out at the rolling depths below. "Well?"

The two boys leapt from the ledge onto the flat rocks which were washed by gently breaking waves. On a calm day such as this, it was possible, if you timed it right, to jump into the receding wash and have it lift you back onto the rocky ledge at the next break. They cast a quick glance at each other in silent recognition of the right moment and jumped together into the wash, laughing gleefully as they were swept back onto the smooth ledge by the next wave. They would not allow the girls to try this game as it was risky and neither of the girls were strong swimmers. Instead, they had to walk along the rocky ledge down to the sands of the beach and enter the water painfully slowly squealing at every extra inch.

"Are yer' coming?" Bluey yelled up to the girls. "Slower than a wet week," he complained to George.

"Yeah," the girls climbed carefully down the ledge, their bronzed legs feeling the way down the grey stone worn smooth by endless wind and waves. Clara wore a new black and white bathing suit which she had bought with her wage from her job at the Laundromat and

Bluey raised his eyebrows and whistled in appreciation before she quickly drew her towel across her torso.

"Stop gawkin'!" she smiled at Bluey nevertheless.

Gracie was draped in her familiar, heavy blue suit faded from several seasons of sun and surf and straining against her fast-developing curves. George noted to himself that he would buy her a new swimsuit for her birthday. Although she would be fourteen soon, she was staying on at school because she wanted to be a secretary and so she had no income at all. He observed her small, pale breasts pushing with increasing impatience at the girlish vest of her suit and thought how different she was from Rats' friend Pam who had pressed her large, soft breasts into him and led his hand to sit against her swaying hip. Gracie caused a rage of conflicting emotions in George, he felt protective of her, knowing and relishing her innocence, even while he resented it at times.

The girls paced coyly next to the boys along the rock ledges to the sand, embarrassed as always for the first few minutes to be half naked but quickly forgetting their self-conscious shyness in the thrill of the cool waves against their bare skin as they squealed in the shallows.

"It's a bit odd here today," said George to Bluey looking along the shore. "There seem to be a few different breaks." He gestured behind them several yards where there was the damp shadow of a recent high wave. "See, it's breaking down here but then it breaks up there."

"Must have been a late, high tide?" Bluey offered before diving for Clara's legs under the water.

Gracie splashed George powerfully and then ran from the water and through the shallows as he chased her kicking a giant arc of water over her as he caught her several yards along the beach. For almost an hour, they swam in the cool waves. They loved to dive through them into the empty sky behind the waves and fall into the ocean again, competing to see who could fly the highest from the back end of the wave. A two or three-foot wave was perfect but only if you got out to just before the break where anything bigger required a deep dive into the swirling bowel of the wave and a platypus kick to get through it without getting dumped. The boys kept one eye on the girls while the other watched for the right wave to catch into the beach and somersault out of before the crash against the sand.

Once they had clambered back up on the ledge, they ate ham sandwiches and drank long draughts of cool water then lay on the warm rock and fell into a sun-drenched sleep. In the early afternoon, George was the first to awaken to the sound of squealing and slowly oriented himself into sitting up position shaking his head dizzy with sun. It was getting annoying, the squealing getting louder and his head throbbing from the heat so he stood up and surveyed the bay. What he saw struck him dumb. The first giant wave had already hit the sandbar where unsuspecting paddlers, many full-clothed, were knocked about with several losing their feet and slipping with the wave from the sandbar into the deep waters of the bay. As George watched, the second even bigger wave crashed into the sandbar breaking a throughway at its centre and beginning the slow but steady crumble of sand as people fell helter-skelter into the wash. The final wave, the biggest George could remember ever seeing, wiped out the remaining ledge of sand and hundreds of flailing, panicking bathers wallowed desperately in the deep churning waters which now reached so high up the beach sunbathers were being dragged into the waves and a heavy surfboat was bobbing, suddenly afloat and unmanned in the dangerous, swirling froth.

"Bluey!" George shook his friend's arm urgently. "Wake up!"

Bluey shook himself awake and stared incredulously for a few moments at the chaotic, sandy churn of the bay littered with flailing bodies. In unison, the boys leapt from the ledge and ran full pelt down to the sand where they began dragging people from the shallows along with other bathers who had escaped the waves. The surf lifesavers had sprung into action and were furiously reeling out their swimmers but there were so many people in trouble, they couldn't keep up. The surfboard riders had paddled into the fray and people clung with ugly desperation to the long boards so that they could not paddle them but only try to stay afloat among the chaos. Many men dived into the mayhem of the water and swam out to rescue those in trouble, often to be clawed at and almost drowned by panicked bathers.

The waves did not recede as they normally would due to their compounded size and the load of sand they had unleashed into the contained space of the bay so the panicked rescue continued for what seemed forever. As George lowered an older woman, fully clothed and utterly exhausted onto the sands, he looked with dismay along the beach to see huddles of people gathered around unconscious bathers pulled from the water. The lifesavers continued to work on the reels with desperate faces and well-rehearsed rhythm that was normally beautiful to watch but today seemed almost comical with so many drowning bathers. He squinted against the sun and surveyed the beach until he located Gracie and Clara near the Pavilion where Bluey and George had insisted they stay. They were hugging crying children in their towels and staring with silent horror at the waters. At last he heard the sirens of the ambulances pulling up at the Pavilion and turned back to the shallows.

It was now that the enormous body of water began to suddenly recede, dragging with it bathers who had almost made it to the shore and on whose tired faces relief turned once again to despair as their legs gave way beneath them and they were dragged screaming back into the deathly and gritty wash. George grasped the hand of a boy just a year or two younger than himself as the sand under them gave way and they were thrown together like tumbled dice under the grinding water. It took all of George's strength to stand against it and clamber again in the swamp-like sand onto the solid beach. He turned to scan the water for the boy but could not find him and was quickly distracted by the needs of others seeking assistance out of the water. Although he had only stared into the boy's face for a few seconds, he never forgot the expression of lost hope on that young face as it was clawed back by the angry sea.

Once the waters had calmed and all the bathers had been hauled from the sea, it was late afternoon and the shadows of those left on the beach had grown long and slender. The last of five inert bodies was stretchered to an office within the Pavilion where they were held until the injured had all been transported by ambulance to hospital. Over twenty people had been revived on the sand spewing seawater from their lungs as they re-entered their lives. The city learned quickly of the news of five dead from the radio transmissions and for weeks it was the main topic of conversation, becoming known as Black Sunday.

The foursome returned on the tram to Darlinghurst in the late afternoon in silence. George held his arm around Gracie who clutched her towel tightly around her shoulders and gazed unseeing at the seat in front of them. Despite the wild tide, the close heat of the day remained so that the air hardly shifted as the green and gold tram ploughed up the rise towards Bellevue Hill. Sweating, tired and scarred, the passengers held their belongings to their laps with a new tenacity, each shocked at the tenuous nature of human existence and reflecting on the random fact of their own survival.

"Fez plis," the conductor took the coins George offered as he swung expertly from the leather holding strap. "You lot get caught up in those waves?" he asked.

"Nah, we were lucky," Bluey spoke for the tram. "Tin-arsed lucky."

When the double decker ferry, *Rodney,* capsized in Sydney Harbour five days later as over a hundred eager Sydneysiders farewelled an American cruiser, nineteen more souls were lost. The city was reminded of its vulnerability to a coastline that had its population enclosed via a pounding Pacific Ocean and a web of harbour waterways. The majestic forces of the bodies of water that made Sydney so beautiful could also make it a terrible and treacherous city.

George had given up on reading novels now he was a working man and fully fifteen years old but he continued reading the newspapers following Hitler's steady reclamation of German territories lost as a result of the War. He learned the names of places even as they ceased to exist outside of Germany, the Rhineland, Austria and Czechoslovakia. He read of the Japanese invasions in China and the evacuation of Shanghai. When he took Gracie on her birthday to see the Marx Brothers at the Kings Cross picture theatre on a Saturday afternoon, the newsreel before the film showed the disastrous explosion of the Hindenberg and then moved on to footage of a smiling Hitler shaking hands with pilots of his Luftwaffe before they took to the skies like a swarm of bees. They watched the second year of war in Spain with Franco's troops charging through dusty colonnades bearing German rifles. Then they were shown images of the Japanese hoards attacking Shanghai and Nanking including attacks on British and American ships killing both military and civilians. The footage of Nanking was filmed from the air and tiny Chinese people appeared to run like ants through the streets fleeing Japanese bombers. George worried that he should not be exposing Gracie to this.

"S'posed to be a comedy, for Gords' sake!" he whispered. Although they laughed until they cried throughout *A Day at the Races,* George could not shake the gloom he felt from watching the newsreel as he and Gracie shared a pot of tea in the Theatre Café after the film. He watched Gracie blow on her milky tea enjoying her pretty pout and wiggling his eyebrows like Groucho Marx to make her laugh but his thoughts were filled with images of war machines, goose-stepping regiments and a dead Chinese child lying on a dirt road.

Jim also read the daily papers from front to back now he was not working down the wharf and he had installed a radio in the front room which he sat close by in order to hear the news and listen to Steele Rudd's *On our Selection* with Harry. Harry's horse Winnie had died at the grand age of twenty-five and Harry had almost died of a broken heart with her. His grocery run had ended now most people bought their supplies at the grocery shops and motorcars were driving horse-carts off the roads. He and Jim now spent more time in each other's company than ever and helped each other with odd projects. They were supposed to be converting the wooden stable into a chook shed for Maggie but they were most often gathered before the radio shaking their grey, stubbled heads and mumbling. As they listened to Prime Minister Menzies announce that Australia was at war with Germany along with Britain on a September afternoon in 1939, they stared into each other's weary eyes in dread silence.

"Jesus wept," said Jim, eventually.

Sybil heard the news during the afternoon shift at David Jones as word spread between the departments like wildfire. Eventually, to address the kerfuffle that was developing in the store with staff and customers all fretting alike, the store manager made an announcement over the loudspeaker system.

"Ladies and gentlemen, it is my duty to inform you that Prime Minister Menzies has announced today, that Britain, and as a consequence, Australia, are at war with Germany. As a result, David Jones will close early today so that staff can be with their families. The store will close in half an hour. Will customers please vacate the store and will staff please prepare their areas for closure."

Sybil could not remember being so miserable as she made her way home through the drizzling rain. The sweet, wet smell of the first flowering jacaranda only made her feel ill and she stomped bad temperedly along the wet, tree-lined avenues of Hyde Park. She was angry but she was not sure who she was angry with. Everything had suddenly changed. The world looked darker and the people around her more menacing as they trudged towards their homes in contemplative silence burdened with the implications of this news of war. A woman in a purple hat wept as she stood in the rain by the Cathedral while a man comforted her. Sybil wanted desperately to be home with her family to be reassured by their presence that the world had not suddenly collapsed. Mostly she wanted to look into Sean's eyes and hold her children to her and vow that the family would see this out together.

As Sybil entered Dowling Street she saw Sean approaching the Pace family home on his way from the wharf where he had been unloading a freighter as the news of the war broke. She picked up her pace and they met at the front of the house. Sean could see the fright in her eyes and held her quietly in his arms as she cried into his dirty jacket. After a minute Sybil pulled her head back and stared up at him. She could not speak. She had forbidden herself the words she longed to say. That she loved him and that she didn't want him to ever go to this war. But she could let her eyes speak and she heard Sean draw a heavy breath as he held her gaze and recognized her pain.

"It's all right, Syb. It's all right." His voice broke and he stroked the wet ringlets that fell from beneath her hat with his rough fingers. Her smell engulfed him, like fresh cream and he jumped as Jim opened the front door.

"You've heard the news, I suppose," Jim watched his son and daughter-in-law untangle themselves without further comment.

There was a gathering in the front room when they entered the house. Harry, Maggie, George and Anne as well as two of the neighbors were drinking tea and listening to the radio. Sybil wiped the rain and the tears from her face and sat between her children on the couch. There was little conversation. Conversation was not going to change anything. Human touch was all that they had to ground them. And tea.

Edith Sacks was getting married because her Charlie was going to war. The Second Australian Imperial Force offered Charlie the first honest pay he had earned in over a decade, a trip overseas and the chance to fire weapons legally. He was not alone in his enthusiasm for war as the numbers of Australian men enlisting for training in the Middle East steadily grew. In pace, the heady drama of parting with a loved-one-turned-soldier drew many couples down the wedding aisle to commit undying love in an environment where dying had suddenly become a very real possibility. It was to be a church wedding at St Comicals and Edith spent weeks musing over a suitable dress.

"Don't worry, I won't be lending one," she laughed at Sybil. "I'll tart up my good frock. Make it look smart. That'll do." Edith spent hours perusing copies of the *Women's Weekly* and *Woman's Mirror* held at the newsstand near the great entry doors off Castlereagh Street. Jake Barnett, the wizened David Jones' 'newsboy' was always happy to let the staff handle the magazines a little longer than the customers as long as the ground floor manager wasn't about.

During her breaks she pored over the pages no longer illustrated with photographs of well-tailored British aristocrats but glamorous Hollywood starlets like Bette Davies, Norma Shearer and Ava Gardner. Their gleaming hair was piled in perfect, high rolls, their lips painted blood red and their groomed eyebrows arched in disbelief from the increasingly coarse paper used to print the magazine stories otherwise dedicated to advice for Australian women in times of war. She skimmed over the rough pages offering instructions on how a woman might fix her own plumbing, preserve seeds from the garden and grow her own vegetables or even start her own orchestra. War had made women invincible, it seemed and home girls were portrayed in contrast to the Hollywood glamour girls wearing overalls and headscarves tackling horses, operating industrial machinery and in their spare time, furiously knitting their way to victory. Her eyes stopped short at a story in the *Mirror* entitled *Where the AIF are*. Letters from Australian soldiers training in Palestine described dessert landscapes, dusty columns of camels and donkeys and ceaseless preparations for a fearsome war that they yearned to join. It was sobering to think of her Charlie off to foreign lands to fight the fascists. It had taken a war to get Charlie serious about her and while she realised that the war may not only start but also finish her marriage, she was not going to let any army interfere with her wedding day.

Charlie had enlisted in the infantry and was training in Bathurst for deportation in August, so it would be a winter wedding and that meant that she would need a coat as well as a frock. Edith worked into the nights after her day shift at the store had finished adding glamour to her Sunday frock, writing invitations on the back of cardboard rectangles which she cut from discarded DJs boxes and applying Sta-Blond with new vigilance to her scalp. Her good frock was a light-coloured beige, not too far off the fashionable ivory. The fitted rayon accentuated her still slim waist and fell in shifting panels to just below her knees. It would look well enough with the strips of lace she was fashioning around the neckline and the cuffs of the puffed sleeves. She had a golden, silk ribbon from Mrs Bradshaw to sew into the hipline and she dressed a plain white bonnet with a short veil and a white paper rose. The wedding was all she could think about and she drove Sybil half mad nattering about frocks, invitations, finger food and most irritatingly, a band to play at the reception which was to take place by some spatial miracle in the two front rooms of Edith's family home. Edith begged Sybil to ask Tom to play with some of his local musician mates.

"Maybe George could play the clarinet with them?" Edith suggested with her chin buried sheepishly in her neck and her pleading eyes working on Sybil's better nature. "Tom would like that, wouldn't he? Go on Syb! You know we can't afford a real band. It would mean so much to me. Make it a real party. You and Tom need to bury the hatchet, anyway. One day. Don't you? I mean, it's been almost ten years!"

"Your double chin is showing." Edith snapped her chin up and shook herself like a wet duck.

Initially, Sybil could only snort at the cheek of it. Eventually though, she thought it through and decided that Edith was right. She did need to make some sort of peace with the father of her children and she had refused to see him long enough for the deepest wounds to heal over. The children had seen him now and then when he visited Sydney for performances and he wrote them odd letters, about himself, of course, and the performances of his orchestra. He asked after them when he signed off and they wrote letters at Christmas to tell him they were well. But she knew that music was the real love of Tom's life; followed by Tom. She did not envy his fancy woman with him being always gone from home and no children between them. It occurred to her, for the first time, that he had done her a kind of favour taking off like he did. Their first years together had been full of the excitement of new romance, moving to a new city, endless musical evenings and parties and laughter, all of which lost lustre once she had the children and realized that while she could give up living for the night and sleeping it off over the day, Tom had no intention of doing the same.

She was happy in Sydney. Secure in the Pace home, earning her own wages at the store, taking charge of her own children, having fun with her friends and being in the constant company of people who loved her. Her thoughts turned to Sean with some discomfort. She liked to think of them as brother and sister but she knew that her feelings for him were not confined to brotherly affection and struggled to resist daydreams where she had never been married to Tom and it were possible she could be with Sean whose deep voice, loud from so many years on the wharves, rattled the cage she had built around her heart and warmed her so that she was only truly rested when he was at home. She could never be with him, she knew, but she could live with him and that was the next best thing. To see him every day and talk as they did, confiding in each other about the happenings at work, about the children who adored him and about the war, of course. The war that had become the only conversation worth having for most Australians.

"Thank Christ for Garden Island," she had sighed when Sean told her he was to be employed in building the Captain Cook Graving Dock that would join the island to the mainland. A project made urgent by the war and expected to take several years.

"It's Pig-Iron Bob you need to thank for that," laughed Sean. "Who would've thought the Prime Minister would be giving me a job after I've downed tools on 'im more than once! Ya' think the graving Dock will win us the war, Syb?"

"No, but I hope it may keep you out of it." She turned on her heel as she did whenever she felt she had stepped too close to him and he stared after her in silence as she tied her apron around her waist and stoked the glowing logs in the kitchen stove with brutal determination.

"Edith wants me to get Tom down to play at her wedding," she called over her shoulder. "Can you believe it?"

"No flies on Edith," called Sean, shaking his head and falling onto the sofa. "Will you ask him?"

Sybil stopped her battle with the fire and stuck her hands into the deep pockets of her apron.

"I don't care about him anymore." She let the words drift in the quiet house in which they were alone on a rare Sunday afternoon with the rest of the family at a rugby match in Moore Park. She walked slowly into the front room. "I'm not angry. I just don't care. That's good, isn't it?"

Sean watched her approach. She swayed when she walked in a long-legged, broad hipped way that he found peculiarly graceful. He could smell her, the same scent that was on his jacket which he kept at the back door and which she used to pull over her back when she had to fetch the wood or visit the dunny in the rain. He returned her gaze and nodded.

"There are worthier things to care about than our Tom." Sean filled the awkward silence between them as he always did with humour. "I mean, there's my dinner, for starters."

.   .   .

Private Charles Hunt looked smart in his service uniform with the cap tilted over his forehead and his boots gleaming expectantly. Only a thin line of sweat gathering above his top lip betrayed his nerves. He was grateful it was a cool day and hoped he could get married without breaking into the full sweat that would ruin his jacket. A parishioner was playing some God-awful racket on the Church organ as he waited before the priest with his mate and fellow soldier, Gary Lyons, who rocked back and forth on his heels and threw him sideways glances.

"Last chance, mate. Wanna' make a run for it?"

Charlie stifled his laughter with some effort and the mood in the crowded Church changed as all eyes turned to the door, the chatting subsided and the organist launched into the bridal march.

Edith stood holding her father's arm at the Church door with the eyes of just about everyone she knew upon her and felt suddenly shy. She clutched her father harder and took in a long breath hoping her legs would stop shaking so she might complete the walk she had planned for so long. She focused on the grinning faces leaning into the aisle from the Church benches and saw Sybil who immediately stuck out her tongue and thereby broke the paralysis she was experiencing. Twelve steps and several minutes later, she was Mrs Charlie Hunt squealing with delight as they were cheered and pelted with rice on the steps of the Church. Edith and Charlie walked down Dowling Street to the family home in Nicholson Street and retired to the upstairs rooms to 'freshen up'. Downstairs, the party started.

Tom led the five-piece band in a gentle waltz to kick off the festivities. He couldn't wipe the smile off his face as his son George blew a competent clarinet accompaniment at his side and had to pause his trumpet part to loosen his tight lips. The crowd filled the front rooms and was spilling into the back yard where green tarpaulins were strung from the fences over the washing line and secured to several branches of the giant Jacaranda tree that had grown through the back fence and was lifting the bitumen in the rear lane. The guests chattered loudly as they sipped beer or punch and discussed the likelihood of rain. Threatening grey clouds were stacked high to the south and a cold front brought a chill breeze off the harbour.

"Winter weddings are always a mistake," Maggie observed cheerily. She pulled her shawl tighter around her shoulders and drained her glass of punch.

"Oh, wasn't Edith beautiful, Grandma?" Anne already stood taller than Maggie. Despite her plaits and her pink Sunday frock and white stockings, she looked more a woman than a girl. Maggie sighed heavily as she observed Anne's excited face. Soon she too would be after a boyfriend and the little girl would be gone.

"Yes, Edith looked beautiful."

"I hardly recognized her," confessed Jim from where he leant on the outhouse wall next to Maggie and Anne. As he had removed his tie and was clutching a large beer he was feeling more himself and nodded his head at the people he knew. Sybil appeared in the yard through the open doorway at the rear of the house and waved at them.

"Come in and see George playing," she called, gesturing inside and disappeared.

"S'pose we should make an effort," Jim put his hand at the small of Maggie's back and guided her between the thronging guests into the house. Anne followed in their slipstream staring at the array of colorful hats that were balanced like exotic birds on the heads of the women at the wedding. There were tall bonnets and smartly angled pillarboxes with bits of feather and lace dangling in the wind so that she felt her winter beret was very dull.

"You're like a blasted tug boat!" Maggie complained to Jim.

In the crowded room the music remained restrained until the bride and groom descended the stairs. Then, there was a great roar followed by a toast to the beaming couple. The band struck the first refrain of *All of Me* so the couple could smooch and shuffle around among the throng. The piano player had a good set of lungs on him and so it was not long before the whole crowd were swaying, rocking and singing along to the increasingly bombastic song list. During a break from the music, once they had swallowed a plate of scotch eggs and fried chicken, Tom invited George to step out for a smoke. They stood at the kerbside in front of the house from which slabs of light and laughter spilled into the darkening, chilly night.

"Crikey! You forget how bloody cold it gets in Sydney," Tom rolled a smoke and lit it then passed it to George. "You're old enough now, son. You're almost seventeen!"

George puffed amateurishly at the smoke and coughed. Tom laughed. "It's just like anything, mate. Takes practice. You're doing well tonight." He patted George's shoulder. "You've got the music in yer'. It's good to see."

George nodded, feeling an awkward smoker and an awkward son to a father he barely knew. "It's just a hobby, Dad."

Tom looked evenly at his son and nodded. "That's good. You stick with the tech study, mate. You'll go a long way with metal work." They smoked in a silence heavy with what should be said but neither capable of filling the profound gap. They did not know one another and each of them digested this as they kept wary company on the footpath.

Edith was getting ready to leave the reception and saying her goodbyes in the back kitchen. The couple were off to the Australia Hotel to spend their first romantic night together somewhere other than the front sofa of Edith's family home.

"Congratulations, Mrs Edith Hunt!" Sybil hugged her friend tightly with tears in her eyes and Edith took her hand. "I won't be needing these anymore," she winked at Sybil as she retrieved a brown envelope from her handbag and pressed it into Sybil's palm. Sybil blushed when she glanced inside to see a row of neatly packaged condoms.

"I don't need these," she spluttered casting glances left and right.

"Keep them at hand," whispered Edith gleefully. "The Americans are coming! Have some fun will yer', woman!" Sybil watched her leave with Charlie to the well wishes of guests who lined the hallway and spilled into the street where the taxicab had pulled up. Sybil couldn't help but reminisce on her own wedding day when she had also been full of joy and hope. As she passed through the front door into the street her eyes fell on Tom and George, the son now taller than his father. Tom smiled at her and she summoned every ounce of her better nature to return his smile. Then she turned her back and entered the house. There, that would have to do.

"Can I get a new hat, Ma?" Anne rushed at her. "Please?" Sybil laughed.

"What a good idea. Why don't you ask yer' father?"

Shortly after the bride and groom departed the heavens opened and sheets of rain poured from the dark sky as the guests scurried inside the cramped front rooms and filled the smoky kitchen crowding around the wood stove. Thunder rolled from the south as the storm that had been gathering all afternoon burst over Sydney. Tom picked up his trumpet and nudged George towards the corner where the band was set up.

"That's our cue. Back to work, mate."

Sean was silent and walked ahead of the family as they made their way home several hours later when there was a break in the rain. He was trying to forget his brother Tom's comment as he was leaving the wedding.

"You've got my blessing with Syb, Sean." Tom had held his shoulder as they fare- welled and looked into his startled eyes with some amusement. "Blind Freddy can see you two have got a thing for each other." Sean had scoffed and sunk his hands into his trouser pockets and shuffled his feet, taken aback by a possibility he had never actually considered despite his feelings for Sybil. Tom winked.

"Just sayin', it's no skin off my nose."

Anne was singing *Stormy Weather* and George hummed an accompanying bass line. She was as happy as she could remember now her father had promised to take her to the shops and buy her a new hat in the morning. Maggie and Jim were discussing what windows they had left open and the likely damage at home from the storm. Sybil picked up her pace and fell into step with Sean.

"You have a good time?" She glanced sideways at him but he just hummed and kept his eyes to the road. She knew him well enough to know he did not want to talk and so she picked up the refrain and sang along with Anne and George with increasingly melodramatic emphasis until Sean could no longer resist laughing and joined in. The family marched into Dowling Street at midnight in full voice lamenting the loss of love and laughing as if it were the funniest thing in the world.

Life is bare; gloom and mis'ry everywhere
    Stormy weather
    Since my man and I ain't together
    Keeps rainin' all of the time, the time
    Keeps rainin' all of the time.

When he went away, the blues came in and met me
    If he stays away, old rockin' chair's gonna get me
    All I do is pray the Lord above gonna let me
    Walk in the sun once more

Can't go on; all I had in life is gone
    Stormy weather
    Since my man and I ain't together
    Keeps rainin' all of the time, the time
    Keeps rainin' all of the time

In the winter of 1940 George learned two German words; *Lebensraume* and *Blitzkreig*. He learned the names of countries even as they fell, Poland, Belgium, Norway. The newspapers spoke of the glory of the French troops in defending Dunkirk as the British Expeditionary Forces were evacuated. French shame followed closely at heel as the swastika was raised atop the Eiffel Tower and broadcast in flickering newsreels of jubilant German infantry and weeping Parisians.

George was busier than ever at the metal works now the war was on as the factory had received commissions from the government to manufacture precision tools for army engineers. Instead of fashioning gutters and pipes for the everyday purposes of directing water, George and his team now fashioned wrenches, spanners, pliers and knives that fitted into regulation tool boxes to support the work of Australian soldiers. It was clear how profoundly things were changing due to the war when their first female apprentice entered the workshop with her hair tied in a striped scarf and her chin in the air daring anyone to try her out.

In addition to his day job, George now had a regular evening gig playing his clarinet in a jazz band at the Cross. His performance at Edith's wedding had connected him with local musicians who sought him out and paid him cash for doing what he loved. As he was only sixteen, he kept a low profile and remained behind stage in the band room between sets rather than join the drunken revelers in the front of the Beat Club. The Club was one of several now drawing eager crowds of military men in uniforms of every variation of khaki. Some were on leave from overseas postings and had seen battle. Others were in training or stationed at the wharf awaiting their orders to sail off to Egypt. All of them sought entertainment late into the night and there seemed no shortage of female company for them on the dance floor and at the baccarat tables laid out across the terraced club floor.

George had met a few working girls in his time and had grown up accustomed to their sideways gaze, their high-split skirts and lounging sensuality in the doorways of Darlinghurst and Woolloomooloo but he had never seen the likes of the goings on out the front of the Beat Club. It wasn't so easy anymore to pick the working girls as pin curls, red lipstick and breasts like isoceles triangles seemed to have become standard issue. Illicit beer, wine, whisky and sherry flowed like a secret river churning through the smoky, dark room washing away the fear and uncertainty that war had brought, often washing away fidelity and caution in the mix.

He frequently ran into his cousin Rats at the Club doing some sort of business that George was careful not to inquire into but seemed to involve a lot of roaming the Cross backslapping, handshaking and standing around drinking illicit beer from coffee cups. Rats was a lightweight compared with the heavy-set blokes that accompanied him who answered to outrageous names like the King of Egypt, Artyficial and Lone Wolf McQuade, but Rats was doing the talking and seemed to be running whatever business it was they were engaged in. Buzzing around this swaggering mob there was always a group of attractive women dressed in sheer, figure hugging evening clothes befriending groups of men and urging them to dance and buy drinks and then perhaps go for 'a stroll'. Pam was almost always part of the roaming party and would come and see him backstage and pull his hair and hug his back so that he could feel her insistent breasts against his shoulder blades. Finally, one evening after the second set was over and the rest of the band were drinking champagne with some big shot British officers out the front bar, Pam stuck her head and leg around the door of the backroom and lifted her penciled eyebrows up and down as she drew off her glove, then her shirt and banged the door closed behind her as she dropped her skirt to the floor and grabbed him by his ears.

As Kings Cross was the connecting point of five roads, it was also the biggest traffic bottleneck in Sydney. The snarl was at its worst in the early evening as the crowds of workers heading home from the city to the eastern suburbs in trams, buses and motorcars encountered the crowds heading in to the Cross for entertainment. A chaotic tangle would ensue so that bad-tempered passengers might stare from the windows of the tall trolley buses and watch the minute hand crawl a full three hundred and sixty degrees around the red disc of the Capstan Clock as fretful drivers tried their best to navigate through the gridlock. On the evenings that he played at the Club, George avoided this approach and took the steep hike up Butler's steps from Woolloomooloo to the quieter Victoria Road where the local residents who were mostly city office workers, musicians, artists, dancers and nurses from Saint Luke's Hospital lived in the grand terrace homes and manors now subdivided into cheap, dilapidated flats with splendidly inconsonant ceiling to floor windows and spectacular views of the sparkling harbour.

After work, George usually took his tea at home with the family after which they listened to the news on the radio. Together they stared into the swirling knots of pine in the kitchen table listening to the reports of London's agony as the Germans bombed the heart out of the British Empire and stared at each other in disbelief as the Nazi war machine marched into Russia disregarding the non-aggression pact. He often napped on the sofa next to Sean or Jim before changing into a fresh shirt and heading out for the evening towards the Cross. From Victoria Road he would hike up Orwell Street past the popular Roosevelt Club and turn up Macleay Street looking in the windows of the ham and beef shop with its glass display cabinets stacked with preserved meats and overhung with swinging salamis. At Harry's barrow stacked neatly with colourful arrangements of fruits and veg he would turn into the stairwell for the Arabian Coffee house where he liked to spend an hour or so before the show drinking brewed coffee and watching the passing parade of characters from between the colourful paper lanterns hung along the upstairs balcony.

Through the leaves of the adolescent plane trees lining the busy roadway he watched men and women dressed in fine suits and shawls on their way to the Minerva Theatre or to the pictures. Fellow musicians carrying black cases of odd shapes and sizes scurried towards the various restaurants, cafes, and clubs where patrons gathered to be entertained. It was easy to spot the refugees or 'reffos' who had fled Austria and Germany and settled in numbers in Kings Cross from their unfamiliar felt hats with their heavy European greatcoats sweeping down to long boots. The odd madwoman or inebriated street girl might stray past singing to themselves heedless of passersby and now and then a flock of boy-girls might glide past on their way to a Potts Point party with elaborately painted faces trailing suffocating wreaths of perfume. Watching people pass from the balcony of the Arabian at the Cross was as entertaining as any actual show George had seen. Sometimes he was joined by other blokes from the band or the Lump who had a got himself a night job as the doorman at the dance club on Kings Cross Road. They would discuss local goings on, the poor behavior of some of the rowdy and drunken crowds at the clubs, the cricket or else the war. Then, as the night progressed beyond the dinner hour, George would stroll down Kings Cross Road through the buzzing neon centre of the Cross to the Beat Club passing the working girls pacing the corner of Springfield Avenue who might smile at him:

"C'mon love, thirty bob to strip to the earrings."

Although he was no longer a boy, George could not help but blush when they addressed him. He pitied these lone girls on the dark avenue with their bright yellow hair and pockmarked skin. Their existence seemed so tenuous to him they were almost like specters. He shuddered to think of the men that they might attract and how they might be treated by these men. He knew that Pam was a working girl but she had the protection of Rats and his mates and seemed always well groomed and well fed. She was not a street girl. Not yet, anyway. Pam was on his mind a lot now that she had 'taught him a thing or two' as she put it. He had not been with a woman before the evening in the band room and had only progressed to long and deep kissing with Gracie who sometimes let him touch her nubile breasts through her blouse so that he groaned in joy and frustration. He knew that the only way to really know Gracie was to marry her and even if he was sure that that was what he wanted, they were both too young for marriage. His evening with Pam had left him feeling excited and guilty. He told no one of their interlude but thought about Pam's warmth and her urgency and the incredible relief he experienced inside her. It was precisely this thought that preoccupied George at the moment that he sliced two fingers from his right hand with the metal cutter in the factory. He stared in disbelief at his two fingers lying among the metal filings on the factory floor still curled together from their hold on the steel sheet as blood gushed from his hand and he dropped the cutter. Suddenly, Jonesy was lowering him onto the work stool and bandaging his hand. Stewy, who had been working at the same table with George put George's hat on his head and they bundled him into the work truck, holding his torniqued arm aloft.

"Should'a worn the flaming gloves," Stewy stepped angrily on the accelerator as he drove them to the hospital with George's arm propped on his left shoulder. Jonesy sat beside George holding the decapitated fingers wrapped in a blood stained white cloth, shaking his balding head.

"I think that horse has bolted, mate."

George was white but silent as he stared grimly at the traffic. Two bloody fingers! He had always expected to lose one, but two was over the fence and he cursed himself for not concentrating and wondered how he would work again even as the extreme, hot pain shot up his right arm and shook him so that he groaned in agony and frustration.

"Lost mine when I was about your age, son," Jonesy tried to comfort him. "You get used to it. I hardly miss it anymore."

"But I've lost two," George gasped.

Jonesy undid the lace of his enormous work boot and pulled out his left foot. He peeled the sock from it and exposed his deformed big toe that had been sliced to half its proper size. He looked sideways at George.

"Wanna' see the other one?"

"God, no!"

"Put yer' flamin' socks back on for Christ's sake," urged Stewy as he frantically turned the handle to open the driver's window.

Over the next few months, as his fingers healed George grew tired of hearing how lucky he was to have only lost the top ends leaving his middle joints to wiggle about expectantly, missing objects he clutched at for weeks as they adjusted to the empty space where his fingertips had been. The worst part of it was that losing two fingers meant that his clarinet playing days were over and he missed the music and the merrymaking of the Beat Club. He still visited the Arabian Café for a coffee and a chat with Lump and it wasn't long before Rats sniffed him out.

"Give us a look," Rats grimaced at the two stumps and sipped the froth off the beer he was holding as they leant up against the curved bar of the Tilbury. "Not pretty! I hear you've stopped blowin' yer' pipe?" He ran his pale, long fingers through his greased black hair and lit a smoke.

"Can't hold the keys," George explained. "S'oright, I can still work."

"Course you can. I reckon you'll throw a punch all right again soon, too. Which reminds me, they need a hand on the door at the Beat Club. Easy job, just making sure everyone behaves. Keepin' an eye on the girls. It's like a bloody saddling paddock some nights up there and some blokes don't know how to hold their grog. Be handy having a bloke like you around. Wanna' give it a burl?"

"I dunno, mate" George drew a careful line in the condensation around his glass. He couldn't tell Rats that his mother would not approve. She was always worried about him associating with 'Ratbags', as she called him.

"He's not the clean potato, son. Anyone can see that. He's got his father's look in his eye. Mad as a cut snake." Sybil was so proud of her son. He had kept himself out of trouble since the Billy McFadden incident and had grown to be six-foot and four inches with broad shoulders and a deep resonant voice. He was handsome too, with a dimpled face, soft, grey eyes and a thick head of brown hair which he kept close-cut for fear of developing the same ringlets as his mother. As he was earning his own living and paying more than his way at home, he no longer sought or heeded her advice on where he went. Nevertheless, he remained for Sybil her thoughtful and well-meaning boy with eyes the colour of a winter cloud and he could do no wrong.

"I'll give it a go, Rats," said George after several moments. "But let's keep quiet about it, eh?"

"Quiet about what?" Rats laughed at his own joke and drained his glass. His bloodshot eyes were shining.

George saw another level of the world of night frolics at Kings Cross from his premium position just inside the door from the street, past the peacock feathers and fancy drapes of the entrance to the Beat Club where he tucked himself discreetly against the back wall sipping lemon squash and watching. The owner of the club was a portly, sweating Dutch bloke named Hans who sat at his reserved table under the stairs leading to another floor where there were a number of rooms which George had no desire to learn more about. From his 'office' under the stairs Hans received his regular visits from the plain-clothes coppers who were ferried in like royalty early in the evening and drained their beer and pocketed his envelopes as they departed, eying off the clientele with benign smiles. At Hans' okay, the odd gentleman would ascend the stairs to the first floor of the Club accompanied by one of the regular girls. George watched grimly as Pam ascended the stairs on various occasions with different blokes. She winked at him, whenever she caught his eye but she had never repeated the interlude in the band room. George was not sorry as he watched Pam flutter unsteadily like a colourful but injured bird around parties of men, sitting on their laps and throwing back the grog. Her eyelids and her make up grew heavier each week and George suspected she had succumbed along with Rats to the twang as they called the local opium.

He worked on weekend nights for extra cash as this was when the Club was packed to the rafters with revelers who elbowed each other for room on the dance floor. George enjoyed the work because of the music, even if the club reeked of hairspray, sweat and a faint odour of vomit. The music always swept all that away and he longed for the days he had been onstage and reflected on his father's choices with a new appreciation. There were many occasions when he had assisted Les, the head doorman, encourage some of the wilder patrons to take a walk outside. On occasion a fistfight would break out and Hans would squeal like a stuck pig.

"Staken! Staken! You bastards!" Even as Hans was still struggling to get his belly out from behind the round table, Les and George would be on the brawl, each grappling a hold around the main protagonists with Rats and his gang moving in in support when they were around. They were usually able to drag the offenders into the street and throw them in the kerb with a warning not to come back but it was nerve-wracking work and the offenders were more often than not in uniform and increasingly accompanied by a gang of mates. Since Japan had bombed the American Pacific fleet in Pearl Harbour, the revelers in Kings Cross were more frequently Americans and they changed the character of Sydney nightlife with their generous spending, endless supplies of candy and perfume and their way with the ladies. You knew a local girl was out with a Yank from the size of the corsage she wore on her breast and the way she would say things like 'Geez' and 'Well, I'll be!' Even Gracie had started with the American sayings which the locals were picking up from the Hollywood pictures and the visiting soldiers.

"Why do yer' say 'Geez'?" George asked her on a Saturday as they lay on the grass under the Moreton Bay Figs in Hyde Park during Gracie's lunch break from her new job as junior receptionist at Nock and Kirby's Hardware offices.

"Say what?" she asked.

George sighed. "Are you liking the job, then?" He changed the subject.

"Sure am," said Gracie in her strongest American drawl. "I'm liking the pay! I'm gonna' save up and buy myself one of them fancy holidays on a cruise ship once this war is over." She gazed over the Bay at a white ocean liner that sat next to the battle-grey Australian and American gunboats like a vessel from another world where holidays still took place. Although Gracie, now sixteen, wore her hair up and used lipstick her profile remained childishly pretty and her skin was as soft as a kitten's ear. George loved to hold her small hand and feel her pulse point at her wrist where she wore the slim, silver bracelet he had made for her.

"I hope yer' not going to fall in love with a blasted Yank?" George commented.

"I s'pose you're tryin' to tell me you like me, then?" Gracie's eyes gleamed and she wrenched her mouth to one side in mock repulsion. "Well, strike me pink! Whatever next?"

George had a good idea of what was next but he was not ready to share his plans with Gracie just yet. Instead he rolled with her on the grass and she squealed.

"Watch me hair, yer' big lug!" They kissed farewell when the Post

Office clock chimed the hour and she smiled at him. "If yer' like me so much, when are you gonna' take me out dancing?"

"It'll be a cold week in Hell when I take you to a Kings Cross club, Gracie." She wrinkled her nose in annoyance.

"How am I ever going to keep myself out of trouble, if I don't see any, George? Why, I wouldn't recognize it! I'm not a child anymore. Just once? If it's all right for you, why is not all right for me?" She smiled at him and put her head to one side before she walked away. He did not want to say what he thought because that would involve pointing out that she was a girl, and a nice one at that. She was getting very sensitive to being called a girl and to any insinuation that she was not his equal. Just as George felt he was beginning to understand women, he felt that they were changing right in front of him.

That Saturday evening he watched a bloke as big as himself pick Pam up like a doll and throw her sequined shape across the room into the mirrored wall where she fell to the ground among giant shards of smashed glass. Even as Pam lay unmoving on the carpet, the bloke ran at her roaring abuse and kicked her in the hip before George managed to get to him. This time, George didn't bother with a hold but threw his best left hook at the bloke's jaw so that he was taken aback a moment. But George watched the raging fury return to his face as he recovered and threw himself forward lunging at George and sending tables and chairs flying around them as they crashed along the floor and frightened patrons who grabbed their glasses and scurried out of the way. George leapt up first and grabbed the aggressor in a headlock against which the giant struggled forcing George to release him with an elbow in the guts. It was George in the end who had to be calmed and held in a lock by Les and the King of Egypt as the offender, now bleeding from the nose and the eye and reeling against Lofty Black the barman, was dragged out the door. Once the ambulance had left with Pam's broken frame on a stretcher and most of the patrons had departed the club in shock, George handed in his notice to Hans and clapped Rats on the back as he left. He held the clean rag Hans had given him to his bleeding head and limped into the early hours of the morning on Kings Cross Road where unsteady laughing groups of revelers stalked taxi cabs up and down the strip, their evening clothes now grotesquely stale in the brightening sun. Gracie was right, just as he was. It wasn't good enough for her and it wasn't good enough for him. He had had enough of the seedy side of the club world. And he had had enough of injuring himself for the time being. The pain of his amputated fingers had returned as a result of the punches he had thrown and it tore up his arm. At least he knew he could still punch an idiot in the head with it. He had got the best of the fight but he felt like he had had a near escape from something worse than a bashing. He felt with grim certainty that Pam would not escape and pitied her.

Several weeks later, when Rats was found dead in Springfield Lane behind the sly grog shop from a series of knife wounds to the chest, Guy dropped his bundle. His wife, Madge had been admitted for a prolonged stay at the Women's Refuge to 'take a cure' so that he was alone when the cops came to advise him. Guy roared and threw himself at the two constables repeatedly so they had to restrain him and lock him up. He didn't throw a single punch but hurled his large body against the cops, the walls, the furniture, like an ungainly whirling top, throwing angry spittle from his mouth. He continued to lunge and roar obscenities whenever approached so that after two days in the lockup the cops had him incarcerated at Callan Park Mental Hospital.

Over the previous months, Guy had descended into a state of living that had frightened even Nick with constant gambling, drinking, drug taking and brawling. The home, always unkempt and shabby, had become decrepit, reeking of stale beer and tobacco with litter decorating every corner. Guy was often incoherent and when he attacked Nick in his front yard, believing him to be 'one of them' but unable to explain who 'them' were, Nick began to avoid him. Guy's sons had stopped going home but Guy still talked to them. He was slipping into a world of his own nightmarish imagination and he had no anchor with which to grip the shore.

When Nick visited Jim and Maggie to explain what had happened, Maggie cried and hugged Nick but Jim just stared at his tea and shook his head. Everyone knew you didn't get out of the nuthouse in a hurry.

George was deeply affected to hear of Rat's death and his Uncle's internment. His mother stared at him meaningfully when she was told the news on her return home from work. She didn't have to say anything but he knew she had hated his night job at the Beat Club and all this misfortune just made her right with her chorus about 'blasted Ratbags', 'bad company' and 'coming to no good'. But George knew Rats never had a real choice. His home was part of the very underworld that killed him and he felt intense sadness but also renewed relief that he had walked away with his life.

"I'm goin' out," he muttered as he grabbed his hat from the hall peg. He needed to see Gracie.

That night behind her parents' house in the dark, warm air they held each other close leaning against the washhouse listening to the cicadas switch on an off. Gracie's sweet scent transported George to a world where violence and ugliness and death did not exist. He breathed her in and stroked her fine hair and she pressed against him and held his kiss so that he gasped when she let him go and pushed her hand down the front of his trousers. She giggled explosively minutes later as George doubled over and fell to his knees.

"Gracie," he looked at her in pleasure and shock, "where did you learn to do that?"

"I've got three big sisters," replied Gracie archly. "And you're not the only one who borrows books from the library, George Pace."

In early 1942, just after scores of Japanese planes dropped their bombs into a sunny Darwin morning killing or wounding hundreds of Australians and stunning the rest, Sydney began turning off the lights. Filter shades were fitted to streetlights, office windows and the headlights of trams and cars so that nothing was clear once the sun sank behind the western mountains. Windows of homes bore the crosses of taped paper and it was getting hard to find the necessary staples to keep life going like petrol which had become rare and expensive, clothing, meat and most critically for Maggie, tea.

"Stone the crows!" she had exclaimed when the rationing of tea began. "How are we supposed to win the war with no tea?"

"Just remember, every cup of tea you don't have is one more for an Australian soldier fighting overseas," offered Sean. Maggie merely grunted as she sat knitting the socks she was always making for the war effort, her fingers working automatically on the thick brown yarn. She remained silent on the topic of the war as a rule, hoping it might go away but it was the dominant topic of everyone's conversation.

Sean was always talking of the importance of the Graving Dock to the war and giving a running report of the battleships at harbour. The Dock was almost complete with the first truck having driven over the road that now crossed the earth-dam that was built in place of the waterway that had once made Garden Island an actual island. Sean, George, Jim and Harry pored over the newspapers following the campaigns of the Australian soldiers, navy and RAAF in the Middle East, Malay, New Guinea. They talked more and more of munitions and guns and tanks, bombers and U boats so that Maggie was able to lose track and concentrate on ignoring the blasted war.

But Sybil was full of it too as David Jones had been transformed by rationing and the loss of over a thousand employees to the war. Each department remained open only until the rationed supply of goods was sold at which time the workers, increasingly women, were redeployed to various tasks in support of the war effort. As undergarments, especially the finer varieties, were in critically short supply, Sybil's department was often closed all day and she became adept at knotting the coarse fibres of endless yards of camouflage netting coming home in the evening stinking of coal tar with calloused fingers and an aching back from lifting the heavy nets.

The relentless patriotism of the store owner, Mr Lloyd Jones, was evident from the sustained pay he guaranteed for employees enlisting in the AIF, the posters on the walls and pillars within the store encouraging all employees to do their bit for the war, the regular evacuation drills where they proceeded in threes to the underground car park beneath the Market Street store which he proclaimed the safest air shelter in Sydney.

With the 'impenetrable' British defence of Singapore fallen away and the Japanese invasion of New Guinea proceeding with alarming speed, the war, once so far away, was suddenly on Australia's doorstep but Australian troops were fighting with the allied troops in the Middle east and the Mediterranean, while those troops stationed in the Pacific, were now prisoners of war in Malay and Singapore. Shock reverberated around the nation as they read the news on the morning of the British surrender of what they had thought an impregnable barrier between their southern land and the Japanese.

Sean made sure that he had an evening alone with Sybil the night he told her. George was out with Gracie and Anne was singing in the local choir while Jim and Maggie had gone to visit an old friend of Maggie's at Manly and would not be coming home until the morning. He waited until they had eaten the lamb chops and peas and potatoes Sybil had prepared and they had cleaned the plates before he took Sybil's hand and led her into the front room to sit on the sofa.

"I've got two things to tell yer," he said looking intently at her and squeezing her fingers.

"Ow," Sybil shook her inflamed hand free and then returned it to his softened grasp, chuckling. "What is it?"

"The first," Sean took her other hand, "is that,…" he stared at the floor searching for the courage he needed. He looked at her face that was so familiar to him and which he had studied for so many years in quiet admiration. "Syb, I think you know how I feel about you…" She remained silent and her smile faded. "I love you." There, he had said it. "I love you, Syb and I want to marry you."

Sybil's mouth fell open and she took a deep breath but no words came out.

"And the second thing," continued Sean determinedly, "is, …I've enlisted, Syb. I'm goin' to the war. I leave in a week for training camp."

Sybil's emotions ran riot with joy, shock and despair so that she started crying and fanning her flushed face with her hand.

Sean stroked her fingers as she absorbed what he had said. "Are yer' happy, Syb?"

She nodded even as she sobbed into his shoulder.

"Blasted war! I knew you would go. I just knew it. But Sean, if you love me… well, if you love me, then you have something to stay alive for, to come back for." Sybil smiled through her tumbling tears and cupped his stubbled cheek in her hand.

"Is that a yes, then?"

"Is it not wrong of us, Sean?" Sybil stared earnestly into his calm brown eyes flecked with orange lights like tortoiseshell buttons. "We're supposed to be brother and sister."

"Tom's given me his blessing."

Sybil snorted. "Oh, he has, has he?" She wiped her face with her rough fingers. "That's very kind of 'im!"

"Syb," Sean grasped her hand again more tightly, "…it doesn't matter about him or anyone else. If we love each other, that is enough."

For reasons she could not explain, Sybil continued to cry but more softly as Sean held her in his arms and kissed her. They dragged blankets from Sybil's room and lay together on the sofa late into the night. They did not make love nor talk much for they each felt as if they were recovering from an illness that had held them in a paralysis for years and now had suddenly departed leaving their bodies shocked and exhausted.

"We'll take this one step at a time, eh love?" Sean reassured her as they sat up on hearing the front door latch. "We'll tell the family when you're ready. Might be best to wait 'till I get back from winning the war." Anne entered the front room, returning from an evening of choir performance and gestured hello as she made for the kitchen.

"Who let the stove go out?" She wailed as she reentered the front room. "Why are you sitting in the dark?"

"We're saving for the war effort," Sybil answered folding the blankets. "You can talk in the dark, yer' know."

"I'm going to bed," Anne yawned. "Maisie's got a new kitten. There's another one without a home, Ma?" Sybil was stupid with the shock of everything that had happened and merely stared at Sean in the dim light of the room. Sean nodded.

"No harm in a young girl having a kitten, Syb. Something warm to hold in the night." He smiled broadly as Anne squealed and hugged him around his neck.

Sybil stared at them as if they were strangers.

MAY 1945

Woken from an uncomfortable sleep in which he dreamt he was adrift in the billowing open ocean, George washed his face, dressed in his khakis and took his breakfast in the ship's mess. He then headed onto the deck to join the gathering soldiers as the first sun broke the horizon with an orange smudge. Men nodded at each other in silent greeting as they looked over their sullen armada hung on the grey water off the east coast of Tarakan Island. The broken mangrove forests that bordered the narrow bay were still smoking from the bombing that had taken place for the preceding week to clear Japanese positions near the landing site. In the growing orange glow of the sun, the island appeared ghostly and abandoned, belying the presence of several thousand Japanese troops who they were to hunt down, capture or kill.

Today was the day that the Australians had trained for months to survive in their camp at Morotai, a northerly island of the Dutch East Indies which the allies had won from the Japanese and developed as a training and supplies base. The troops had rehearsed the planned amphibious landing over the last three days during their voyage to Tarakan island. George was well-drilled in the maintenance and use of small weapons, camouflage, map-reading, and the particular skills required for jungle warfare but his main task was to operate the heavy machinery that they had brought with them to repair the Tarakan airfield. It was the capture of the airfield that was the primary target of their operation. This small airstrip which the occupying Dutch had built to support their lucrative oil production industry was to serve as a critical base for airstrikes on Java, the next phase in the allied recovery of the Pacific islands. They had been allocated six days to capture, repair and open the airstrip for American air squadrons.

Through the long and grueling months of training they had slept in sweaty, scrubby tent camps fronting a jungle perimeter where snakes and straggling Japanese soldiers roamed unpredictably. The Morotai camps backed onto idyllic sandy beaches lined with coconut palms and a glinting ocean infested with coral sea snakes and out of bounds for the tired, overheated and frustrated Australian battalion. The two parallel airstrips around which the camps were laid were in ceaseless operation with hundreds of aircraft landing and taking off so that the camp was never at rest and the sky was alive with propellors, smoke trails and screaming engines. They had been overjoyed to finally leave for the Oboe One assault on the island. Anything was better than waiting.

There was much apprehension among the troops on the deck watching the island target floating in the smoke and haze. Yesterday's rehearsal of the landing at a beach across from the island had gone badly with four men drowned in the muddy backwash that sank one of the clumsy, fold-up landing boats. The American lifejackets, it turned out, were able to keep a fully equipped Australian soldier afloat for only seven minutes.

Assuming they survived the landing, they then had to survive the assaults of an enemy that they had been assured would show them no mercy. George had witnessed the capture of several Japanese soldiers who had breached the perimeter of their training camp in Morotai where they had shot and injured two infantrymen before being captured. The three ragged soldiers in filthy uniforms were marched past jeering troops with their eyes to the ground and their boxlike brown caps pulled low. The whole battalion had heard the horror stories of Japanese summarily executing and often torturing enemy soldiers that they overwhelmed and they were despised. Fanatical soldiers, touched by the sun God and believing in their own infallibility as a divine race was how the Japs were described in training. The Japanese soldier was considered enduring, patient and covert and therefore dangerous but he was also a poor marksman, prone to panic and to bunching making him a good target for automatic weapons. The training manual also mentioned the persistent dunk odour of the Japanese and advised that they could be smelt out but George could not get a whiff of these men as they passed. They appeared like any other miserable bastard who had been captured by the enemy.

George performed the last minute check of his pack for the standard 50 rounds of ammunition, two grenades, his half tent and blanket, groundsheet, gas cape, mess and toilet gear, water sterilising outfit, mosquito lotion and Malaria tablets, first aid kit, spare clothing and rations for three days. Despite his lost fingers, he had mastered the Bren gun with its generous trigger which he could work with his stubby fingers. He had proved a deadly aim in drill but George was painfully aware that he had not yet shot at a man.

As the armada awakened the dark waters with churning engines and began the approach to the island, the bombers returned overhead and blasted the Bay before them with bursts of fiery black and orange creating a wall of fire along the coast just as rockets and mortars were fired beyond the beach from the decks of the gunboats flanking the landing craft.

"Here we go into Hell again," murmured Corporal Ben Moxham, a member of George's squadron, who had seen service in France in the Great War and was working as a squadron engineer. 'Retreads' were what they called those blokes who had served in the Great War and then showed up again for the next one. They drew a special level of respect from the younger soldiers and Ben had taken a fatherly interest in George knowing he had not seen action before.

The sweet, acrid smell of cordite blended with the salt-water wash and the stink of anti-mite cream with which they had doused their uniforms as the laden men clambered unsteadily like migrating turtles over the ship's rails down the scrambling nets and into the lurching 'alligator' landing vehicles pulled alongside.

"I hope it's not a repeat of Gallipoli," George grunted.

"Nah, it's gonna' be a walk in the park, mate" remarked Lofty Green, a lanky gunner from Queensland. "Didn't you hear the big brass. Be over in a month. A short visit, that's all we're payin."

"The only thing I've seen short is leave, cigarettes and beer," replied Ben as they settled into seated rows within the landing craft already sweating in the tropical morning. The machine guns tracked in steady circles surveying the smoking beach as they headed in silence into the bay. Ben laid his palm on George's right knee to still the shaking that he had come to know was habitual. They smiled at each other in the lurching dark.

"Stillness in the jungle is a virtue," Ben winked, quoting from the training manual.

As they made their way across the calm water, George was struck by the unexpected course his life had taken in the last six months to land him in this boat at this Bay with these men. It was only six months ago that he had finished his apprenticeship and Jonesy had offered him full employment at the metal works. The old metalworker had been disappointed but also pragmatic when George had told him that he was going to the war.

"We'll miss you round the shed. But there'll be a place for yer' when yer get back, mate," Jonesy had shaken his hand with both his rough paws. "They don't mind you're two fingers short, then?"

"I'm going in the Airfield Construction Squadron with the RAAF," George had explained. "Can't fire the rifle properly but I can help build an airstrip and I can look after me'self." The rest of the work mob at the shed, now made up of the older men and the new female apprentices, had clapped him on the back as he had left for home with a grim set mouth to tell his family and Gracie about his visit to the enlistment office.

Gracie had shed a tear or two but then she smiled in her lop-sided way and pulled his ear fondly as they sat on the warm front step of her parent's house in the afternoon sun. "I didn't expect George Pace to miss the war," declared Gracie. "I just hope the Japs miss George Pace! I need you back here in time to marry me while I'm still young and beautiful." That was the best thing about Gracie. You couldn't rattle her. And she never minced her words.

"I'll keep that in mind, Gracie," he had kissed her warmly and they had watched the sun sink over the rusty, corrugated iron roof tops of Woolloomooloo.

Sybil, however, had not taken the news so well.

"No!" she had wailed. "Not you!" She had threatened to refuse him the permission he needed being less than twenty-one years of age and it took some convincing to get her to relent. It was Jim who convinced her in the end.

"He's a man now, Syb. He's a fine man and you can't blame him for wanting to do his duty."

Sybil had cried for a whole evening even as she declared how proud she was of him really and he felt terrible knowing she was already worried about Sean, somewhere in New Guinea, hopefully still alive. She had turned to drinking beer every evening. He knew she was getting the grog from Ted her mate at *the Fitzroy* but he hadn't the heart to comment.

"I'll be fine, Ma. I can look after me'self." Those were the last words that he had repeated to Gracie as he held her small hands at the wharf watching the seagulls circle the battleships. Those words that were his mantra through the hard months of training and now played in his head on the lurching boat shoulder to shoulder with his squadron. His job now was not only to look after himself but also his fellow section members and he glanced sideways at the faces of his comrades strained with concentration as they stared between the shoulders of the man in front, waiting for the command to scramble over the side into the blue mud.

He remembered that his grandfather had wiped away tears when he farewelled George at the Quay busy with soldiers, bright flags fluttering in the breeze, couples embracing and women holding handkerchiefs to their eyes. "You and Sean are the best things to come out of this family," he explained to George over the noise of the military band. "And now the war is taking both of yer'. It's hardest on yer' mum. Come back safe, son." George noticed that Jim's old eyes were sinking further into his head and his grey eyebrows grew in increasingly wild abandon from his leathery forehead. He wondered how long it might be before he saw his family again and swallowed a sudden swell of emotion as his mother embraced him.

"I can look after me'self, Ma," he whispered again. "I'll be right. And I'll write. Don't fret."

She could not look at him further and walked away from the wharf even as he kissed Gracie on the lips and hopped on the gangplank to the ship. He had turned to wave at Gracie and watched his mother disappear between the frosted glass doors of the Ladies' Lounge at the Woolloomooloo Hotel. All that seemed years ago when it was barely six months and here he was about to wage war.

As the fleet of churning alligators approached the narrow beach, the clearing work that the sappers had done the previous day blowing up the steel posts and barbed wire obstacle course built by the Japs to protect the beach became evident and a sixty-foot gap emerged allowing the alligators to draw together, their giant treads working the shallow water into a porridge of mud and sand. Thick cloud and smoke made visibility poor and the strong scent of dredged sand and broken vegetation blended with the fumes from the vehicles. George could see the alligator in front of them try and fail to clamber the steep embankment so that the troops leapt from the vehicle into the muddy shallows, cursing as they sank up to their waist in oily, thick mud.

"Gonna' be a wet one," remarked Lofty anxiously as they watched the lead platoons scramble from the waters and head cautiously up the beach back lit by the bursting rockets now being flung inland by returning flocks of screaming aircraft which lit up the Dutch oil tanks like giant candles.

At his Sergeant's command to disembark, George leapt over the side of the alligator and steadied himself in the mud that clutched his thighs even as the tide turned, falling back from the steep bank of the beach and stranding several alligators suddenly in deep mud from which they could escape neither forward onto firmer ground or back into the water. As he pushed forward in the column of men against the heaving torrent he saw again the face of the young man swallowed by the receding monster waves at Bondi but his section made the shore and hurried to assist the unloading of one of the transport ships. With no enemy fire apparent, it seemed that the weeks of bombing undertaken in preparation for the landing had worked to clear the Japs from their positions along the beach so that the landed troops could focus on unloading from the transport ships the many tons of machinery, munitions and supplies supporting an invasion of several thousand men.

George held his place in the human chain of filthy, wet men passing crates of water and ammunitions along to the beach. Their slouch hats bobbed up and down as they worked so that from the top of the beach, their column appeared like some giant, undulating sea serpent. The beach itself was now busy with heavy machinery and the shouts of Provosts trying to create order in deteriorating conditions as the tanks and bulldozers that were floated ashore ripped through the heavy mesh laid over the sloppy sand. Bogged RAAF trucks blocked the main exit from the beach to the roadway that lead to the airfield creating havoc as further vehicles crowded onto the beach from the waves of landing craft.

"Like mustering mosquitos", observed Lofty as he watched a Provost directing confused drivers.

"It's a dog's breakfast," George agreed. They watched a team of sappers couple a tractor to a truck bogged at the high end of the beach. The screaming tractor managed only to pull the bumper from the truck even as shots rang from the forest where the lead patrols were scouting. Unperturbed the sappers linked heavy chains around the truck's axle bending it like a banana. They linked more chains around the cab which flew from its chassis so that the sappers were left staring perplexed at the skeleton of the truck stuck firm in the unrelenting mud.

"If this wasn't so serious, it would be bloody funny," commented George as he passed a heavy box of artillery to Lofty.

A small group of slight, native Indonesian men and women observed with apprehension the chaos of the landing from the forest fringe. George squinted at them with some curiosity as the platoon continued to work their line. One had lost a leg and the remainder appeared half-starved. Would they welcome this invasion, he wondered. What did all this mean to them? Before the Japs, it was the Dutch. Now it was a mob of Australians and Americans unleashing further chaos on their little island. Poor beggars were caught up in a war that had nothing to do with them.

"They don't look too sure about all this," Lofty remarked.

"They got no say," George responded thinking of Terry. "Like always."

From along the roadway where vehicles were lining up to escape the beach a series of loud explosions marked the mine-clearing going on in order to create safe passage to the airstrip. News reached George's section as they rested to take water that the lead patrols had encountered Japanese pillbox resistance and the first casualty had been taken by a Jap sniper.

"Well, it's on," Ben had remarked as they took their warmed bully beef, beans and sweet potato dinner from the cook, affectionately known as the Poisoner, and collapsed under the brush shelters they had erected for a night's rest at the beach perimeter before heading for the airstrip in the morning. The air hung close and wet and oversized mossies buzzed relentlessly around their ears as darkness intensified and the soldiers' thoughts turned to their mates in the lead patrols who would spend a tense evening in the jungle.

"Tomorrow we will see some action, young George," Ben commented. "We've gotta' fight for that airfield. Are yer' ready for it?"

"Is the Pope a Catholic?" grinned George. He took first watch and sat late into the night listening to the lapping ocean and the rustlings in the jungle. The sky had cleared briefly and stars blinked uncertainly through the remaining smoke haze over the Bay as a reminder that this battle too would pass and that they would soon restore a peace that allowed for star-gazing and bathing and making love. He let his mind return to Gracie, the smell of her freshly washed cascade of hair, her laughter and her delicate pink lips whispering in his ear. As he closed his eyes, he smelt the water tank at Dowling Street and knew they were in for rain. The first drops fell in loud splats upon the broad palm leaves with which they had covered the slung shelter roofs under which the rest of his section were trying to sleep. Within seconds the rain was torrential and cursing soldiers shifted their positions in the sand to avoid the water pouring down the shelter roofs.

As another smoldering dawn broke on the beach the men consumed strong tea, tinned fruit, beans and biscuits as they readied for their advance along the road now christened the Anzac Highway that led from the beach to the airfield. The rain in the night had further softened the sand so that the George's boots sank inches under him as he trudged behind Happy's dark bulk up the beach. Happy was so named as he kept to himself and rarely smiled. When he spoke, which was also rare, it was usually to observe with glum fortitude, the impossibility of whatever it was the section or the battalion were trying to achieve.

"Happy as a Bastard on Father's Day," Ben had observed and the nickname had stuck.

Happy was from a farming family back of Orange and could shoot any kind of gun at any moving target and bring it to the ground. He had left his small town for the war as the local hero of the rugby team, charging through or over a scrum and over the line, unstoppable with his great bulk. Like George, he was trained as a gunner but he had not had the same technical training and so he was partnered with George to carry the Owen gun slung across his meaty shoulders and protect the section as they worked on the airstrip. They were an imposing partnership as the tallest and youngest men in the group hauling the biggest guns. George liked Happy's silences. He knew that, like stillness, silence was also a virtue in the jungle and he could count on Happy to watch, listen and shoot. Happy's fair freckled face and blunt nose reminded him of Bluey. He often wondered about Bluey and how he was doing in the navy. He was fighting somewhere in the Pacific also. At least, George hoped he was. It was impossible to know.

Ahead of their section, minesweeping continued with the word spreading back that there were more mines and booby traps planted along this strip of road than the whole of the Pacific put together. Regular explosions sounded their path and the men stepped in wary formation along the dirt road framed by long ditches aflame in places where the oil from the exploding Dutch tanks had leaked and gathered. The strengthening sun combined with the smoke to turn the sky red so it seemed that both the earth and the sky were burning. Ahead of George's section, the men threw themselves suddenly to the ground and signaled a halt having heard movement in the brush alongside the road. Three horrendously wounded Indonesians were discovered hiding in the scrub and a message was sent for the stretcher-bearers. A hobbling native woman of slim build and indeterminate age appeared on the road dressed in rags with part of her face blown off. She stared uncomprehendingly at the passing column of soldiers holding a bunch of leaves to the open wound where her cheek had been.

Progress was slow along the highway for the column of men accompanied by Matilda tanks and shadowed by tractors, trucks, diggers and graders. Around the airstrip were three high ridges that were the key targets for the Australian forces to take from the Japanese in order to secure the airfield. As George's Airfield Construction Squadron proceeded towards the strip, regular reports told them how the lead patrols were progressing in their assault on these positions. The 2/24th supported by the force of the 25-pounders operated by the 2/7th had now taken two of the hilltops occupied by the Japanese with the loss of seven men and ten wounded but the Japs had suffered over fifty casualties, mostly burned in their pillboxes by grenadiers. The airstrip remained beyond their sight but the sickening stench of cordite, burning vegetation and Japanese flesh permeated the air and George wetted his scarf and tied it over his face. When the training manual had said the Japanese smelt pungent, he didn't think this was what they had in mind but he couldn't help but reflect on that particular section of the manual as his stomach turned.

There remained a further ridge to secure before they could approach the strip so they stopped to smoke and wait anxiously in the pumping heat for word to arrive for their advance. They heard occasional machine gun fire from further along the highway and stood alert for snipers. While George's squadron were prepared to fight, their main task was to provide a workable airstrip and their skills in doing this meant they were precluded from the lead assaults. The airstrip came first, at all costs. Without it, the entire mission was pointless and the lives of Australian soldiers wasted. So, the Airfield Construction Squadron had to be delivered to a secure airfield as a primary objective for the entire battalion. Accordingly, each member of the squadron felt the grave responsibility of opening the strip to aircraft as soon as humanly possible to allow the RAAF and the USAAF to clear out the rest of the Pacific. More than this however, the squadron needed to fulfill the mission that gave meaning to the dead and wounded Australian soldiers now being transported past them in jeeps to the medical station at beach headquarters.

George could feel his anger building as he watched a jeep carry several groaning and bloody soldiers past their position. His mouth hardened and he gripped his gun a little tighter. He was relieved to feel the anger he knew he would need to take it to the Japanese, to shoot and kill the bastards. All he wanted now was to get on with it. The waiting was torment.

"How much longer d'yer reckon we'll wait, Ben?" George asked as they stood with their backs against the tractor that George was to operate and watched over the baking jungle.

"How long's a piece of string, mate?" Ben responded with his rifle held ready at his hip and his eyes studying the brush with unblinking concentration.

"Well, we've only got six days to fix this bloody airstrip, so they'd better get a move on," offered Lofty from his position at the far side of the tractor.

As he spoke, a runner arrived to let them know the Japs had

abandoned the third crest and the ridges alongside the airfield were now captured. The squadron could at last resume their convoy of giant machinery and occupy the airstrip. They were warned that the jungle was full of tripwire and booby traps and Japanese snipers remained scattered unpredictably among the surrounding vegetation.

"Good luck!" The runner left to carry the message down the line. As he trotted along the dirt road a shot rang out and he lurched suddenly sideways like a puppet with a snapped string and fell to the ground.

Ben held George back as the section nearer to the dropped runner crashed into the jungle from where the shot had been fired. A rifleman made his way on his belly to the fallen runner and dragged him into the ditch along the road.

"They've got him," Ben assured George.

"All right men," the Sergeant signaled sharply for an advance. "We're off!"

"Like a dirty shirt!" Lofty reiterated, grasping his rifle to his chest and taking his position at the rear of the tractor.

The stuttering of machine gun fire sounded from within the jungle where the sniper had shot from as the engines roared into life and George fixed his Bren gun onto its tripod at the front of his tractor and drove it onto the highway to join the slow procession of mechanical beasts come to tame an airstrip. Happy stood on the stepping board of the tractor scanning the jungle with the Owen gun poised. George could not think of anyone he would rather have travelling with him down this road but he kept his head low as they progressed towards the strip shadowing the Matilda tanks and the forward platoons who waded through the muddy, leech-infested ditches alongside the highway. When they turned the bend and finally laid their eyes on the distant airstrip still several hundred yards away, the enormity of the task struck them. They took it in turns to gaze through the field glasses at the bombarded strip with water-filled potholes the size of trucks, huge rocks scattered by explosions and torn earth where flat runs were meant to be.

"We've certainly got our bloody work cut out for us here," commented Ben.

"We've got Buckley's," Happy offered barely moving his lips.

Most of Woolloomooloo and half of Darlinghurst turned out for Harry's funeral service and then moved on to the Pace home in Dowling Street for the wake once the simple pine coffin had been driven off on the back of a draped lorry to catch the last train for Rookwood. Harry had passed in his sleep, leaving this world with as little fuss as he had lived in it. Mrs Vinelli, his landlady and neighbor to the Pace family had become concerned when Harry hadn't come down the stairs that morning and had called on Jim to go up and see what was the matter. She hadn't stopped crossing herself all morning.

"All that's left of 'im is a dent in the mattress," Jim had murmured when they went through his meager possessions and cleared his room after the undertaker had been and carted his body off. Maggie squeezed his hand.

"I'll miss yer', mate," Jim declared to the dip in the bed and then turned to follow his wife down the narrow stairs balancing the cardboard box holding Harry's measly possessions.

"Only one thing worse than a blasted wedding, and that's a funeral!" Jim declared working his tie under his fresh collar. He hated anything formal and the worst thing was, he knew Harry hated this sort of thing even more but Roy had insisted on forking out for a funeral and a decent wake even with the war rationing on. A covered truck pulled out the front of the Pace family home the morning of the service and two burly men unloaded several kegs of beer, crates of soda, legs of ham, plucked chooks, boxes of tomatoes, jam tarts, lamingtons and enough loaves of bread to feed a rugby team.

"God's trousers!" Jim declared. "Where has all this come from then?"

The two blokes just winked. "From Roy for Harry's farewell." They drove off leaving Maggie, Jim, Sybil and Anne staring in wonder at the pile of contraband.

The funeral was simple with Father Scott delivering a mercifully short sermon about the blessedness of the meek and the persecuted with a couple of hymns thrown in and then the desultory crowd dispersed with most of them trailing towards the Pace home. Roy was looking taller these days due to the platforms he now had built into his woven leather shoes and the Brylcream holding his greying hair stiffly aloft over his leathery face. He was certainly not suffering on account of the war.

"A man's still gotta' get his hair cut," Roy responded when Jim remarked on his well-cut suit and the generous spread he had donated for Harry's farewell.

"Harry was me mate and he deserves a proper farewell." Roy's face was set in concrete from years of squinting at a sun-blasted horse track and so his grief was only evident from the wetness in the corner of his eye and the pile he spent on the wake. A pile everyone knew came from the shifting telephone rooms he now had set up around the Cross and Darlinghurst taking bets from those too busy or broke to get to the track.

"Shame he's not here for it," added Jim. "Woulda' been the best feed he's ever had!"

The wake continued through the afternoon and Sybil grew tired of the questions about George and about Sean. Questions she could not answer. Where were they now? Were they all right? Would they be back on leave soon? Was she terribly proud? As the sun began to fall, she took her chance and disappeared into her room, relieved to escape the old cronies left reminiscing about Harry and his horse and his vegetable cart. In her room, she flopped onto her bed and undid the corset that gripped her thickening torso with a sigh. From her handbag she took the lamington, the chicken leg and the three jam tarts and ate quickly and silently staring at the rag rug, washing down the sugary crumbs of tart with swigs of cool beer. There was so much missing from her life now. She was desperate to fill the emptiness inside her. "My darling boys," she muttered to herself as she drifted into a sound sleep interrupted only by the odd hiccup.

· · ·

George's squadron did not make the airfield that day but were ordered to pull their heavy vehicles off the road to make way for more Matilda tanks summoned by the lead patrols of the 2/24th who had encountered Nippon Ridge. Although this ridge was several hundred yards beyond the airstrip it was heavily defended by the Japanese and gave them a clear view over the airstrip which they continued to bombard with machine gun fire. George watched in horror as an Australian platoon closing in on the ridge flew into the air like a flock of flustered birds as the Japs exploded massive depth charges they had laid along the strip at the base of their fortified ridge. Five were killed outright and many wounded with the survivors struggling forward to the jungle at the base of the ridge where they dug in for cover and sent back runners for smoke screens in order to cover a withdrawal. The Japanese were rolling grenades down the ridge as if they were marbles. Several Matildas lumbered across the airstrip through the machine gun fire to where the platoon sheltered to collect the wounded and deliver them back to the roadside Aid Post. George and Happy helped unload the stretchers and lit smokes and passed mugs of tea to the wounded men streaked with swamp slime and blood. The medics patched and tagged them as best they could before loading them into the bouncing jeeps headed for the main dressing station at the beach. With the light fading the remainder of the lost patrol had no choice but to dig in at the base of the ridge and sit out a long and sleepless night.

"Poor bastards," Ben muttered.

From the beach a sudden explosion and burst of flame caught their attention and the squadron learned that a light aircraft had hit a log while trying to take off from the makeshift beach airstrip the sappers had cleared that day. The pilot had torn from the wreck a human fireball and the beach airstrip was abandoned. George shared a meaningful, silent stare with Ben, Happy, and Lofty. The longer the delay in getting the airstrip up and running, the more Australian lives would be lost. As they took their bully beef and biscuits and settled in to camp by the road for the night, the young Padre approached and squatted near George.

"You fellas all right?" he asked. "It's been a hard day." George squinted at his pale, young face in the dim torch light and reflected that the Padre did not seem more than a year or two older than himself.

"Feel about as much use as tits on a nun, Padre," Lofty commented. "We need to get to that airstrip." The Padre smiled despite himself and nodded before moving off into the darkness.

The first light saw Nippon Ridge bombarded with 25 pounders and obscured in smoke and flying dirt and dust even as two more platoons approached cautiously creeping across the exposed airstrip from crater to crater, stepping high into the vegetation to avoid trip wires and booby traps. When they relieved the remainder of the lost platoon from the day before they circled the ridge and reached the top around midday. There they discovered to their surprise that the Japs had abandoned their position in the night leaving only the headless corpse of a local woman with her sorry pile of clothing lying beside her. On searching the Dutch pillboxes that the Japanese had sheltered in, the Australians uncovered a map of the island produced by Dutch oil surveyors. The map showed in great detail the various villages, swamps and tracks across the islands as well as the areas where oil reserves and oil storage tanks were established. Over the next few days this map reached every unit in the battalion and George folded a copy into his breast pocket.

Now the Nippon Ridge was clear, George's squadron were finally free to re-start their convoy of tractors, dozers, mobile shovels, ditch diggers and caterpillars and get on with repairing the devastated airstrip. But as George was to discover, that was not the end of the Japanese.

Despite every effort, and with Charlie home twice now for leave, Edith had not fallen pregnant and was worried she never would.

"What if that blasted nurse made a balls up of me piping," she hissed at Sybil over a glass of lager in the Fitzroy Lounge late on a Saturday afternoon.

"Now, now," Sybil counseled. "You don't want to jump to conclusions."

Ted approached with fresh beers for his favourite fillies as he liked to call them. It was only ever Sybil and Edith and perhaps the odd Sheila out with her bloke that ever sat in the 'Ladies Lounge' which was really just a partitioned section of the L-shaped public bar of the Fitzroy. As women were not allowed in public bars and required a male escort to enter pubs at all as a rule, Ted had knocked up a partition made from broken up soda crates and hung a picture of Errol Flynn on it. The lounge offered two armchairs with oversized arms and worn floral velvet upholstery with a low timber table between them and an old leather two-seater sofa across the end wall. There was no room for anything further. Sybil kept a dishcloth in her handbag so that if the cops ever came in she would start wiping the table. Edith said she would just tell them to get stuffed and that her boyfriend was in the front bar.

"Any one of them would vouch for me," she assured Sybil smoothing her hair which had been set like concrete that morning into two large rolls arched over her brow making her several inches taller and quite devilish.

Nowadays, the front bar was busy with American, British and Australian servicemen. They were all hungry for female company and each had their leave allowance to spend. Edith spent more time leaning on the bar chatting around the partition to the soldiers with one leg swinging in the air than she did chatting with Sybil who focused on the crossword seeking Ted's help with some of the tougher clues. Inevitably, these soldiers would offer to buy a round of drinks and Edith would scurry back to Sybil with a couple of sherries.

"Come on Syb, they wanna' go dancing. There's no harm in that."

"What about Charlie?" Sybil reminded Edith alarmed by the colour in Edith's cheeks and the looks she kept flashing at the tall American soldier with his head stuck around the partition.

"It's only dancing," squealed Edith. "The night's a pup. Let's go and have a bit of fun. That tall one's taken a shine to me and he says he'll shout a bottle of champagne!"

Sybil saw Ted watching them through his black-rimmed spectacles from the other side of the bar. His large milky blue eyes seemed even sadder than usual and Sybil felt sorry for him. He was always doing things for her, giving her free beers and sharing little delicacies of food that he was able to get despite the rationing. He listened to all her problems and she had bent his ear often enough. She knew he liked her more than he should but he had never put the hard word on her and she felt she owed him her friendship. Ted was tall although a little stooped in the shoulders and was not unmanly although no-one had ever called him handsome. He had tried to enlist not long after the war first broke out but was rejected on account of his poor eyesight. He did his part for the war effort packaging supplies for the soldiers on behalf of the Comforts Fund in the evenings. He was a softly spoken and intelligent man not much older than Sybil with long, gentle fingers and a ready laugh. His hair was a shambles with tufts at the sides and the back of his head that he arranged over his bald dome in odd patterns. He may not have been the manliest creature to look at but he had thrown many a larrikin out the door of the pub onto the street and, despite his limited vision, he didn't miss a trick.

Sybil crossed to the bar with the empty sherry glasses and handed them to Ted.

"On the hard stuff?" he quipped.

"Be a shame to waste it," she replied. Ted sank the dirty glasses into his washing tub under the bar.

"I got a coupla' nice meat pies and a cream bun out the back Syb, if you fancy a bit of a feast after closing. Or are you girls headin' out with them Yanks?" Ted eyed the Americans on the other side of the partition. She hadn't had a cream bun since before the war and licked her lips before turning back to Edith.

"I can't come, Edith. Me corn's playin' up."

"Honestly, Sybil, I don't know why I bother with you anymore. I'm not going to be sitting around wasting my life waiting for this blasted war to end. For cryin' out loud, you're not even married to 'im!" She slammed the door of the Ladies Lounge on her way out. Sybil blushed and Ted smiled kindly.

"Have you heard from either of the lads lately?"

"George wrote last week and he was fine. Missing the home cooking, of course but he said he was learning all kinds of new things. Nothing from Sean," Sybil responded. "Not for a month now."

"Ah well," Ted replied wiping the bar with a rag. "The mail only gets out of the north of New Guinea by a bloody miracle. I'm sure there's a letter on the way."

Sean had survived for almost two years crawling on his belly through the jungle muds of New Guinea living off tinned peaches, bully beef, beans and his own body fat. He was no longer the well-built, kind-hearted wharfie but a hard-hearted, lean and deadly rifleman with a burning hatred for the Japanese. He had escaped death and capture, beating the dysentery and the jungle madness that had taken so many of his comrades at Shaggy Ridge, but still he crept along jungle trails, this time in Bougainville, relieving the American infantry in tracking the remains of the Japs still fighting a war they were no longer winning. As they had landed at Empress Augusta Bay to begin this 'mopping up' campaign, Sean had observed the thick jungle leading up from the shore to the smoking volcano and watched the team of natives help unload the landing craft with a feeling of foreboding. Surely, this was the island of Kong.

They had been attacking, chasing and killing Japanese soldiers for four weeks now. Cut off from their supply lines and desperate, the Japanese soldiers were increasingly unpredictable and he and Bags, or Baglen Owen, a Welsh Australian rifleman who had the disconcerting habit of singing loudly in Welsh while he shot up the enemy, were silently stalking a small troop of Japs that they had disturbed on their way across the Soraken Plantation which led to the all important Peninsular. Sean and Bags were leading their platoon in the throbbing heat of the afternoon, crawling noiselessly through the grass towards the creek bed where they knew the Japs were dug in. Suddenly, two Japanese soldiers bolted from the undergrowth twenty yards ahead of them and made for the creek. Sean rose with his rifle to his shoulder and took aim but paused to check his sights. The two Japanese soldiers continued to run, their bare arses jiggling in the glaring sun and he could not help himself. He laughed. It may have been his laughter that caused him to miss. It may have been this most unusual sound of joy in the deadly jungle that drew the bullet from the Japanese sniper, but Sean fell. The bullet hit him through the forehead so that he still had the smile on his face even as Bags shot both of the bare-arsed runners in the back and fell to the grass to check his mate. Sean's platoon charged the position from where the shot had erupted and they lined up the fourteen Japanese corpses by the creek before nightfall. They had dug a deep hole for Sean and Bags sang, of course, but this time his beautiful tenor filled the twilight with the words Sean had taught him as they had trekked long, weary miles along the Frontierres range:

Oh my name it is McCarty & I'm a rorty party

I'm rough & tough as an old man kangaroo

Some people say I'm crazy, I don't work because I'm lazy

And I tag along in the boozing throng, the Push from Woolloomooloo.

The remaining members of the platoon shook their heads and turned away as Bags said his farewell, "Hwyll fawr, bytty." He pocketed Sean's tags and opened his diary, to gaze at the tatty newspaper cutting which had been lovingly covered in sticking tape and fixed inside the cover of the diary. It was a photograph of a vampire, a pirate and a beautiful woman in a red gown. He placed the diary in his breast pocket. Sean had written it whenever they had a spare moment and had made Bags promise that he would get it to his young nephew serving in Tarakan, if anything should happen to him.

"It *was* pretty funny, mate! Those yellow arses." Bags wiped his eyes and slung his rifle over his back as he trudged behind his platoon along the creek.

It had been three more days of stop and start along the beleaguered

Anzac Highway before George's squadron made the airstrip. Fighting had been fierce and they had lost over a hundred men and many more injured just to be able to hang the Australian flag over the airstrip.

"The longest three bloody miles in history," George had commented to Happy as they finally shut down the tractor's engine alongside the sorry airstrip that lay before them, cratered for most of its three thousand yards with holes so big that two tractors might fit within each of them. Allied bombing over the preceding weeks had efficiently destroyed the very object of the entire mission. The squadron of men walked the strip assessing the craters and stepping around the great piles of sand and rubble blown from them, shaking their heads. At one end of the strip, the giant craters were filled with dirty, stagnant water from the last rains, and at the western, lower end, putrid swamp water that leeched up at high tide from the surrounding swamplands.

"Smells like a bandicoot's arse," Happy mumbled.

"What kind of drongo would build an airstrip on a swamp?" George asked in wonder.

Beyond the swamps, the idle Dutch oil derricks stood erect like metal skeletons of a dead industry in the otherwise monotonous jungle that swept away from the strip and then up along the steep slopes where Australian troops continued the desperate battles for the ridges, evident in frequent gunfire and plumes of dark smoke and reported the next day in numerical reports of yards won, men lost and enemies killed.

"Well, no use flappin' our gums." Ben removed his shirt and headed for his bulldozer. "I reckon we'd better get on with it."

Repairing the strip became a matter of desperate and grueling experiment for the entire squadron who worked in three shifts across day and night to get the strip operational. In George's platoon, Ben worked the dozer to push the sand and rubble back into the craters so George could pull the rollers over the filled holes only to have them sink as the mud foundation gave way. Heavy vehicles of all types got bogged down in the mud and their deep tracks coming and going over the strip only made the dirt softer so that, after several frustrating days, a new approach was adopted and two platoons were dedicated to quarrying gravel and sand from surrounding hills to truck to the airstrip. The Dutch Civil Affairs Unit supplied hundreds of natives to help fill the craters with anything at hand. They threw lumps of concrete, piping, timber, boiler plate, old machinery, steel plates and forty-gallon Japanese oil drums filled with sand into the hungry craters in order to establish ground firm enough to roll and grade. At night the natives were trucked back to their village camps as the next shift of the construction squadron readied to take over the work. The airstrip was something to behold at night, lit up like a Manly ferry with giant industrial lights and music blaring from loudspeakers to keep up morale. Bing Crosby, Perry Como and the Andrew Sisters competed with the wild percussion of the empress cicadas and the clicks and staccato burps of relentless swamp frogs. And just when it looked like they might be making some real headway, the sky would open and the rain would fall in thick sheets sinking new craters into the strip and returning the western end to a quagmire.

The morning after one such night of heavy rain, George's platoon returned to their machinery to find Ben's bulldozer sunk in the mud at the side of the strip. The roof of the driver's cab was the only visible part of the dozer left. They stared in disbelief for a moment and then Ben looked at George who was generally responsible for rescuing bogged vehicles with his tractor.

"Not a hope in Hell, mate" George offered before Ben even spoke.

"Gawd struth! This strip's got the bloody mockers on it!" Lofty spat as the regular morning formation of Kittyhawks patrolled over their heads. "Those blokes should be landing here about now. You couldn't land a blasted balloon on it!" Lofty gave voice to the frustration they all felt as they headed back to report the loss to squadron command.

George had never seen so much Marston Matting in his life as was piled up along the sides of the strip and he dragged endless plates of it on top of the firmer patches of the strip that appeared to be holding as the repair works continued. It was monotonous, hard labor performed in relentless heat and humidity over days that became weeks. His skin was almost the color of the natives except for the patches where it peeled from his body and his hair was stiff with sweat and bleached almost blonde from the sun. They all worked shirtless now and only bothered to dry between their toes to stop the tinea after showering at camp before falling into their cots exhausted. Despite the hardship, they knew they had it good compared to the frontline platoons still fighting on steep ridges in impenetrable jungle against a desperate enemy who would never surrender.

At the airstrip, they experienced only a few minor incursions by marauding Japs and it was George who saw the movements in the scrub as the afternoon light faded on another hot and hazy day. They were stationed at the western end stamping down yet more gravel dumped there from the quarry. He gestured his team to down tools and lie low as he grabbed his gun and slid silently from the tractor cab to the dirt. Happy had learned to read him like a book and was by his side as George scurried to the jungle cover at the perimeter of the airstrip. He was sure he had seen a flash of pale Japanese uniform in the brush and he and Happy silently stalked into the jungle with Ben following close behind as Lofty tore across the strip to share the word. George's heart pumped so hard he glanced at Happy to see if he could hear it but Happy had seen something and moved away from George gesturing beyond a fallen tree and for George to circle around. The jungle was so thick, George couldn't see more than a few yards ahead at any one time and his boots sank deep in the swampy ground. He kept still and tried to ascertain Happy's trail beyond the fallen tree from where he heard a sudden whoop-like call. As he inched closer to the tree, he struggled to lift his boot from the swamp and looked down only to see it firmly wedged inside the rotting torso of a Japanese soldier. At that moment Happy fired his Owen gun into the jungle and a body dropped in the foliage just as another sped further into the greenery. George shook his boot free of the maggoty flesh and pulled himself out of the swamp waters onto a mangrove root where he vomited silently and violently before wiping his face and forcing his feet back into the swamp water to resume the pursuit.

It didn't matter. It couldn't matter. There were the living to think about. Behind him, he heard the water move and swung around to see Ben stealthily tracking him crouched over his rifle. George indicated to the west of their position and they moved with slow, steady care in the hushed jungle sweeping aside the giant ferns and elephant ears, straining for any sound or sight of Happy or a Jap. As they stepped into a fern gully and deeper, dark water several blasts rang out from just above them and a Japanese soldier crashed through the heavy creepers and fell backwards into the shallow swamp. Even as he fell, he fired several shots from his rifle before Happy burst from the jungle in pursuit. George fell on the Jap, knocking his rifle from his hands and held his own Bren gun to the soldier's head as he rose to his feet. The soldier's filthy face was twisted with pain, fear and something else. George struggled to place the look on the young soldier's face which seemed to him familiar even as he kept his gun pointed steadily at his nose. He knew he could not have met this soldier before but there was that look in his eyes. And then it dawned on him; the look on his face was that same look he had seen on the face of the boy at Bondi beach just as he was swallowed by a wave.

"We should kill the Bastard," Happy panted as he and George held their guns pointed at the cropped head of the writhing soldier who bled from inside his shirt somewhere while Ben stripped him of weaponry. George hated the young face he saw before him but he knew that the reason he hated the Japanese so much was their brutality. He had heard all the stories of gory executions, torture and ill treatment of soldiers, civilians, women and even children that the Japanese had engaged in across the whole Pacific. He hated them for this inhumane brutality, but he recognized that if he were to remain different from them, there had to be *something* that defined that difference. He knew how common it was for Australian soldiers to shoot wounded Japs but he could not justify it.

"Nah," George shook his head. "That's what they do. We're fighting them for what they do. We've gotta' be better. He's buggered anyhow."

"He would'a shot yer' as quick as look at yer'". Happy responded and the three soldiers stood struggling with their rage as they stared down the barrels of their guns in the dripping, sweating green cathedral of ferns as the swamp frogs bellowed in joy at the gathering dusk. Happy kicked the soldier. "Get up, yer' mongrel!" The soldier staggered to his feet.

Ben pushed the butt of his rifle into the soldier's back. "It's your lucky day, mate! There's a Christian among us!"

They marched him slowly, pulling him back to his feet when he fell, back to the airstrip where they surrendered him to the infantry duty platoon.

"There's another one, but he's dead," Happy offered the warrant officer who received the injured Jap with a raised eyebrow. "'Bout thirty yards in the jungle off the north-west side of the strip."

"You ever seen anyone taken by a wave, Ben?" George asked as they shared a cup of tea outside their camp tent after chow that evening.

"Can't say I have," answered Ben drawing heavily on his smoke.

"There was a boy I almost rescued," George said quietly. "Black Sunday at Bondi. Just a bit younger than me, I guess. I had his hand in mine. I had him,... for a moment. And then a monster backwash..." George paused for while feeling the nausea rising in him again. "Anyway, he had this look on his face. Just like that Jap soldier. Like he never saw this coming but he knew he should'a seen it coming. You know what I mean?"

"Swallowed by a wave, eh?" Ben ground his smoke into the dirt and gazed at his boots. "Maybe that's what's happened to us. The whole lot of us swallowed up in this blasted war that we never saw coming even though it was flamin' obvious it was coming. I thought the last war woulda' put an end to war but there's no stoppin' progress!" He laughed sardonically and patted George's twitching leg. "You did the right thing today, mate. That was a good decision ... for all of us in the long run. When we think back on all that we have done." Ben rubbed his grey-stubbled chin. "That will be one of the moments we might be thankful for." He stood and stretched his back moaning. "I never want to see another single piece of Marston Matting in my life. Time for some shut-eye, eh?"

Although the Japanese soldier was sent to the casualty clearing station and tended, he died from his wounds in the night. George was not surprised.

"Well, at least we didn't waste another bullet on him," Happy offered.

George was made responsible for supervising a team of natives provided by the Dutch Civil Authority to assist in filling and leveling the strip at a point where his platoon were struggling to make firm ground. That was how he came to meet Lukas Bram, an official with the Dutch Oil Company who was working as Petroleum Supervisor with the Dutch Civil Authority to help defeat the Japanese but, perhaps more importantly to Bram, to restore the flow of six million barrels of the finest oil in the world. Bram had introduced himself to George and Happy at the end of a hard day's work when they trucked a load of natives back to the Dutch camp. He was a slim man with long, greying hair neatly combed into a ponytail and long limbs that he moved with an exaggerated slowness that reminded George of a spider. They shared a hot cup of tea on the verandah of the Dutch administration building and Bram told them a bit about the famous Pamusian oilfields which lay inoperable nearby but which he hoped to restore.

"I can say," Bram had assured them, "…tat two strrrong men like you could make a lot of money worrrking for the Dutch Oil Company. After tis trrrouble is overrr." Bram waved his arm in an arc. His heavy Dutch accent reminded George of Hans at the Beat Club and he looked upon him with some suspicion.

"Doing what?" Happy asked.

"Why, mining!" Bram smiled broadly at them. "Mining for oil!" He waved them farewell as George turned the empty truck around and they headed down the uneven dirt road back to the airstrip. They remained silent for much of the way other than for the involuntary grunts forced from them by the bigger dips in the road. The evening was falling and the sky was hung with clouds like giant apricots. Each was thinking through what lay in store for them if they were lucky enough to return home. And each of them was imagining what a lot of money might look like.

Sybil was almost home from work on the Wednesday afternoon in June when she sensed something wrong at the house. The blackout paper covering the front window to the street gave nothing away, but she had an uneasy feeling as she entered Dowling Street with her hands thrust deep in her coat pockets against the cold. With George and Sean gone, it was not the same busy home and the blacked out windows made it dimmer than ever inside. As she hung her coat in the hall, she heard Jim pleading.

"Mags, darling, my darling... come on now, girl..." Jim sat on his knees on the kitchen floor before Maggie who stared motionless and speechless into space. He rubbed her plump hand softly and pumped it as if trying to bring her to life. Sybil ran into the kitchen and Jim looked at her in a way that caused her to freeze. She saw the opened telegram on the kitchen table and looked from Jim to the letter on the table and back again. Jim stood painfully to his feet placing Maggie's inert hand on her apron and approached Sybil who felt the blood drain from her face and stepped away from Jim.

"No!"

"It's Sean," Jim hastened to explain. "He's ... gone, Syb. He was shot dead. The Japs got him. Our boy is gone." Jim let the tears fall unchecked down his grizzled face and Sybil saw for the first time how he had become old and small. She turned on her heel and grabbed her coat as she flew out the front door. Sybil walked with the tears streaming down her face for a long time down around the wharves, directionless, unable to stop but with nowhere to go. She felt that if she stopped, it would become real. The unthinkable would become real. Her Sean. His playful brown eyes shot with gold, his strong arms and booming voice, the sun in his hair, his laughter, his thousand kindnesses, his love for her and the children. It was gone. All gone. She could not accept it. She walked determinedly so that the reality of it could not catch up with her until she began to tire and her feet dragged. It was then that she noticed a tall man following her at a little distance in the darkness. She eyed him suspiciously and made to cross the road from the harbour side when the man called out her name.

She peered closer at the shadowy figure as he removed his hat and several tufts of hair sprang upright. "Ted?" she asked.

"Yep, it's me Syb. I came to watch out for yer' I heard the news. 'Bout Sean." Ted murmured apologetically. "I don't want to bother you, love. Just wanted to be around in case I could help." Sybil stared at him for a moment and then collapsed against him with the sobs breaking from her like relentless waves. He held her and let her sob and punch his chest as they stood beside the lapping water in the moonlight. "You know I am always here for yer', Syb. Always."

On George's twenty-first birthday, the Germans surrendered. While that did not mean a great deal to the men still fighting the Japanese across the Pacific, the entire battalion on Tarakan were granted one bottle of beer for each man and there was an appreciative silence among the men as they drank the cool, amber liquid with slow deliberation.

"Happy birthday, George. What a shame you gave to celebrate your coming of age with the likes of us in a place like this. But at least the Germans have made it a grand day for yer'," Ben laughed. Happy and Lofty each patted George on the back and he smiled despite himself. The beer reminded him of home and made him sentimental. In his cot that evening, he stared at the recent photograph of Gracie which she had sent him and which he kept in his diary. She had that coy, mischievous look in her eye as if she were teasing the photographer and she wore her hair down over bare shoulders. She looked like a woman and not the girl he remembered. She had written about some new job at a Sydney radio station which she was very excited about. She signed off with love but George noticed her letters changing, or was it him that was changing? She seemed further from him and ephemeral so that increasingly he had trouble picturing her face. He thought of Woolloomooloo, the family home, his mother, his grandparents and sister, the Cross and Jonesy and the gang at the metal works and it all seemed like a dream when he knew it was hard fact happening three thousand miles away.

"It is not so easy to returrrn," Lukas had shaken his weathered head when they had told him they would keep his job offer in mind. "If you want to make the money, it's here and now in Borrrneo. I can say, it is a question of supply and demand. We need skilled men now. Nort later. Well, ... now beink when we have finished with these bluedish Japs!"

The next time George drove the natives to the Dutch Compound he spoke again with Lukas Bram under the groaning fan of his dilapidated office in the whitewashed administration building. When George explained he was a qualified metal worker, Lukas raised his long eyebrows and offered George a year's salary for three months' work paid in pounds sterling starting as soon as his service duties ended on Tarakan. When George indicated he would have to offer Happy the same, he hesitated only briefly before agreeing. "Ya, ya! But you must start soon."

George was careful to hide his shock at the generosity of this offer. "We're trying to win this flamin' war Lukas, but it could last a bit longer than you think, mate."

"We will vait." Lukas folded his arms and placed his boots on his dusty desk. "My men frrom Califorrnia are arriving next week to starrt to the rrepairs. We are cornfident. You must be cornfident in the frontierrr, Georrge!"

As George and his platoon continued the grueling work of filling, leveling, and grading the airstrip, the infantry pressed on in the continuing, bloody fight for the Ridges. *The Tarakan Times* filled them in on the progress of the troops at the forward positions. The Airfield Construction Squadron had cleared a thousand yards of strip adequate for the light Austers to fly each morning over the island and gather information on the enemy's movements. Grey American fighters from Palawan Island roared overhead most days dropping napalm bombs to clear the jungle which exploded in giant black clouds lit furious white and orange at their core. Then the Australian troops would press ahead into the burning, stinking wastelands pursuing the Japs as they abandoned first Snag's Track, then Freda, then Joyce and then Margy. But these battles were not easy and not foreseen. The solemn memorial services were held almost daily for those soldiers lost in these battles and of those who survived, many were damaged either physically or mentally and lay in recovery struggling to escape the enemies in their minds. The planned brief six-day assault drew out to six weeks of desperate fighting until finally, the Japanese stronghold of Fukukaku fell in mid-June and the remaining Japs scarpered into the jungle heading for the north of the island to get as far away as possible from the allied patrols and camps. As if a trigger had been pulled with the fall of Fukukaku, the heavens opened and it rained for seven hours dropping one hundred and forty points of solid water on the airstrip, undoing a week of work in a day and dampening the joy of the Japanese capitulation for the Airfield Construction Squad.

Constant boat patrols now scoured the north coast of the island looking for Japanese on the run and as George relaxed with Happy over tea and biscuits and a game of bridge at the YMCA, the favourite gathering place for men on a break from duty, he listened to an account from a bloke from the pioneers who had been patrolling the strait on a barge when they had encountered three Japs in a canoe several miles off the Tarakan coast.

"There they were, naked as the day they were born, paddling away like there was no tomorrow. So, we sang out to them 'Ko-sun-say-oh', 'Ko-sun-say-oh', you know. Surrender. But the little bastards just kept paddling. So, we fired a warning shot over their heads. Didn't make no difference. They just kept paddling. We fired a second shot, closer this time. Then they did something, … well, they knelt all close together in the boat, like they were one, and you could see one of them pull the pin on a grenade that they held between them. Well, after a short while, it was clear that the bloody thing was bung and wasn't gonna' blow. So, they picked up their paddles and started paddling again." The pioneer shook his head as if he still found it hard to believe his own account.

"What happened?" asked George.

"We shot 'em up." The pioneer looked evenly at George. "They had no food, water, clothing or weapons in that boat. Nothin' other than that dodgy grenade. But they wouldn't surrender. Looks like they believed the garbage they've been fed about us being cut-throats and cannibals. Don't reckon we will catch too many alive."

It was the next day that, George received the letter from his mother. He was just out of a shower after a day on the airstrip and flopped onto his cot and opened the envelope. His mother wrote a good letter, full of stories about David Jones, the local goings on at Woolloomooloo, his sister's swimming trophies and the failures of Jim's garden plot. This letter was different. It was a lot shorter than usual and the first paragraph made his head spin.

My darling George,

It is with a broken heart that I write to tell you that we have lost our darling Sean. We received the news from the AIF two days ago and I wanted to let you know as I know how much you loved him. He was taking part in the mop-ups in Bougainville when he and his platoon encountered a group of Japs who they pursued and he was shot in the head and died. He served with honour and has been awarded some medals. They have buried him in New Guinea. I cannot tell you how this has broken me. Your Uncle and I were closer than I have been to anyone besides you and your sister and I cannot forget him. But I am so proud of him. And proud of you, son. It's because of him and you and all those other good Australian heroes who are fighting those blasted Japs that we can continue to live free lives. I am so sorry, son. I am not up to writing much more today. The skies are grey and the wind is cold and it is just how it should be for misery. Take care, George. I couldn't bear to lose you. Come home to your mother in one living piece!

Mum xxx

.   .   .

George was crushed by this news more than he could have imagined. His Uncle Sean had been like an older brother to him. It was impossible to think he would never see that smile again. He stood up from his cot with no idea where he wanted to go. He twirled on the floorboards, re-read the letter and punched the wall with his bare fist several times cursing the Japanese and cursing the war. They were just getting the upper hand. They were near the end. Sean had almost made it through. After two years of fighting! To die so near the end like that. It wasn't fair. He felt the distress his Grandfather and Grandmother must be feeling and moaned. He decided to run and headed out of barracks to the road that led to HQ. He would send a telegram. There was nothing else he could do. He ran in the sweltering, wet heat of the late afternoon his tears indistinguishable from the sweat that ran all over him. He promised himself that, no matter what happened, he would stay alive. He would survive this blasted war.

The blokes in the communications hut offered their condolences and sent his telegram and they suggested he could call a telephone line in Sydney if he wanted to plan, so he told his mother to be at Mrs Mill's shop to take a call on the Saturday afternoon at 2pm. He told her to bring Gracie, if she could.

His mother answered the phone with an uncharacteristically quiet voice.

"Hello?"

"'Lo, Ma, it's George." He heard her struggling with her grief before she could speak. In those few moments of quiet, he felt the pain she was in like a knife in his belly.

"It's good to hear your voice. Are you going to talk to me?"

"Of course I'm going to talk to yer'. Oh, George, it's so good to hear your voice. I am so happy you're alive!" She started crying. "Yer' Uncle Sean,…"

"I know Ma," George said quietly. "I can't believe it. I got your letter two days ago. It's a terrible shame but he died with honour, just as he lived. With honour."

"He was the best man I knew," Sybil whispered.

"Yeah," George responded. "He did his bit for all of us, Ma. We're winning this war!"

"Yes, we're winning the blasted war, son. And I live for the day you will come home again."

"Yes Ma, but not just yet. The war is not over yet, but once it is, I've had an offer of some work here in the oil fields. It's a good opportunity, so I might stay a bit longer and see what I can do. There's a bit of money in it and I expect jobs will be scarce in Sydney once all the service men start returning home."

"You're right there," Sybil conceded.

"How's the work at DJs?"

"Well, I'm thinking of giving it up. Ted's offered me work at the pub. He's been very good to me, son… a good friend. Well, more than a friend actually. He told me he wants to marry me," Sybil uttered the words with little emotion.

"Of course he has," George smiled down the phone. "Everyone could see he always thought the world of yer'".

"Well, I shan't be deciding on that for a while yet."

"How's Grandma and Grandpa?"

"Maggie's slipping now Sean's gone," Sybil sighed. "She 's having trouble accepting it. She keeps talking to him…"

"Give her my love, Ma. And Grandpa. I promise I will come home to yer' before another year is up. Is Gracie there, Ma?"

"Yes, son. You keep yourself safe now. And write me a long letter. I love your letters." Sybil passed the phone to Gracie.

"George?" Gracie's familiar songlike voice wakened so many memories.

"Gracie," George smiled. "And how are you poppin' up?"

"Oh, George, it's so good to hear your voice. Is it really you? You sound like a big soldier!" Gracie giggled and then remembered herself. "I am so sorry about your Uncle Sean, George."

"Yeah, he will be sorely missed. He almost made it, too. Blasted war has cost too much!" George checked the anger in his voice. "So, tell me what you are up to, girl?"

"Well, George, there is so much to tell you. About the radio station, you know, where I'm working. Well, the weather reader got sick and so I read the weather, and the producer liked it and well, he has me reading it all the time now. And he wants me to be part of a radio show they are putting together for a tour. It's so funny, George. The show, I mean. Hilarious. Mr Andrews likes the way I tell a joke or two when I am reading the weather, you know, how the weather is so boring. George, I am sorry, I am going on but I just wanted to tell you because, well it's a long tour and I may not be here if you get back…." Gracie trailed off and George was quiet for a few moments.

The evening before he had lay in his cot pondering whether he should take up Lukas Bram's offer once the war was done, and how he might break the news that he wouldn't be coming home yet to Gracie. Eventually, he had said to himself, if you don't take this chance, you will always wonder what might have been. And living with what 'might have been' did not sound like much of a life, so he had decided. Now, he heard those words leave his lips as if they belonged to another person. "Well Gracie, it's a great opportunity and if you don't take it, you will only wonder what you might have done."

"I do love you, George," Gracie continued.

"You can tell me that the next time yer' see me and hopefully I will be holding a big bunch of flowers and you will be dancing and singing on a fancy stage with a bunch of toffs applauding yer'!"

Gracie squealed.

"There is some oil business going on up here with the Dutch, Gracie. I might be staying around for a bit. There's good money in it so, … you go on yer' tour, love."

George hung up the phone and left the communications hut with a nod of thanks to the operator. He walked in the baking sun and dust along the dirt road that cut through bedraggled jungle towards the airstrip. They were nearly done here, he could feel it. The Japs were on the run and the strip was about as good as it was going to get. He promised himself that he would never again try to build an airstrip on a swamp and he marveled that they had got it operational at all. Now, the allies were poised to take the rest of the Pacific and win this blasted war. It was cruel that his Uncle Sean had given his last just when they were on the verge of victory. A monkey watched him from the high branches of a palm tree cracking seeds and impassively shoving them in its mouth. So many men dead, now being dug up and buried again in the official Tarakan War Memorial graveyard that was built over the Japanese shrine which the Australians had burned to the ground. So many lives given for a very ordinary airstrip. It would be a bitter victory for the men on Tarakan.

Were he and Gracie done, he wondered. He had been apprehensive about telling her his plan to stay on and work for Lukas. After all, he had said he would marry her and he thought she might expect him back now that the war was over. Actually, she had told him he would marry her, he recalled. That was the truth. And he had said he would keep it in mind. He smiled at the thought of her telling jokes on stage. Yes, he would keep it in mind. Gracie wasn't someone you could forget.

EPILOGUE

The young soldier who had lain immobile and unconscious for almost two days in his cot suddenly moaned and blinked. Nurse Wilson studied him for a moment unsure she had not imagined his movement but saw him blink again and sprang to his beside.

"Private Pace, Private Pace, can you hear me?" Nurse Wilson took his hand and rubbed it warmly. "You've come back to us," she smiled. "You were knocked out by a mortar. But you are okay. Can you hear me, Private?"

George slowly realised that the noises in his head were not in his head at all but surrounded him. He began to track movements in the room and could vaguely discern the face of a woman in a white uniform. He blinked to try and clear his blurred vision. Then he vomited.

Nurse Wilson washed him and helped him sit up but he could not stand without a blinding headache and his vision remained blurred. The Doctor examined him and re-assured him that he would regain his vision and lose his headache and dizzy nausea in the next few days. In the meantime, he was under strict orders to just rest. So, he stayed in his bed drinking tea and eating whatever he could get his hands on enjoying a bit of catch up conversation with the nurses and the injured patients in the ward.

The big news was that the war was over. The Yanks had dropped their hydrogen bombs on Nagasaki and Hiroshima while he had been out cold and the Japs had surrendered. The next news he wanted to catch up on was in the pile of mail next to his bed. As his vision was still unclear, he asked Nurse Wilson to read him from the envelopes and was pleased to learn that he had two letters from home but his skin crawled when she told him there was a parcel from a Sean Pace which it turned out held a soldier's diary with a letter tucked inside.

George asked Nurse Wilson to read him Sean's letter.

Dear George,

If you are reading this, it means that I have copped it and am dead and gone. I always knew the war might put an end to me but I couldn't let it finish my story. I wanted to finish that myself. Enclosed in this mail there should be a diary, if Bags has done what I asked him. It's not a diary, nor is it a history. It's just a story. I know you like a good story from all the novels you read when you had your broken leg and I sometimes think a good story has more truth in it than any history.

It's my story, mixed up a bit with your story and the story of any other lad from Woolloomooloo, I suppose. I borrowed bits from you and others I know and I made a lot up to fill in the gaps. But you are the hero George, so I have sent it to you and you may share it with whomever you choose – and that may be no one. It's all one to me, being dead.

I wanted you to know that I hoped to be a father to you and Annie. I loved your mother like nothing else on Earth but I held my feelings back for many years so as not to cause her trouble. In the end, we shared our feelings before I left for the war and we agreed that, should I return, we would wed and put aside all the wretched doubts and fears we had carried with us that our love was not right. Love is always right, I suppose.

I wrote this story in the bloody boredom of the nights and the days that pass so slowly before and between the battles. It's covered in sweat and tears and mud and the like as it has ridden with me through all kinds of mad scrambles through New Guinea. Of course, I don't know all of your story, so I have had to fill in some gaps with imagination and claptrap. I heard about your going off with the Eighth Airfield Construction Squadron. I followed what I could with the happenings in Tarakan. I had to imagine a lot of that chapter, of course, but I hope it is at least a possible account of what happened to you. War is such a monotonous misery and these Pacific jungle islands seem so alike I felt I could well imagine your experience in Tarakan. More than anything, I hope you are alive and well.

I cannot know how my own end came but I wrote one that I liked the sound of. It actually happened like I wrote but the Jap's bullet just skimmed my slouch and I lived to laugh about it and to write the end to the story. But not much more, it seems.

This story is my way of staying with you and Anne, my parents and most of all your beautiful mother. My way of winning the war. Stay good to your Ma, George. I have always known you were a good soul since you were just a tike and took the crippled Radcliffe boy under your wing. And I know as well as anyone that if Woolloomooloo cannot turn a man bad, nothing can.

Your loving Uncle Sean.

George felt the worn binding of the book and asked Nurse Wilson, if she could read him from the first chapter.

"Well, all right George. Things have calmed down a bit now the blasted war is over. But I may have to interrupt the story when I am needed. She settled into the bedside chair and opened the scarred diary. "Now, Let's see ..."

Although George recovered his eyesight by the next day, he asked Nurse Wilson to continue the reading as the other recovering soldiers in the ward were following the tale with interest and she had a lovely reading voice. There were a few tears and some laughs. In the dark of the second night, once Nurse Wilson had finished the story, his neighbour asked, "Is Gracie real, George?"

"My oath she is, but her name's not Gracie." He smiled to himself in the dark. He had always known Sean and his mother held a torch for one another but he was glad she had taken the job Ted had offered her at the pub. She may have loved Sean more than she should love a brother but Ted worshipped the ground Sybil walked on and even Sean seemed to be on Ted's side in this story he had written. And what a story it was. He knew that he would read it again and again and each time he did, he could be with his Uncle again. Sean's story was a gift to him and the rest of the family and he couldn't wait to share it with them once he got home. But first, he had a possibility to explore.

When he walked from the medical compound two days after opening his eyes on the world again, he nodded at the guard at the perimeter and squinted at the Dutch oil derricks in the distance. "How do I get to the Dutch administration offices, mate?"

An Infinity of Days
in the
Psychotic Atomik Empire

Gregory Alan Norton

Plain View Press
P. O. 42255
Austin, TX 78704

plainviewpress.net
sb@plainviewpress.net
512-441-2452